KU-310-928

The All True Adventures (and Rare Education) of the Daredevil

Daniel Bones

OWEN BOOTH

4th ESTATE • *London*

4th Estate
An imprint of HarperCollins*Publishers*
1 London Bridge Street
London SE1 9GF

www.4thEstate.co.uk

First published in Great Britain in 2020 by 4th Estate

1

Copyright © Owen Booth 2020

Owen Booth asserts the moral right to be identified
as the author of this work in accordance with the
Copyright, Designs and Patents Act 1988

A catalogue record for this book is
available from the British Library

ISBN 978-0-00-828255-4

This novel is entirely a work of fiction. The names, characters
and incidents portrayed in it are the work of the author's imagination.
Any resemblance to actual persons, living or dead, events or
localities is entirely coincidental.

All rights reserved. No part of this publication may be
reproduced, stored in a retrieval system, or transmitted,
in any form or by any means, electronic, mechanical,
photocopying, recording or otherwise, without the
prior permission of the publishers.

This book is sold subject to the condition that it shall not, by
way of trade or otherwise, be lent, re-sold, hired out or otherwise
circulated without the publisher's prior consent in any form of
binding or cover other than that in which it is published and
without a similar condition including this condition being
imposed on the subsequent purchaser.

Set in Bembo
Printed and bound in Great Britain by
CPI Group (UK) Ltd, Croydon

MIX
Paper from
responsible sources
FSC™ C007454

This book is produced from independently certified FSC™ paper
to ensure responsible forest management.

For more information visit: www.harpercollins.co.uk/green

The All True Adventures
(and Rare Education) of the Daredevil
Daniel Bones

LIBRARIES NI
WITHDRAWN FROM STOCK

ALSO BY OWEN BOOTH

What We're Teaching Our Sons

To Gav

BOOK 1

On What Happened to Our Mother

Our father, like all fathers, is a brutal man, and that's as good a place as any to start.

He comes from a poisoned legacy of poor fighting men, damaged alternately by wars and the absence of them, with the horrors visited on each generation being passed down to the next, and so on, and so on. The old man himself, into his thirties now and having never seen battle, has chosen instead to make warfare of his life, and with those closest to him – being mainly myself and my younger brother – cast in the role of his enemies.

Our father is six feet tall and almost as broad, drinks every day and whatever he can get his mouth around, and in the year 188— has been using his fists and feet and the square of his head to visit terror upon us for as long we can remember.

Monstrous in his self-pity, he cries in his sleep for everything he has suffered and everything he has lost.

The story our father tells, when he tells us anything at all, is that our mother died either from fever or a cancer, taken while my brother was still nursing, and I was not much more than 3 or 4 years old. If this is the case then whatever memories I might once have had of her must have been knocked out of me, for I'm unable even to picture her face.

There are other versions of the tale, too, told quietly in our village. These suggest that our mother might have died while giving birth, or been knocked down by a horse a few weeks afterwards, or fallen from a cart or a boat, or, suffering some great sadness brought on by the aftermath of childbirth, possibly took her own life by wandering out onto the salt marsh at the turn of the tide. Or worse, that she may have taken the logical decision to save herself and abandon us, running away to take up with a better family, with better sons and daughters than we are.

And we are not above conjecturing either, my brother and I, that our mother may have met an altogether darker fate at the hands of our father.

None of it would surprise us. We live, in a manner of speaking, out on the edge of the marsh, at the very end of a spit of land, at the end of a slightly larger spit of land, by the mouth of the River D—, and no one in our village ever makes it to a ripe old age, or a rotten one either. Even reaching middle-age is considered a notable feat. People die of drowning, or of exposure, or of fevers, or of consumption, or of choking to death on meat, or of drink, or by lightning strike, or at the hands of their friends and neighbours. One winter half the village froze to death in the space of a week, and by spring hardly anyone could remember their names.

Everything we own in the world, our father, my brother and I, is contained within the one room of a former blacksmith's workshop – its solitary window half stopped-up with rags and paper – in which the three of us sleep and eat and our father repairs nets and wheels and broken furniture and anything else he can charge for. Outside is a small vegetable plot in which I struggle against the salted mud and sea air to grow anything, and also a pen for a single pig, and a tiny strip of beach, just wide enough at high tide to land a rowing boat. At low tide there is only the treacherous, stinking mud, and, eventually, the oyster beds beyond.

The other houses of the village are strung along the spit, which is bounded by tidal waters on either side for its quarter-mile length before it joins the mainland (itself low-lying enough for the next five miles to be only tenuously considered separate from the estuary, especially during spring tides). They are the houses of oystermen and fishermen and subsistence farmers and salt workers and takers of bribes to look the other way, and men who are a combination of all those things when and as necessary. There is also a school for their children until the age of ten, and a church for their souls thereafter, and an inn for everything else in between.

In the spring the oystermen sail to Jersey to catch brood oysters and bring them back for cultivation in the local beds out past the mudflats, and in the summer contraband cargoes are rowed ashore at all hours of the night, and for the rest of the year we cling on to the unreliable land and are occasionally washed away in storms, and that's our life.

I am either 15 or 16 years old, and I've been earning my own living for the past three years as an apprentice craftsman, oysterman and fisherman's mate, as well as cooker and cleaner and traveller up the river to the market on Wednesdays, and a generally useful set of limbs, besides. I am fit and quick and clever and subtle, can turn my hand to making and fixing most things that come through the workshop, know how to kill a pig and dig a garden and steer a boat and catch a fish, and my experience with the opposite sex is limited to a few minor experiments with some of the more adventurous older local girls, including Susan, the vicar's daughter, with whom I am, for the most part, in love.

I am tall for my age and have two good blue eyes and can read and write, and for as long as I can remember have been both mother and father to my younger brother, and also mostly to myself as no one else ever volunteered for the job.

PROSPECTS

My brother is 6 years old the first time he runs away. I find him after a night and a day of searching, hiding out in a wrecked barge on the flats five miles up the river, and when I bring him home our father beats him so hard he can't get out of bed for a week. The next time he is gone for three days, comes back sunburnt and half dead of thirst, his lips bleached white by the salt, and he won't say where he's been. Thereafter his disappearances become common enough not to be remarked on, except for the punishments they inevitably engender, which in turn inspire further abscondings.

Over the years there is not a hedgerow, upturned boat, sty, fisherman's hut, barn, milk shed, abandoned church or graveyard in the county that my brother doesn't spend at least one night in. And always with the result that I end up treating his wounds, papering his bruises and washing the blood from his eyes, and asking him why he doesn't stop, to which he replies, 'Because I don't want him to *win* ...'

Every Sunday morning our father sweats off his Saturday night drinking in church with all the other sinners. On Sunday afternoons he goes back to bed, and I take my brother out on our little boat and teach him about the tides and the weather and animals and what philosophy I have learned, and we perform the same pantomime of escape.

'What if we just kept going and rowed all the way to Holland?' he asks. 'They'd think us dead and never come after us. And we could live thereafter like princes and kings.'

And I reply, 'But we don't speak Hollandaise …'

Still, I let us drift a little further out each time, out past the sandbanks and the oyster beds, floating on the current that might draw us towards a better future, and allowing my brother to hope for a few moments longer, before I eventually turn us for home, aware as always of the reality of the world, and a coward, too.

At 10 years old my brother is in his last year at school, and can recite epic poems by heart and draw an apple so realistic you'd think you could pick it up off the paper. Thanks to the fine attention of the vicar's wife he excels at English and mathematics and geography and other things that are also of no use to anyone for fifty miles around. By the end of the summer he will be put to work and expected to forget everything else. He owns: shoes, a winter coat, pencils, two knives, and three lead soldiers which he keeps on an alcove behind the cot we sleep on.

At fifteen or sixteen, I can usually be found in the evenings walking on my own, or outside the window of Susan, the vicar's daughter, after my brother has gone to sleep, our father is down the pub and the world is near enough straight and true for at least a couple of hours. I own: shoes, coat, a scavenged Döbereiner's lamp found on the marsh used for lighting cigarettes, and a locket (also found on the marsh) which is rusted shut.

'And what then?' says Susan, the vicar's daughter, passing me the cigarette back, and returning to leaning her arms on the window ledge.

'And then we'll live like princes and kings,' I say.

'I suppose I'm the queen in all of this, huh?'

'If you came with us.'

Out on the marsh an owl shrieks. There's a moon up some-where, behind dark mottled clouds.

'If I come with you, I want to be the president.'

'Marry me, then.'

'You're too young for me,' says old Susan (sixteen). 'Also you have no prospects.'

'Nobody round here has any prospects. You don't have any prospects.'

'Give me some more of that cigarette, then,' she says, and then inhaling deeply and crossing her eyes, pretending to go faint, adds, 'My but you are a fine and handsome young man, Daniel Bones, and I must admit the honest thought of your hands all over me ...' before being overtaken by sweet laughter and coughing, at which point her father shouts from somewhere in the house and I wisely scarper.

And then I walk home again past the sleeping houses, the black shape of the water somewhere out there too, and I find my brother sleeping soundly in the darkness of the shack with his lead soldiers in his fists, and I lie down next to him, put my arm around him and move his head onto my chest, and lie awake in the dark waiting for the sound of our father's return, and the next apocalypse.

How My Brother's Arm Was Broke

Even monsters have their finer points.

Our father's is an attention to detail and a delicateness in his craft so raw it would break your heart. To see him at work is to see the man he could have been.

A wheel repaired by him, or a chair, or a jewellery box, is to all appearances an improvement on the original. Joints are stronger and more flush, spokes truer, mechanisms run more smoothly. His tragedy is that none of this is necessary. Good enough will do, especially out here at the edge of the world, where even the finest repair work can never fully change the facts of the damage already done.

Our father's only possession, other than his tools, is a replica wooden sailing boat which he rescued and repaired from some wreck or foreclosure, and which we are not allowed to touch. He dotes on the boat, cleaning and polishing it every few months, attending to the tiny intricacies of sails and rigging and gear.

On Easter Sunday, warm April weather blowing up from the south after three days of rain and currents running in two different directions out on the estuary, my brother takes down the boat while our father is in church and I am out running errands and – whether by accident or design he never explains, but you'll have your own suspicions – smashes it on the earth floor.

I've fought with my brother enough times with fists and wrestling holds and rocks and lengths of wood to know that he's a determined opponent, but even I'm astounded by the ferocity of his defence as our howling, grief-racked father attempts to beat him up and down the spit, in front of most of the entertained village. The fight seems to go on for hours.

It's only when the desperate boy finally sticks his knife into the monster's chest, causing our father to respond by snapping his son's arm over his knee, that things are brought to a conclusion.

It's then my responsibility to wheel my brother, laid out on a cart, by road to the local doctor, who is at home and, it being a day ending with the letter 'y', drunk too, but who still makes a decent job of setting the bone, and we're done with the round trip in a few hours. While we're gone our father pulls out the knife that's in him, goes home and attempts to destroy what isn't already ruined of our home, including pissing all over our bed, and then heads out again to the pub, but not before flattening my brother's soldiers on the anvil, and it's only on making this discovery that my brother finally allows himself to cry.

That evening, my brother eventually sleeping with the help of a substantial quantity of rum, I sit on the edge of the estuary weighing up my lack of options. The sky is still luminous with dusk, and the water is so calm that the vast bowl of stars lighting up one by one above sits reflected on the surface, letting me stare down into a better world than this one.

All is quiet except for the sound of the birds out on the marsh, and I am considering the possibilities of poisoning or drowning our father, or alternatively my brother and myself, and which would be the greater sin, when I catch the manure scent of drifting cigar smoke out on the water and make out the shape of something that I can only assume to be a seal on its way up the river. Except that the thing is making too much of a perturbation to be a seal, and soon enough the incoming ripples pull apart the perfect picture of the universe that I was contemplating.

A swimming man?

In fact, as it draws closer, I make out that it's a man all right, not swimming but gliding along as if in a very low Eskimo kayak, indeed flat on his back in the water in some sort of inflated suit, head up only, and propelling himself along by means of a short, double-ended paddle. A few yards behind him is towed a small canvas litter, in which are secured possessions or supplies.

'Ahoy!' the man shouts, startling me out of my wondering. 'Is this the River W—?'

'No,' I shout back, 'the W— is two miles back that way. This is the D—.'

He's far from the first to make the mistake – and says, loudly, 'Goddammit!' – but nevertheless he comes in anyway, unwelcomed, pulling up to rest a few feet from the landing, which lets me get a better glimpse of the rubber contraption covering him from hood to foot, secured with various straps and attachments, and a tube by his mouth seemingly to keep the floatation device full of air, although it's currently a cigar that he has clamped between his teeth.

'Dangerous to be sailing these waters this close to dark,' I say, feeling the need to assert some authority in this situation, though as casually as I can. 'A barge or oyster boat could run you down and not even know it.'

'And why,' he comes back, with a strange accent, and not just on account of the cigar held in his mouth, 'would a barge or oyster boat be out at this time of night?'

'They might be about other business than barging or oystering. Either way you'd be wise to adopt some sort of running light.'

'You may be right. How would I go about that, do you think?'

'A lantern, projecting by means of a pole, from your left foot there. In the same way you have a socket on the right for that currently lowered sail strapped along your leg. Simple enough to fashion in a basically equipped workshop, is what I think.'

And I'm proud of that, want to make it clear who owns this little spot of beach and spit of nothing, boldly return his look as – I realise now – he is sizing me up.

'Are you a strong swimmer, lad?'

'Not the strongest or the weakest.'

'But you can swim?'

And I say, 'Of course, like a duck. Hard to grow up here and not know how to swim.'

'And yet,' he says, 'it's a skill frowned upon by sailors, who argue that the facility only prolongs the acceptance of death in the event of shipwreck or falling overboard at sea. For what, in all that blank immensity, is one going to swim *to*?'

I'll soon enough get used to this tortured and ludicrous manner of speaking, even come to enjoy it, wielded as it is in all its intricacies to both entertain and confuse in equal measure, but still …

'No sailors round here,' I say, 'only oystermen, who I've yet to see farming on the open sea.'

'Quite. And a smart lad you are, too.'

And with that he comes ashore, laying down his paddle and getting to his feet with my assistance, the water pouring from all the crevices of his rubber suit, and shakes my hand with his rubber-gloved one.

'So where,' he asks, 'might an exotic traveller find a place to sleep for the night about these parts?'

13

PRESS-GANGED

And this, of course, is the famous Captain Clarke B., of either the United States of America or Ireland, depending on whose story of his background you believe, and news of whose exploits has reached us even this far from civilisation.

The adventurous Captain Clarke B., daredevil inventor of the life-saving inflatable suit that you were introduced to in the previous chapter, who had only a few months ago swum ashore on the west coast of Ireland in the middle of a storm, having already demonstrated his invention on the great rivers of the American continent and now embarked on a promotional tour of the waterways of Europe.

The charming Captain Clarke B., who addresses the small crowd gathered on the muddy, oyster-shell-strewn ground outside the inn the next morning (after sending Little Pete, the innkeeper's son, to half a dozen neighbouring villages in the hours before sunrise to announce his presence here and around) and about whom rumours are already spreading, chiefly that he may have spent the previous night in bed with either the innkeeper's wife, or daughter, or both, and this has gone a long way to winning us simple village folk over before he's even started his speech.

Six feet tall, not yet forty and still handsome enough, with a weirdly high-pitched voice, 'Ladies and gentlemen of this fine parish,' is what he opens with, and the air is still cold enough that there's a crisp edge to it, and a crunch to the mud under our feet too. 'I have swum the mighty rivers of the Missouri and the Mississippi and the Rio Grande. I have crossed giant oceans and seen flying fish and whales breaching in the Pacific at dawn' – 'oohs' and 'aahs' from the crowd here – 'I have navigated terrifying rapids and mighty cataracts, saved only by the efficacy of my patented life-preserving costume' – pointing to the suit itself, which is standing up on a frame by his side, and to which we all nod, knowingly – 'and this last week I have single-handedly travelled the length of the Thames from its source to this place at the very edge of the sea …'

He pauses here to let people realise that he's talking about them, about us, about our little village. I exchange glances with Susan, the vicar's daughter. A small, warming cheer goes up.

'… and in three days' – holding up a copy of the London paper with a picture of himself in it, in retrospect probably a paid advertisement – 'I am due to attempt a crossing of the treacherous English Channel and land upon the coast of France!'

A chorus of 'Boo!'s goes up here at the mention of the historic enemy, momentarily throwing the captain off his stride. Nevertheless he rallies, and embarks upon the section of his performance about how, although his insignificant life means nothing, if, through his scientific work, he might save the lives of others – fishermen, sailors, brave members of the Royal Navy – by the adoption of the technology contained within his suit, then all will not have been in vain, and asking us to think what we might say to our own various loved ones, lost to the waves over the years, offered the chance to explain how we had given

15

up the opportunity to save others like them by dropping a coin into the hat *even now being passed around* …

Well, even my father, that sour old arm-breaker, is reaching into his pocket by this point. Giant Pete, the innkeeper, is trying to push fistfuls of notes into the captain's hands, his daughter shyly smiling and toeing the shingle, and no sign of the wife. And then comes the kicker.

'But who among you might assist me on this adventure?' the captain shouts, and we all stop and turn and go 'Wha …?'

And then the captain's eyes fall on me, as was his plan all along, and he points me out, making sure everyone can see.

'What about you, sir?'

Me?

'A strong young man to journey with me across the wild continent, to support me in my life-saving work, and take the name of his village to the farthest corners of civilisation – and paid a wage, of course!'

'Of course!' everyone shouts.

Trapped, I look around, trying to spot my brother, don't find his eyes anywhere, meet instead the adoring gazes of some of my former classmates, the raised and sceptical eyebrow of Susan, the vicar's daughter. And then Giant Pete the innkeeper comes forward and throws his giant arms around me.

'He accepts!' he shouts. 'Of course he accepts!' and suddenly I am being lifted and carried along by the hands of my friends and neighbours, passed along the crowd and through the doors of the inn, where I am laid along the bar – and *there's* the innkeeper's wife now, with a definite glow about her it must be said, and she's already drawing the first of the very many glasses of beer that will be poured down my throat that morning – and so is my fabulous, awful destiny sealed.

When I come to, hours later, I am laid out in the middle of

the marsh, my face in a bed of glasswort, with dim memories of it being buried earlier in the warm bosoms of more than one of the women of the village, and my brother sitting on the cracked mud some yards from me with his bandaged arm laid across his knees. It's already late in the day and the tide is coming in.

'You're famous,' he says.

'That wasn't my intention,' I answer.

'But all the same.'

'I'll send for you,' I say, struggling to get up. Across the marsh the water is advancing quickly. 'As soon as I've enough money. I don't know any other solution to our situation.'

'Let me come now.'

'It won't even be a year.'

'You know I won't survive that long.'

'Children can survive anything. We both know that.'

He laughs, darkly, 'Ha!', then wipes his eyes, wipes his nose on his sleeve. Sniffs.

'One year,' he says. 'That's a promise, now.'

'One year,' is what I reply.

But, of course, it doesn't turn out like that.

Goodbyes

And so, over the next few days, plans are put in place, and lectures delivered to me by Captain Clarke B. on the importance of life-saving at sea, as well as stories of his previous escapades, and maps of the continent are laid out on the tables of the inn, and due diligence is carried out, including demonstrations of my swimming ability and boat-handling and navigational skills.

For the most part our father maintains his distance from both my brother and I, being largely in the pub.

The day of our departure my brother is up and about early, broken arm and all, and is nowhere to be found, so I go for a walk through the village to pay my respects to the place, tip my hat to people here and there. At the end of the street I find Susan, the vicar's daughter, sitting on the front step of the vicarage in her best dress, shading her eyes against the morning sun.

'I've been fucking Joseph Parsons,' is the first thing she says. 'I thought you should know.'

'Are you going to marry him?' I ask.

'I don't think so,' she says. 'I've been fucking his brother Jeremiah, too.'

'Is that the one who they say can catch bats out of the air with his bare hands?'

'I've seen him do it.'

'It's a rare talent. You could do a lot worse.'

'Well,' she says, 'it was nice to know you, Daniel. Good luck on all your adventures.'

'You too, Susan,' I say, and mean it too, and then we shake hands and that's that.

I spend the rest of the morning putting the last of my affairs in order, weed the garden and pull up three rows of early radishes, say goodbye to the pig, which doesn't seem much interested in my grand plans. I take the boat out to look for my brother up and down the estuary, hear reports of him a couple of villages over, then a couple further on from those. I eventually give up and head back, imagining him already at large out in the territories, causing trouble and writing new legends for himself. I sail back up our river, pull up the boat onto our beach, say goodbye to the both of those too.

At noon I find my father, not sober, at the bar of the inn. Having already handed over responsibility for the garden and the pig to my brother, I can think of nothing I need to discuss with the old man himself. Staring at his broad back from the doorway I cast around for an identifiable emotion but am unable to work out what, if anything, I feel. I'm about to leave again when he says, without turning around, 'You won't be back.'

I wait for him to go on.

'You were always your mother's children, both of you,' is how he continues, eventually, apparently to no one in particular. 'None of you ever gave me a chance.'

And there's an emotion, after all, suddenly so vast and deep it threatens to swallow me and maybe take half the bar and the surrounding landscape down with it too.

'If you hurt him again …' I say, and I don't complete the sentence only partly because I hope it will feel more like a threat that way, but also because, in truth, I have no idea of what else I should add, not having lately been in the threatening business.

At this he finally turns around and meets me with his red, monster's eyes, sinks his beer while holding my gaze.

'You'll what?'

But then there's the ruckus of the man himself, being driven up outside in the coach he has been lent by some local dignitary, drawn by four horses no less, and our brave captain's gear safely stowed on top, who comes into the bar now and claps a gloved hand on my shoulder – 'If I may borrow this excellent young gentleman …' – and steers me outside, and that's the last time I see my father, alive or dead.

'All ready, lad?'

'My brother …' I start to say, wanting to ask the cap again if and why we can't take him with us, but don't. This is a man with letters of introduction from counts and dukes and kings of European nations – which we will be using to secure our passage across the continent. Who am I, a coward from a village at the edge of the world, to make demands of someone endorsed by nobility, however stretched their current circumstances?

Captain Clarke B. having made our village inn the base of his operations – the proximity of the innkeeper's wife and daughter, and the allowance our little river has afforded him to make last-minute tests of his equipment both playing a part in this – gives a small send-off for us, and speeches, and also a painted banner wishing us success and godspeed, organised by the vicar's wife and her young pupils. I recognise my missing brother's hand in there, in the steady curls on the letters, and reach in my pocket for the deformed shape of the lead soldier he solemnly gave me to take on my journey (I, for my part, having given him the rusted locket in return, knowing he had always admired it), as

I'm passed around to say goodbye to people who I'll forget within three months.

There's a toothy wind getting up on the water as we leave, though nothing of a sky to speak of, low grey cloud solid as far as the eye can see across the endless marsh and few licks of colour about on the landscape this early in the year, and for the next couple of hours we sit in the moving coach smoking and watching the flat horizon, the pair of us, the captain oddly silent in his military greatcoat, and I, I suppose, still hoping to spot the figure of my brother somewhere out there, running to catch us, and feeling the huge weight of guilt dragging like an anchor rope at my coward's heart, until the known world disappears behind us and I'm lost and swimming towards nothing I can see or understand.

All I Have in the World

Our journey to the capital that day takes the best part of the afternoon, and by the time we come into the city I am bone-shaken and already half exhausted, though amazed enough by the sight of things to be eagerly leaning out of the window, staring at the great buildings and the painted signs and the traffic and endless numbers of people. Most of all I am disoriented by the lack of a horizon.

Our equipment, stowed on the roof of the carriage, includes:

» One collapsible canvas boat or dinghy, large enough to take one crew member (me), plus supplies and gear, and a retractable short sail to be used if necessary, the whole thing when rolled up being able to be carried, just about, on one shoulder
» One rubber life-saving suit, plus paddle, also rolled up
» Tools for repairs in a canvas military bag
» Pamphlets and flyers advertising the captain's exploits, with information for potential investors, secured in a cardboard case
» Another canvas bag containing the captain's various uniforms, including full evening dress and shoes

For my part I have the clothes I'm wearing, plus a shaving kit in my pocket which was presented to me by Susan's father, the Reverend Pritchard.

For the last hour of the journey Captain B. has changed into a giant white fur coat which I imagine to have been taken from a polar bear, and which is impressive enough to make a few people turn and stare when we pull up at the cab rank outside the railway station and he steps down from the coach. He sweeps into the giant station building while I struggle to unload our equipment with the help of the driver, and carry it in stages into the great noisy departure hall, where I find the cap again, alone and looking briefly confused, casting about the crowds of thousands of hurrying travellers, which is likely more people than I have seen in all the rest of my life combined, in search of an explanation.

Finally, the captain spots a skinny man in an oversized coat and bowler hat approaching hurriedly – 'Ah, here's our man, Mcinerney' – who soon arrives and shakes the cap's hand, while still looking around.

'There have been …' he says, this Mcinerney, lowering his voice and looking at me suspiciously, '*complications.*'

'What complications?' says Captain Clarke B. 'This is my apprentice, Daniel Bones. You can speak as clearly and honestly in front of him as you would me.'

'What happened to the last one?' says Mcinerney.

'Never mind that.'

The man stares at me for a while longer, before shrugging.

'Complications with one of the endorsement deals,' he says. 'Largely being that we lost it. And so the money. And so the suite at the station hotel. And so the train tickets,' pausing here to let the captain take it all in. 'And so on.'

'I see,' says the captain, and places a finger against his own chin for a very long time, hard enough to leave a mark.

I, it has to be said, am largely too much distracted by the magnificent vaulting iron and glass ceiling of the station, this being the first of its kind I've ever visited, and also the billowing clouds of steam, and the screeching of train wheels and whistles and so on, to fully comprehend the situation, and so don't entirely follow how we come to leave our gear in the care of the luggage office, and repair to the bar of the station hotel, where I am equally impressed by the polished table-tops and zinc bar and the other, well-to-do drinkers, and a plan is hatched over a couple of beers between the captain and his man.

Soon enough, hands are being shook and Mcinerney departs, leaving the captain seemingly carrying the absolute weight of the world on his shoulders all of a sudden. A few minutes later the two of us are invited by a frock-coated member of the hotel staff to take the lift – *the lift!* – to one of the highest corridors of the hotel, where the captain knocks on a particular door, and we wait. The captain turns to me and puts a gloved finger to his lips and I nod.

Eventually the door is opened by a well-presented, rich-looking woman – rich-looking to me, anyway, in her bearing and the jewellery at her neck and so on – somewhere upwards of the captain's age, who sighs when she sees the subdued cap.

'Clarke,' she says, flatly.

'Eleanor.'

'It's still "Mrs Ravenwood".'

'Of course.'

'What happened to the last one?' she says, tilting her head towards me.

Ignoring her question, he asks, 'May I come in?'

She considers it for a few seconds before nodding and open-ing the door to the captain, who follows her into the room, telling me 'You'd best wait here' as he closes – and going by the sound of things, locks – the door behind him.

And so I wait, standing by the door, for what may be an hour or so, while occasional hotel guests leave or enter the other rooms along the corridor, and I try to look unconcerned despite being higher above sea level than I have ever been before, and wonder what else I'll see before this day is over, and realise at last how hungry I am, having not eaten since breakfast.

Eventually the door opens again, and a defeated and some-what dishevelled-looking cap exits the room, before turning to me and asking, brightly, 'Do you have any money yourself, Daniel?'

Which is how we come to spend all I have in the world, being the contents of a collection held in my honour by Giant Pete the innkeeper, on two third-class tickets for the last train to Dover, into which we are squeezed along with our equipment and a great mass of other people, for whom the sight of our captain in his polar bear fur provides great entertainment for the duration of our noisy and uncomfortable journey through the dark Kent countryside, before eventually arriving to an empty, closed-up Dover Central station, in the middle of the night.

The Crossing

The day itself starts in the damp half-darkness of five o'clock in the morning, with the captain shaking me awake from my spot on the beach, where I have been struggling to sleep wrapped in my coat for the past few hours. Together we drag our gear across the wet shingle and back to the train station, where the captain changes into his rubber suit and a deal is apparently struck with the guards to let us board the incoming London-to-Paris morning train – the train we were originally supposed to be on – and ride it the one stop to the Admiralty Pier, where passengers for France disembark for the crossing, and where, hopefully, we will still be expected.

And out on the Admiralty Pier there's a reception all right. As we step off the train there's a crowd of well-wishers and important people with umbrellas, and newspapermen in black hats and overcoats against the light rain, and the captain stops to throw his arms in the air, and does look impressive wearing the fur coat over his rubber suit. There's a small stage, and a slightly wet banner advertising 'The Fearless Frogman' and illustrating his many adventures – I note that at least *something* was successfully arranged in advance – and as the cap takes the stage a brass band is playing, which he thanks before giving mostly the same patter as he gave in our village, right down to the hat going round, into which the gathered pressmen don't put much.

While I carefully assemble the canvas boat and sail, with one eye on the changing details of the sky, the captain poses for photographs in his life-saving outfit, extolling its many virtues and providing quotes for the press and potential investors on 'our great adventure' and 'the benefits for all mankind', and shaking the hands of dignitaries and charming their wives too. More than one young woman throws herself into his arms, and has to be peeled away from him, weeping hysterically. Then with the assistance of a couple of young lads I take the boat down the steps and into the harbour, followed by the cap himself who gives a last wave before getting into the water with his paddle, and we're off, and as we move away from the sea wall my flimsy boat almost turns over in the wake of a couple of tall ships before I get used to the strange handling of it.

The day is still overcast as we pull out of the harbour, the captain towing me behind him on a thirty-foot length of rope, and the water is green and dark with a sickly white foam. The channel is filled with more ships than I've ever seen. Boats of all sizes are out for the trip, from steamers and clippers and cruise liners to fishing trawlers and sea barges and dinghies, even a couple of ironclad warships which intermittently let off deafening broadsides with their guns pointed safely in the direction of France. Within two miles of port, three rowing boats overloaded with onlookers have already capsized in the swell. From the deck of a hired paddle steamer the members of the world's press watch our progress from reclining chairs, toasting us with cocktails, as party-goers on pleasure boats let off rockets and threaten to swamp my tiny craft by coming too close while attempting to light the captain's cigars for him.

For his part, Captain Clarke B. mostly weathers the attention in good humour, being exactly in his element, in all possible senses. Every few miles he slows his steady paddle stroke to drink a restorative brandy and smoke and wave to the audience, while I pull up alongside and supply whatever other provisions he requires, and so pass the first few hours of the day.

By the afternoon we're into the middle of the channel and the tide has turned against the wind, shortening the sea and bringing up the swell. I can see the inexperienced sailors on even some of the bigger boats getting sick, and I'm struggling to bail out my little ship, which, it's becoming clear, was not designed for the open water. The captain is still shouting out, 'Hurrah!'s and 'Ho!'s punctuating each particularly tough stroke of his paddle, but his words are mostly lost in the wind, and we have a hairy hour or so in which I have the luxury of regretting my eagerness to come on this voyage, before the conditions eventually clear again.

Then, with the tide back on our side, we have an easy enough run towards the lighthouse at Cape Grey Nose on the coast of France, the early-evening sun at last breaking through the clouds behind us and beginning to light fire to the sky as we touch the beach, where a small crowd is gathered to congratulate the captain, a string quartet striking up, in fact, as I step from the boat and the man himself already shaking hands with the local mayor, and I realise on hearing that new language and seeing my giant shadow fall on the sand that we are, remarkably, ashore on the new continent.

Well, soon enough we are bundled into some carriage or other, and carried through the lanes lined with tall hedges and pretty stone cottages to what seems to me to be the grandest house I've ever seen, which is the home of the mayor, with a pointed roof and shutters on the windows, and where it is apparently decided that I'll sleep in the orchard to keep an eye on our gear, which is all right with me. The captain, distracted by the mayor and his wife, briefly shakes my hand before going inside, leaving me to unload our equipment and set up for the evening.

And so, after a solitary supper of bread and cheese, I bed down among the apple trees, eyed from the other side of the orchard by a single French cow, to which I say, 'Hello there,' before realising she most likely doesn't understand English. All the same I'm glad of her company, and am reminded of my pig and my brother at home a thousand miles away, as I lie watching the bats tumbling through the air above me, and beyond them the millions of alien stars hanging in the foreign sky, and I don't fall asleep for a very long time.

The Most Important Thing

That same cow wakes me early the next morning by softly licking my face, so we sit together for a while watching the sun come up over the bare apple boughs and all my new world.

Out in the lane in front of the house I can already hear farmers and traders about, and I recognise the sounds and smells of a market day. After finishing the last of the cheese and bread, I wash up in the water trough and comb my hair and go round the back of the house, where by smiles and gestures at the kitchen door I cadge a cup of strong coffee from the staff.

Then I stand at the gate drinking my coffee and watching the comings and goings of the market people, until Captain Clarke B. himself appears next to me, dressed as if for a day at the races, a cigar already in his mouth.

'To France,' I say, raising my cup, and he puts his hand on my shoulder.

'And then the world,' he says, and we stand there for maybe a minute, considering our place in all of it, before we're being bundled into the mayor's open carriage again for a tour of the town and other commitments besides.

As the day proceeds and I take in the strange details of foreign hedgerows and trees and shopfronts and the shapes of post boxes and pavements, it becomes clear that this mayor's interests stretch beyond local politics. We visit a small quarry on the edge of town, and a toothpaste factory, and a railway building project, and a meat-pie packing concern, among others, as the mayor holds forth in French and the cap attends to his every word.

Oblivious to much of what is going on, I enjoy the French sun on my face and these new sights, before we eventually end up back at the town square, where the captain is to perform.

But instead of a stage there's only a stall in the middle of the busy market, and it soon becomes clear that the cap is meant to compete with the noise and colour and smell of the other stall-holders selling chickens and lamb's livers and giant cabbages and sausages and cow's tongues and cheese and horse-meat and rabbits and rough cloth and pig's cocks.

'A glass of water first, perhaps?' our captain asks, having surveyed the scene. 'Or wine?'

'When you're finished,' the mayor tells him, firmly, in English. 'Right you are.'

And so the cap begins his presentation, with the mayor's man helping to translate for him, but it's not the words but rather the performance that wins the day.

First, at his stall, the captain requires the translator to collar an apparently arbitrary woman shopping nearby, asking her, 'Are you, *madame*, aware of the horrible price paid to defend your daily freedom by the brave boys of your country's fine navy?' and, by some remarkable coincidence, it turns out that this very woman *lost a brave son at sea only last year*, and, as a result, the cap demands that she be given the meat she is at that moment trying to buy, for free (which does not delight the shamed butcher, as all eyes turn to him, but what can he do but agree?) before our man goes on one knee to thank this fine woman for her son's service.

31

Further members of the crowd are plucked out at random then, each bringing their own terrible story of loss, and the increasing interest of the other market shoppers, before the humble Captain Clarke B. remembers himself.

'And who am I,' he asks the market-goers, 'to demand of these good people to revisit their heartbreak in so public an arena?'

It's clear that no one knows.

'I am nobody,' the captain agrees, 'except a servant who is striving in his small way to make a difference, perhaps to save a life. A nobody who has thrown himself over waterfalls and into gigantic seas, who has battled ocean beasts and foreign navies too, in pursuit of scientifically proven truths. A nobody' – and remarkably his voice is almost breaking here, overwhelmed as the man is by his own insignificance in the face of the great work he does – 'who would only ask you to take a minute to consider this life-saving suit, and listen to a few words about the bright cleaning efficacy of LeClerc's patented Gentian Tooth Powder …'

That night the mayor takes us out to the most expensive restaurant in town, requiring me – this being my first trip to any sort of restaurant – to borrow an outfit from the mayor's son, who is a pale, gloomy boy of eighteen. I am seated between the mayor's son and the captain, who is, in turn, seated next to the mayor's wife, a formidable woman ten or fifteen years the cap's senior, who is wearing the grandest jewellery that I have ever seen, and who spends the evening delighting in the charming Clarke B.'s entire attention, and best broken French.

At some point in the proceedings, when the lady mayoress has excused herself momentarily, the captain turns to me, asking, 'Did you see all those people today, Daniel?', to which I admit that I did.

'And on the beach yesterday? And do you agree that all of them would likely need, at some point, to drink beer and eat pies and clean their teeth?'

'I suppose so, yes,' I say. 'It seems an undoubted fact.'

'So not only does the mayor get to promote his business interests but his town, too,' the cap goes on, 'and the local businessmen also make money out of that, and he is commensurately rewarded by them as well, and everyone is happy.'

'Right,' I say, because I am quick. But not all that quick.

'You're going to see remarkable sights and get a rare education, lad,' the captain tells me, leaning in close, the reek of wine on his breath, 'but never forget the most important thing about our journey.'

'The life-saving properties of the suit?' I say.

'The audience,' he replies. 'Like our lady mayoress, here. Always remember that we are at their service. If they aren't happy, we can't get what we want.'

'And what do we want?'

He looks at me and blinks, as if he hasn't understood the question.

'Did you see the size of that necklace she was wearing?' he asks. 'That alone would fund our work for a year.'

At the end of the evening we are taken for a walk in the spring air — the mayor, his wife, the sullen son, the captain and I strolling along the river front — as the captain explains more of his plan to our hosts. As we pause to lean over the railings and watch the dark, fast-flowing river heading back towards the sea, I look upstream, dizzy from the French wine.

I roll a cigarette, wonder what happened to my lamp in all the comings and goings of the last few days, and the mayor's son leans over with a lit match, to which I say, 'Mercy,' and hand him the tobacco.

'I hate this shithole town,' he says, in English, surprising me, as he rolls his cigarette. 'There's nothing to do except try to fuck girls and write poetry. And the girls don't like me anyway.'

'This is my first day in the country,' I say.

'You should go to Paris,' he says. 'Everyone there is a poet. A poet or a bank robber. Everything else is a waste of time.'

Not knowing what to say to that, I keep quiet.

Then he says, 'So is your friend completely trying to screw my mother right under my father's nose, then?'

That night the captain is banished to sleep in the orchard with the cow and I, and the next day we're on our way before dawn.

The Autobiography of Captain Clarke B., Part One

'According to legend,' says Captain Clarke B., 'I grew up on the banks of either the O—, or the M—, or the S— River, where I spent my childhood *more in the water than out of it*. By 5 years old I had already developed the athletic skills that would bring me fame and fortune, and my nascent spirit of adventure soon showed itself when, at the age of eight, I ran away from home on a coal barge bound for New Orleans, returning five weeks later with a newly adopted sister and a pet alligator.

'At fourteen I joined the navy,' says Captain Clarke B., 'easily persuading the enlisting office that I was older than I was, on account of my muscular build and imposing figure. I went on to serve with distinction on a steamer in the Civil War, during which time I made the first sketches of my life-saving suit. Although unfairly court-martialled due to my being named in a divorce case, my military expertise and need to earn a living led me to fight in the Franco-Prussian war, and also the War of the Pacific between Bolivia and Chile, and with the navy of Benito Juárez against the French invasion of Mexico, before I embarked on my adventuring career and travels of the world.

'The tales of my exploits on the water are well known,' says Captain Clarke B., 'and also the stories of my many romances, including with princesses and heiresses and society beauties. I have fought more than one duel in defence of a woman's honour, and have come to the rescue of countless others in the more savage parts of the world, despite thus far having never met the woman who could tame my wild spirit and tempt me to rest from my travels and bring my journeying to an end.

'Besides,' says Captain Clarke B., 'until my life-saving invention is adopted for general use among the world's navies, I consider it my responsibility and privilege to keep working to bring it to the world's attention.

'I have seen men killed,' says Captain Clarke B., 'by shellfire and bullets and fire and explosive concussion and septic disease and hanging and blood loss following amputation and shock and shark bite, and again and again and again by drowning. I have myself endured shipwreck and torpedo strikes and sniper fire and ambush and hand-to-hand combat, as well as shark and sea lion and electric eel and rattlesnake attack, and also two months in a Mexican prison, until I have been forced to wonder what it is about myself that sees me chosen to survive.

'I am a friend to presidents and kings,' says Captain Clarke B., 'and am equally at home moving among the great and the good as in the company of the humblest workingmen. In my later years I will likely wear the many medals awarded to me by the leaders of great nations, and smoke cigars in dark panelled rooms. I will not drink before three in the afternoon. In publicity photos I will wear a military greatcoat or fur over a white shirt and bow tie. I will wax the tips of my moustache and part my hair on the left. I will open amusement parks and patent a variety of water-related adventure ride devices.

'And what I will have learned through all my adventures,' says Captain Clarke B., 'is that a man's destiny is defined only by the edges of his imagination. That we make the world anew every day, with our every thought and action. That we are limited by nothing except the size of our ambition and our will.

'As God is my witness,' says Captain Clarke B., 'I put my trust in the value of individual human determination to shape the greatest of all possible futures.'

So recorded by Daniel Bones, France–Belgium–Holland, April–May 188—.

An Education

For the next month or so, then, we travel the waterways of northern France and what are called the Low Countries, journeying from town to town on canals and rivers, across swamps and the occasional lake, the captain paddling his life-saving suit and I following in the collapsible boat, powered by oar and sail, my eyes wide open to the new world.

I am initially surprised to find that the manner of our tour is considerably more improvisational than I had expected, as we turn up without invitation to perform at farm shows, and open-air celebrations, and the opening of bridges and factories, and the odd wedding, and even a couple of birthday parties, as well as at markets and demonstrations and during the witnessing of particular feast days, and anywhere else that might have us. Indeed, a couple of times we are run off before we've even had a chance to unload our gear. It seems that word of our trip has not penetrated very deeply into the continent after all.

At the two or three towns where our arrival has actually been announced ahead, there is usually a stall in the town square or bandstand to be put to use for a speech by the cap, which includes the introduction of the suit and its life-saving capabilities, and tales of the captain's adventures, and whatever series of promotional announcements and endorsements have been agreed in advance with our sponsors.

Thereafter, the captain will undertake stunts and activities on the water for the entertainment of the small but appreciative crowds, including the smoking of cigars, and the firing of rockets, and the performance of a number of submerging rolls during which our man will hold his breath underwater long enough to make women faint, before triumphantly righting himself again to polite applause, while I make my way through the thin crowds with the hat.

Following this there may be other events at which the captain is interviewed by the local press, or he may be invited to hobnob with the local great and good, the cap being rolled out to prove the wherewithal and society connections and wealth of some business- or land-owner or other – or, as is often the case, his smitten wife – usually leaving me in charge of our gear and having to negotiate with the locals as best I can using the few phrases I've been able to pick up, including *bonjour* and *combinaison plongée* and *argent* and *l'homme grenouille* and *les pauvres marins, perdus en mer*.

Everywhere we go we meet surprised bargemen and farmers and fishermen, who stare in amazement at the cap and his suit, and who undoubtedly help spread the word about our adventure. We startle horses and cows, are chased by dogs along riverbanks and towpaths, disturb clandestine lovers and entertain swimming children. In towns and cities, people line the bridges to watch our approach, and we are often greeted as celebrities. Further from the centres of civilisation we are treated with suspicion, the captain's costume and broken French being enough to convince some people that we are likely spies. On more than one occasion the cap is forced to produce his letters of introduction in order to talk us out of a potential arrest.

Wherever we encounter more physical obstacles, such as locks or weirs, we portage the boat, carrying it out of the water to the next appropriate spot on the other side of the blockage, which never turns out to be more than a few hundred yards at most and where we continue our voyage, people watching our progress with amusement and excited children running alongside.

I soon become adapted to the rigours of life on the water, growing new callouses on my palms, and a strong back besides. Water being the ideal medium for transport, my days in the boat for the most part are not difficult, with only the weather and the danger of being run down by coal barges providing regular challenges. There's time to contemplate the world and its mysteries, and to remember incidents from my youth which seem now to belong to a different life, and to write letters to my brother detailing what I've seen and felt, and to watch the country go by with all its styles of landscape and architecture, and also to sail alongside the cap and chat about his life and his opinion on things.

Captain Clarke B., I discover, considers himself to be a capitalist, and a man of the modern world and of science and progress, and a supporter of the rights of women, and for the most part a republican, despite his close personal relationships with many of the continent's minor royals, and also a believer in equality between the races, and – having studied many of the religions of the world – of the survival of the spirit after death, 'But in what form, who can say?'

I learn that he begins every day with a series of esoteric exercises designed to facilitate the flow of the blood and oxygenation of the brain, that he preaches the importance of a balanced diet and regular bowel habits, and for my part I impress the cap with my skills on the water, and my ability to spot the best fruit and vegetables at town markets, and by showing him how to catch trout and other fish, which we often cook for dinner on the riverbanks. The captain asks me only a little about my own life, and I venture to tell him even less.

At night we sleep in fields and in woods and on beaches, or, when our hosts provide for it, sometimes in hotels (of which more later) or inns or private houses. And we wake every day to sunshine or rain or mists or storms, to warm or cold weather and forecasts promising better or worse, and get back on the water all the same.

And while it's not always clear, to me at least, quite how any of this is getting us nearer to the ultimate goal of saving lives at sea, or when I am to start seeing the wages I was promised either, true to Captain Clarke B.'s word I am certainly getting an education, and for the time being that is enough for me.

A Gentleman of Leisure

There is a ghostly fog sitting on the canal the day we paddle into G—, and the town feels deserted. The dark stone sides of the medieval buildings looming out of the mist feel like the walls and battlements of haunted castles. The damp air so muffles the sound of our oars that we surprise the guards at the tollgate, and have to argue with them for half an hour before they raise the barrier and we are allowed passage. In the grey cobbled streets and squares beyond, people flit in and out of our focus like spectres.

At the Grand Hotel, where we are to stay, I marvel at the uniformed porters, who the cap calls bellboys, and at the well-appointed guests going back and forth in the marble lobby, and the beds which have already been made up in our room, and the promise of a bath later, and of a breakfast in the morning too.

'Our creditors are very generous men,' the cap tells me, 'though not without their faults.'

At the front desk I am handed a letter from my brother, which reads as follows:

Dear Daniel

It is raining here. Next month or the month after that I am to start working as an apprentice oysterman. I kissed Helen Dunning and ran away for a whole week. Ha! How is the weather there? I will ask Mrs Pritchard to post this for me.

Your brother Will

I read it over again, trying to recreate the world behind those words, and to imagine myself in my brother's company, and wonder where he is at this moment.

That evening we have dinner in the hotel restaurant, and the captain warns me to watch myself about town, and of the various characters and types to avoid, including pickpockets and anarchists, and tells me some tales of duels and gunfights he has witnessed in the American West, and how to shoot a man from a moving horse, and other useful things.

Our meeting the next morning is in the town cathedral, where we wait in one of the alcoves for the arrival of the cap's men. On the stone walls there are hung realistic paintings featuring kings and queens and figures of Adam and Eve and other characters from the Bible, and many I don't recognise besides, including numerous barely dressed women. There are also paintings of battles and war, and the captain and I are stationed in front of one of these when we are joined by three men in suits and overcoats.

'Strange to think,' says their leader, examining the scene, 'that people have been fighting over this one small piece of Europe for thousands of years.'

'And by all accounts will continue to do so,' the eager captain adds. 'You'll have heard the stories about the German navy manoeuvring up north?'

'Which is where you come in, of course,' the man says, with a sceptical tone. 'Five years is a very long time to wait for a return on our investment, Clarke.'

'I'm sure men of vision such as yourselves understand the value of –'

'And what do you think, lad,' the man asks, turning to me, 'of the esteemed captain and his invention? Would you consider it wise to risk your money with him?'

'I think the captain is a great man,' I say, 'and his suit one of the scientific wonders of our age.'

'Indeed,' says the man. 'Well here's a reward for your loyalty, then. Give him some money and the day off, Clarke. We have a lot to discuss.'

And so, reluctantly, the captain hands over a few coins, and I am excused my duties to spend the gloomy afternoon in a rough approximation of a gentleman at leisure, strolling around the town and admiring the many bell towers and churches and bridges, and the tall, thin, brightly painted houses with stepped roofs. I also invite myself to drink a few of the local beers in some of the dark panelled bars that look out onto the canals, and watch the rain falling onto the water, and read my brother's letter again and again.

It's late in the evening and I am very reasonably drunk when the cap finds me in the tiny waterside pub where I have been trying to explain to a working woman – who has not understood a word I say but has been professionally indulging my melancholy – about my home, and our journey, and my brother. The brave Clarke B. wrests me from the lady's attention and takes me back to the hotel, warning of an early-morning appointment.

That night, as we lie in our beds after turning out the gas lamps, I hear the captain's voice in the darkness.

'You will have noted those paintings in the cathedral,' is what he says. 'The women, and such.'

I admit that I did, for they were hard to ignore.

'I would urge you, Daniel, for the sake of your health and sanity,' the cap continues, 'to put aside any ideas that may have been planted by those images.'

I don't tell him about the ideas that Susan, the vicar's daughter, and some of the other older girls in the village used to plant in me, or how we sometimes acted on those ideas either. For all that, I am still, technically at least, a virgin. And so, instead, I lie there in the dark, trying to think pure thoughts, and listening to the tightly controlled breathing of Captain Clarke B., until we both are asleep.

The morning of the demonstration finds us up and out at dawn, and me nursing a sick head as we arrive at an empty stone warehouse which backs onto a disused dock. Inside, a crowd of twenty or thirty sullen men of many nationalities, all of them sweating and sour-breathed on account of travel or intrigues or lack of sleep, eye each other – and us – suspiciously.

I recognise the tang of violence in the air, the sickly promise of aggression, and realise I've almost missed it these last few weeks. On the far side of the room a group of young girls – younger than me, anyway – wait for the end of the proceedings, with nervous or blank expressions on their faces. A couple of them have bruises and black eyes poorly disguised by make-up.

And then here are our men from the cathedral yesterday, arriving with handshakes and cigars and formal embraces for some of their guests, leaning close for whispered conversations with others, and a nod for the subdued cap who I help into his costume then down the ladder at the back of the building and into the cold, black canal water.

The crowd watches with guarded interest the demonstration of the various facilities of the suit, including – a new one on me, this – the planting of an underwater explosive device, or mine (deactivated and quite safe, we are assured by the cap), on the side of the building. Indeed, the whole performance seems more geared towards war and the offensive possibilities of Captain Clarke B.'s invention than the saving of lives.

At the end of the display there is a stand-off as one of the spectators comes forward to put his boot on the head of the cap as he tries to climb out of the canal, forcing him back under the water. This happens four or five times, to growing laughter from the rest of the audience, and the exasperation of the captain. I look to our sponsor, who, after apparently enjoying the situation for a while, eventually sends his two men to haul the spluttering adventurer out of the water.

There follows a short word between my employer and his creditors, and then a number of private conversations during which the dripping cap is personally presented to select guests, before we are ushered out of the building again, our part played. On the way out, one of the young girls meets my eyes with a desperate expression I have seen before, and to which I have no useful way to respond.

As the captain changes out of his rubber suit in the alley at the side of the warehouse he says, almost to himself, 'It's a shame all right, but what's there to be done?'

I have no idea how to answer him.

The Famous Widow Timmermans

By the turn from spring to summer we have been on the move for over six weeks, and out in the vast reclaimed swampland where the map shows the River Rh— branching a hundred times before reaching the sea, the frogs are singing in their millions, day and night.

We see: canals full of sea-going barges and bigger ships coming in the opposite direction too, carrying endless goods and raw materials and other items of trade and commerce, plus people heading from the countryside to towns and ports and opportunities beyond.

We see: giant drainage projects powered by windmills bigger than any I have come across in England, with miles of new land being slowly raised from the sea, as if ratcheted up from the depths, inch by inch, almost before our eyes.

We see: travelling shows and fairs and markets and political demonstrations, with exotic animals and singing and banners and performances, and swelling camps of itinerant or protesting workers outside every town and city.

And everywhere giant blue skies filled with battleship clouds that remind me of home.

There are worse things, too.

» In A——, an adrift iron-hulled ocean liner slowly smashing its way through a sea lock and towards a row of worker's cottages, five men already having been killed in the accident that originally set the unstoppable ship loose, and no way on earth to prevent further disaster other than to just get out of the way.

» A farmhouse on fire on the edge of W——, and the family of the farmer sitting by the road with all their possessions, including a brass bed, watching the building burn.

» An overturned horse-drawn tram outside S——, the result of a collision with a smaller, faster carriage, with the various passengers still sitting around on the cobblestones or pavement, stunned, with broken arms and bandaged heads, their bags strewn across the road, and the tangled-up horses being shot one by one.

Now and then the captain asks if I am very much affected by this or that sight, but I tell him that injury and death is nothing new to me – and, in truth, I am mostly reminded of mass strandings of whales and dolphins, or jellyfish washed up after a storm. For his part the captain keeps his distance, looking distinctly like he has eaten something that disagrees with him.

And we are on our way to visit the Famous Widow Timmermans.

The southern Dutch, we discover, are a canny, unimpressed people, and as a result we put on fewer shows than expected during our time in their country. When we do perform it's to smaller numbers too, and the lack of business soon starts to put a hole in the cap's financial plans. After a couple of nights going hungry I begin supplementing my market shops with some minor pilfering, and soon become adept at rustling chickens from canal-facing back yards, a practice I keep up until the night

I only narrowly avoid being shot while frantically paddling away from the scene of the crime under the cover of darkness.

Outside the port of R— we attach ourselves for a few days to a circus, which has, in turn, attached itself to a huge ongoing workers' festival, which is occupying a disused polder or drained field surrounded by water on the edge of town, where tents and stages and information tables and stalls offering hot food have been set up, to which we gladly help ourselves, and there are talks on the international plight of the workingman, and rousing songs and poems performed by passionate young men and women, and a collection in support of striking dock workers and their families.

'And what of the plight of those lost at sea?' the cap adds, and draws a small crowd for his own presentations.

It's during one of the captain's afternoon performances that a disturbance breaks out in the camp, 'Likely caused,' so the cap explains later, 'either by anarchists or paid agitators or under-cover detectives, or a combination of all three.' The action takes the initial form of a staged fist fight, which then develops quickly into a mass brawl involving broken wooden staves and thrown bottles and the lighting of fires, at which point the local police, who have been waiting a couple of fields over for exactly this opportunity, come charging onto the polder on horseback, trampling women and children and anyone else who can't get out of their way, into the grass, while failing to do much about the fires which rapidly consume most of the tents on our small man-made island. I almost go under one of the horses myself but am pulled out of the way by a young woman who I recognise from her earlier poetry reading, but before I can thank her, we are separated by the panicking crowd.

There follows a chase across the fields and into the surround-ing streets, and much bloodshed and cracking of heads, not to mention a minor stampede by the escaped circus animals, who include a mangy lion which has been tranquilised with alcohol for the past twenty years and manages to spend five hours enjoying its liberty before being shot dead while trying to break into a nearby pub.

Meanwhile the cap and myself attempt to make our escape from the scene via the network of dykes and drainage canals that divide up the area, paddling low in the water with our gear floating in front of us, and are almost away when we are spotted by a local farmer who gives us up to the authorities, likely for a guilder or two.

And so ensues a night in the local gaol, which I, unable to understand most of what is said to me by the authorities, spend convinced I am to be deported back home, or worse. The cramped and strange conditions are only made bearable by the cheery company of our assumed co-conspirators, who accept the cap and I as fellow members of the international oppressed working classes, and gladly share their bread and water with us. I sit up until dawn rehearsing what I might say at my trial, trying to imagine what I might have done differently, and wondering how I might appeal to the better natures of the judiciary, the legal system, the jury.

It's with some surprise, then, that I find myself being released from captivity first thing in the morning, along with the still half-asleep Captain Clarke B., the two of us being politely led out onto the quiet street where a sporty new carriage is waiting for us with an open door, our possessions already loaded onto the roof.

Seemingly used to this sort of treatment, the cap climbs into the carriage without question, and I follow, to find a well-dressed and spectacularly self-assured middle-aged woman sitting opposite us, in a cloud of the most wonderful perfume I have ever smelled.

'Hello, Bunny,' she says to the captain, before leaning forward to throw her arms around him and kiss him hard on the mouth.

The Famous Widow Timmermans.

How I Learned to Ride a Bicycle

The Famous Widow Timmermans's house – *one* of her houses, there are also properties in France and London and the East Indies – is a beautiful white wooden building in a quiet, leafy town to the south of D—, which we reach after a short journey in the carriage, during which time the captain and our rescuer are barely able to keep out of one another's clothes.

I am left in the extensive kitchen, where the housekeeper sits me at a table laid with meats and cheeses and fruit, and encourages me to eat my fill, which I do happily, while the lovebirds disappear rapidly upstairs. I am still eating an hour or so later when the two of them return, both wearing exotic-looking silk robes and little else, and join me at the table.

'Thank you for your patience,' says the Famous Widow Timmermans to me, spreading jam thickly onto a slice of bread, while I try to avoid staring into the gap in her loose robe. Then, by way of an explanation, she adds, 'My fortune affords me certain freedoms to which I have become very accustomed. It turns out that once you reach a particular level of wealth you can largely do whatever you like.'

'I'm sorry for the loss of your husband,' I say, because I'm not sure how else to respond.

'Don't be,' she replies. 'It was a long time ago. And the business is worth a hundred times what it was when he was running it.'

'And there you have it,' says the cap, apparently continuing an argument that I've not been party to. 'It was exactly your individual vision which created the opportunity to –'

'Don't lecture me on capitalism, Clarke,' says the widow. 'I'm Dutch. We invented it. The *historical situation* created the opportunity, not me. All I did was exploit the turn of events. I'll be very happy to hand everything over to the revolution when the time comes.'

'And what of your freedoms then?' he says.

'*Then* I won't require a fortune in order to be free, in relation to my sex, or who and how I love, or anything else,' she says, and then turns to me. 'Isn't that the whole point, Daniel?'

I look to them both.

'Yes?' I say.

'I like this one,' says the widow, pointing at me with her knife. 'He's smart.'

We spend the rest of that day about town as guests of the Famous Widow Timmermans, including being taken to a couple of department stores where the captain and I are equipped with new boots and clothes, and then out to lunch, and then to a local museum where the widow is sponsoring a new wing and an exhibition of art from the country of Japan, of which we are given an exclusive viewing. Appropriately, there are many paintings of waves.

Everywhere we go, shop assistants and waiting staff and museum curators fall over each other to ensure we have the best service, the best table, the best of their attention. Noting the amounts that have been put on account on our behalf today, I ask the widow how long she has been an investor in the cap's enterprise.

'Ha!' she laughs. 'An investor. Yes, of course.'

In fact, we are briefly given an overview of the widow's business interests when we are joined later in the afternoon by one of her managers, who reports on recent developments on the African continent, concluding with discussion of a possible overseas trip, to which the widow complains, 'This is getting to be a habit.'

That night we dine again at the widow's house, and the talk turns to our future plans, and the looming challenge of the Rh—, and all its dangers, including the Mighty Falls.

'But that's what our journey is all about, eh Dan?' says the cap at one point, raising his glass to me. Being aware that he has never called me 'Dan' before, I take the moment and fold it away, close to my heart. Then the widow puts her hand over the captain's, and it is clear that his attentions are required upstairs again.

I am shown to my own room, which has a shelf by the bed to put my brother's lead soldier on, and a slatted wooden blind on the window, and works of art like those from the museum, and I spend an entirely undisturbed night's sleep for perhaps the first time in my life.

In the morning I get dressed and wander out into the gardens at the back of the house to enjoy the feeling of the wet grass under my bare feet and the sound of birds. I find a new bicycle by the coach house and attempt to learn to ride it, falling off a number of times before the widow herself, freshly up and still in her nightdress and robe, comes out of the house and to my aid, instructing me in how to steer the vehicle and steadying the saddle between my legs with her hand while I gain my balance. A few more circuits of the coach yard and I've got it.

'You're a quick learner,' says the impressed widow, and I agree that I am. She studies me for a while.

'There are no illusions between Clarke and I,' she says.

'I understand,' I say.

'I wonder if you do. I mean that our relationship is a very simple, transactional one. He has a lot of stamina for a man his age, and he knows how to fill my sails. That's all of it. I don't have to trust him, and that works just fine for both of us. With you two, things are more complicated. And I'd advise you to be careful.'

I'd like to say that I take note, at that point, of the widow's words, and so am prepared and ready for everything that is to come later, with my own strategies and plans sketched out in case of disaster, and supplies of hope and energy laid up for when everything else has deserted me. But in truth, moments later I'm riding in circles around the yard again, the warning temporarily forgotten, going faster and faster as my confidence grows, with the wind now in my hair, and the growing feeling that I am invincible.

And so I clatter heedlessly on towards my fabulous future, which is coming whether I see it or not, and which I will be forced to address, either way.

A Race

The day before we are due to move on, the Famous Widow Timmermans takes us on a trip to the beach, which is an hour or so away by carriage, the journey spent mostly discussing politics and business and the Coming Revolution. A couple of times I notice the captain staring out of the window as if his mind is already on the voyage ahead, eager to be on the way.

The small seaside town is orderly and clean, with brightly painted houses behind white picket fences, and horse-drawn trams going about, and well-dressed people promenading up and down along the seafront where the widow buys us all ice-creams and asks me what I think of mine, and of the town too. I tell her that I like it all very well, and comment on the remarkable neatness of it all, and how there's something about the place I can't quite identify.

'There are no poor people,' says the cap, a little too sourly, and the widow gives him a sharp look, but all the same that's exactly it. Still, she doesn't remind him that here we are standing up and walking around in clothes bought for us. And, of course, I don't remind him either.

The beach itself has been arranged with hundreds of high-sided wicker bathing chairs facing out to sea, and also white tents and white-wheeled carriages in which holidaymakers can change into their bathing costumes. Here and there painters have set up easels to capture the remarkable scenes of leisure, and the endless skies above, as if the whole experience has been laid on solely for the pleasure of us favoured few.

It's only when I look a half-mile or so down the beach that I see the fishing boats pulled up onto the sands, and men with nets, and the general, everyday industry of the town, and realise that I know this bitter sea after all, even if I no longer recognise it. I stare at the horizon and try to imagine my brother and what he might be doing somewhere over the curve of the earth, a hundred or a million miles away, and how I might explain any of this to him, and wonder if he's looking back at me and think-ing the same things too.

When the captain and I emerge from the tent in our new striped bathing suits, the widow, who herself has changed into a modest black costume, says, 'Well, look at you two,' and I am suddenly very aware of her gaze, and am not un-proud of the newly muscular shape of my body in the tight woollen suit.

I notice the cap's face darkening for a moment too, before he claps me on the shoulder and announces that we should go for a swim, the two of us, 'Just to that buoy and back, what do you say, my boy? Easy enough for a strong lad like you?'

In fact, it's a manageable enough distance, not more than two hundred yards from the shore, and so I agree, and we're soon in the water, and as we head out, matching each other stroke for stroke, I realise that this is the first time we've swum together. But once we're out past the surf the captain suddenly puts on a burst of speed and I'm forced to push hard in order to keep up, which, in turn, only seems to spur Clarke B. to swim even harder, and I have to double my efforts just to stay abreast of him. I try to meet the cap's eye, in order to ascertain what the game is here, but he has his head down now, only lifting his face clear of the water to draw breath on every third or fourth stroke, his powerful shoulders ploughing through the swell, and I have to do the same or fall behind.

When we get to the buoy, both of us reaching a hand to it at the same time, we are gasping for breath and my muscles are cramping in protest. We tread water, clinging to the swaying ironwork for a few minutes, neither of us saying anything while attempting to recover our energies. I make out the widow on the beach and wonder if she has watched our performance so far.

And then, some unspoken agreement reached between the captain and I, we're off again, heading back towards the shore at a fine lick, and once again I do my damnedest to make sure he won't pull away from me, and it seems we'll have a perfectly matched finish – my youthful energy and enthusiasm equalling the cap's experience and superior will – if we don't both die in the attempt.

In fact, as we near the beach I'm beginning to sense the slightest advantage, despite the pain in my lungs and arms and legs, and I allow myself to wonder if I might not beat my man – which is the exact moment when the cap throws an arm straight out and catches me full in the face, almost breaking my nose and nearly drowning me for good measure.

By the time I have regained my senses, and cleared the blood from my eyes too, and started swimming again, the man himself, who hasn't stopped or even looked back, is almost at the shore. As I stagger from the surf he starts clapping, apparently in earnest, and shouts, 'Bravo!' and declares, 'I was concerned I might have to come back and rescue you!'

The widow, seeing the state of my face, gives me a handkerchief, and I tend to my injuries sullenly, while the triumphant Captain Clarke B., studiedly oblivious, towels himself down.

That evening we go to dinner in the newly built seafront hotel, where we are given the best table in the house, and, bruised and swollen face and all, I enjoy the stares of the other diners as they enviously consider the three of us. I also take a guilty pleasure in the ongoing bickering between the cap and our host, which mainly seems to revolve around the sacredness or otherwise of private property, and the extent to which revolutionary ends might justify their means, and other things I don't understand.

We have just reached the point in the proceedings, apparently regularly played out between the pair when they've had too much to drink, at which the widow accuses the esteemed captain of trying to con her – she, of all people! He, unable as ever to avoid reverting to type! – when we all notice the wild-eyed young man in a shabby coat coming towards our table, shouting in Dutch, and both the cap and I instinctively get to our feet and place ourselves between the stranger and his assumed target.

The widow, unflappable, raises an eyebrow and puts down her fork, and calmly addresses the clearly distressed gentleman in their shared language, keeping him occupied long enough for the hotel management to arrive and manhandle him, by now pathetically resigned, away again.

Then she stands up and bows deeply to the rest of the agog room, swaying slightly, before taking her seat again.

'A misunderstanding,' is all she says to the captain and myself by way of an explanation, and then resumes her argument with the cap.

So I don't mention that I have seen the man twice already that day, had noticed him shadowing us both in the town and at the beach. And I keep my own counsel too, not half an hour later, when, having excused myself to go to the bathroom, I see in passing the widow's driver handing the same man a brown envelope in the hotel lobby.

Late that night I watch the captain and the widow as they sleep off the booze in the carriage on the way back to the widow's house, their heads leaned together in stupor, occasionally lit up by the sliver of a moon racing us as we speed across the dark countryside. Just for a moment I let myself wonder how different my life might have been had these two strange and wonderful characters been my parents, and how they might have felt about me, and who I might have become as a result. And then I think of my brother and bury my feelings about everything else.

It's only when there's a particular flash of light as we pass some inn or other that I realise the widow has her eyes open and has been staring back, watching me in silence with an expression I can't figure, the whole time.

In the morning she is gone on business before we wake, and so we set out for the German border without saying our goodbyes.

ƁORDERS

A letter from my brother, which I pick up at the post office in the German town of W—:

Dear Dan

How is it in Europe? I hope it is fine.

Well our father has been up to his usual tricks, and got himself barred from the inn for fighting, and his eye blackened too. I then paid the price for that, but gave as good as I got too, I reckon.

And Helen Dunning says she loves me, but I think she only has an eye on getting hold of your old locket.

How many languages do they speak over there? Davey Cooper wants me to ask you.

Your brother Will

A letter from me to my brother:

Dear Will

Thank you for your excellent letter! Give my best to Helen Dunning.

I don't know how many languages there are in Europe, but each time we enter a new country we have to learn again the words for things. In Germany the captain is now the Furchtloser Froschmann and we are Leben retten auf See. In Holland we were levens redden op zee and he was the Onverschrokken Kikvorsman. What we may be in other countries I don't yet know, as the cap hasn't filled me in on all the details of our trip.

Tonight we are camped on the banks of the River Rh—, outside the German town of W—. Sleeping out like this is fine when the weather is good, but not so much fun when it isn't, but the cap says we must save our money for when we need it, and so we don't spend much on overnight lodgings if we can at all avoid it. We take turns to stay awake and keep an eye out for bandits, which they have here just the same as back home.

Will, the cap is a remarkable man and I am learning a great deal from him, about science and philosophy and history and other things too. We have seen amazing things and expect to see many more. It is strange to cross borders and see how people live in different ways, and to realise how big the world is, but also how people are just the same.

I miss you and cannot wait until we can travel the world together.
Your brother
Dan

Men of Science and Invention

The Rh— is a filthy river, and we have been on it for more than a week now, slowly making our way upstream. If there is a furnace of European industry, says the cap, then this is it.

Each town we pass is full of yet more factories than the last, and bigger too, the huge buildings climbing up the steep banks of the mighty river, their smoking chimneys like forests of giant trees, only dropping black soot over everything instead of leaves. The waterfronts are a solid wall of boats loading and unloading, and in places the water is thick with strange scums, and also the bloated corpses of cows and pigs floating downstream from the slaughterhouses, and sometimes worse. At D— we pass the scene of a factory explosion, where at least a hundred bodies are laid out on the dock under sacks. Elsewhere there are long queues of the living lined up every morning outside the factory gates, desperate for more of the same dangerous work.

The captain and I sleep in flophouses or on half-sunk abandoned barges, and we wake up every morning covered in a fine yellow dust, and the chemical stink goes on all night and all day. Still, the cap's optimism is undimmed, and we are on our way to the University of C—, where, after years of lobbying, the esteemed Captain Clarke B. has finally been invited to demonstrate his work.

'The finest people, Dan,' he explains proudly. 'Men of science and invention, like ourselves, who will appreciate the work we're doing.'

Happy to be included in the captain's reckoning, I try to ignore the vision of hell that we are passing through, despite the hacking cough I have developed, and my itching skin.

In the event we are almost undone before we've had the chance to present ourselves. The day we are due to arrive at the university there is a weird green haze in the air that only thickens as the morning progresses, and soon enough we can no longer see either bank of the river, and – my eyes and nose streaming – I am forced to tie the widow's handkerchief around my face in order to breathe.

Struggling to pull my oars through the water I discover the entire surface of the river is covered with floating dead fish, and other animals from the river bottom besides. I shout to warn the cap but, being lower in the water, he has already realised the situation and, indeed, is having difficulty keeping his head above the foul sludge. Trying to get lower in the boat myself to escape the choking green air, my vision beginning to blur, I start to wonder if this is how I'm to go out, and how long it might take for the bottom of the canvas boat, and soon after my own body, to be dissolved.

And I realise, too, that we are being carried backwards on the current, the captain hanging on now to the side of my boat, trying to steer us towards where he imagines the bank might be – almost crawling over the tide of fishy death to do it – as I continue to paddle, and both of us on the verge of losing consciousness, until by some miracle we bump against the crumbling wooden dock and are landed.

We lie gasping for breath at the bottom of the steep, muddy riverbank, and, as the fog clears, look up the slope to see the magnificent soaring spires of the university building looming over us.

'The seat of learning!' declares Captain Clarke B. triumphantly, before turning to vomit.

Well, it takes us a good ten minutes to come to our senses, and a further twenty to drag all our gear up that slippery hill, and by the time we reach the top we present a fine, stinking sight to the beautiful young man dressed in a high starched collar and robes who has apparently been waiting there for us, observing our struggle.

'An angel!' I declare, sinking to my knees, still half stupefied from the river fumes.

'Captain Clarke B., I may presume?' says this young man in a thick accent, ignoring me, and the captain stands up and straightens his rubber costume, brushing away a crayfish that has been tenaciously clinging to his hood. He swells out his chest and says, 'None other.'

'We can get someone to help your boy with … that,' says our new friend, pointing at our partially collapsed boat.

'Please don't trouble yourselves,' replies the cap. 'This is my associate Mr Daniel Bones, and he's as strong as he is smart.'

'As you say' – casting his dark Germanic eye over me, apparently not much impressed – 'and so: please follow me.'

The three of us troop off in the direction of the medieval buildings, where we stow the boat with a gatekeeper, and the captain throws a bucket of water over himself to wash the suit down, and we are allowed to enter the university by way of a covered cloister which skirts a beautiful garden filled with cherry trees.

We are led through a series of echoing halls lined with glass cabinets in which are arranged exotic stuffed animals, including brightly coloured birds and crocodiles and monkeys and snakes and others I don't recognise, placed in dioramas representing their natural habitats. In other display cases are the skeletons or reconstructions of giant lizards among strange-looking trees and plants, with painted backdrops showing erupting volcanoes and boiling skies behind them, which the cap stops to admire.

'The Komodo dragons of the South Pacific, if I'm not mistaken,' he says.

Our guide looks at the captain, back to the creatures in the case. 'These beasts have been extinct for millions of years,' he says.

'No,' Captain Clarke B. corrects him, 'it is a common misconception, but they are very much real. I have heard tales of them eating men.'

I note another tank containing lifelike figures of men and women in traditional dress from around the world, including Eskimos of the north, and Africans and Chinese, and, having heard of this sort of thing, I ask if they are made from wax.

'These are genuine specimens, brought back from our scientific expeditions,' says our host, apparently offended. 'Preserved by our experts.'

'These are people?' I say, horrified.

'No. They are *specimens*. Do you have trouble understanding your own language?'

In the circular lecture theatre in which the cap is due to perform he is introduced to more robed academics and I, mostly ignored, unpack pamphlets and maps for the demonstration. The damp, green-tiled room feels like it hasn't seen light in a hundred years. The captain, clearly overjoyed to be in his element, discusses science and philosophy with his peers, and there is much laughter from our hosts, and then it's time for the cap to take the stage and the audience to take their seats above, and for my mentor to talk of his travels and his important work and his continuing requirement for funds.

It's at this point that things start to go wrong.

First there are interruptions, with various professors and students shouting out questions such as who has reviewed the captain's results and what his thoughts are on the works of certain noted philosophers and so on. The cap does his best to gamely deal with all of this, though even I can tell that some of his answers are vague and meandering, and the questions specifically designed to trip him up. Then there are apparent jokes, shouted in German, at the cap's expense, which lead to much laughter and applause. And eventually things come to a head when the crowd begins to chant 'The walrus! Bring out the walrus!'

It takes ten of the university porters to manoeuvre the giant glass tank into the theatre. Inside the tank, which is filled almost to the brim with foul water, an ancient, mangy walrus, clearly near-starved and afflicted by a number of skin diseases, stares out through rheumy, half-blind eyes. It only has one tusk.

For once, Captain Clarke B. seems lost for words. He turns from the animal to the crowd and back, looking for an explanation. The silence, except for the snuffling and wheezing of the poor asthmatic beast, is complete.

Then someone stands up and shouts, 'Into the tank to fight the walrus!' and the rest of the audience take up the chant of 'Fight the walrus! Fight the walrus!'

For a moment I almost think the cap might do it, that he might climb into the tank and attempt to wrestle the wretched creature to death. The two of them, the famous Captain Clarke B. and this ancient, moth-eaten anomaly, face each other and seem to share a moment of recognition.

But eventually the cap says, quietly, broken, 'I can't fight the walrus.'

At which point the animal lets out a tremendous, triumphant fart, sending a cascade of bubbles to the surface of the water and releasing a poisonous stench into the hall, and, as if on cue, the audience begin raining books down on the captain's head.

It's only after we've packed up, defeated, and been escorted back to the gate, that I ask our angelic guide, 'Why?'

He considers me for a moment, coldly, before answering, 'You come here, knowing nothing, and then ask for *money*? You poor little fool.'

And then the cap, having weathered everything else thrown at him today with infinite patience but apparently being pushed over the edge by the insult to *me*, lays out my tormentor on the ground with one beautiful punch, for which act I can't help but stupidly love him.

'Now, if you'll forgive us,' says Captain Clarke B. to his prone victim, 'my associate and I must be on our way.'

And so we are.

What Makes a Man

As if to reward us for our humiliation at the University of C—, next begins the part of our journey that I will describe in my letters to my brother Will as the most idyllic of our trip, as our itinerary takes us finally away from the horrors of the Lower Rh— and into that part of the river called the Rh— Gorge.

Here the great river cuts through steep mountains, to the sides of which cling numerous tumbling vineyards, as well as sheer cliffs topped with magnificent castles. My life up until now having almost exclusively been lived on the horizontal, I am hugely impressed by this new landscape, not least because the entire aspect is reminiscent of the fairy tales we were taught by the vicar's wife back in my school days.

For the first few days on this new part of the river the captain and I try to paddle our way upstream, but find the current so strong as the river rushes through the narrow landscape that we are often in the evening scant few miles further on from where we set out at dawn, and utterly exhausted from the effort too, not to mention having only just avoided being run down on more than one occasion by the giant pleasure boats plying their trade up and down this stretch of the water.

69

It's then that the cap hits upon an idea to change tactics, and strikes a deal one evening in a waterfront bar over many drinks with the much-travelled captain of one of these cruisers, a paddle steamer, to take us a few tens of miles upriver in return for our becoming part of the day's entertainment.

'Both you and the lad?' asks this old sea dog, who is a veteran of sailors' chat after a forty-year career on the waves, and consequently speaks about eight languages.

'We're a pair,' says Captain Clarke B, proudly clapping his hand over mine.

'Aye, but a pair of what?'

And so it's agreed that, in between our already planned appearances at towns along the gorge, there will be shipboard talks and demonstrations from Captain Clarke B. and His Trusted and Capable Assistant, to the groups of eager tourists, punctuating their daily whirl of wine tastings and castle visits and the sampling of local foods, with both thrilling and educational fare.

'For when do we come alive,' as the cap says to me that first balmy night, the two of us smoking cigarettes and cigars up on deck into the small hours, watching the reflections of the lights on the far shore break up on the surface of the dark water, 'if not in front of an audience?'

In truth we end up making good on both ends of this deal, the cap being able to send me around with his well-travelled hat at the end of each of our lectures to further raise funds to aid our important work – 'Help save lives at sea!' I beg them, and so on – and also the man himself winning substantial sums most evenings at the on-board card tables from the aspiring poets and idling English lords and sons and daughters of the landed gentry who make up most of our custom.

And we are not, it seems, above occasionally securing more

70

private donations from travelling rich widows and other women of independent means either.

It's in this manner, hopping from boat to boat so as not to outstay our welcome, that we begin to make our leisurely way south, towards our destination and destiny.

I admit I am thrilled the first time the captain introduces me as his adopted son, impressing a group of prison-reforming Christian ladies on a Cook's tour out of Manchester by explaining how he rescued me from a lifetime of crime, violence and the eventual, inevitable noose, and how my feet have ever since been always on the upward path.

The group briefly become our patrons, and us their guides, leading their daily explorations of the surrounding countryside, the cap or myself attempting to communicate with the locals in an invented approximation of French and German, and making up names for indigenous birds and flowers that we are unable to otherwise identify.

During long afternoon vineyard tours the captain thrills our audience with tales of our trip and the dangers ahead, including the terrible Rh— Falls, where he is due to attempt the first successful trip over the cataract itself – 'not for nothing is this particular geological feature better known as the Widowmaker!' – leading to gasps, shudders, fainting, and so on – and meanwhile I invent stories of my childhood to make my upbringing sound even worse than it has so far been.

I tell of my early years of indentured servitude and horrifying, almost unbelievable abuse at the hands of an East Anglian criminal gang, and of the gunfights with the coastguard, and the string of bank robberies committed across Essex, Suffolk and Norfolk, and my usefulness as a breaking-and-entering man, the famous unsolved murders I may or may not have been involved in, and the cap's wit and bravery in winning my freedom by challenging the monstrous gang leader to a test of Bible knowledge.

As a result, I bring in more contributions to our cause, besides being clasped tightly to a number of stout bosoms, and, between the two of us, it seems the captain and I are becoming a fine double act.

It's at the end of another long night spent taking card-money from another group of eager young rich heirs and heiresses that the cap invites me to join him at the stern of the anchored ship to see in the dawn. Above us the rising sun is starting to touch the clifftops with gold, and geese fly low over the still, quiet waters, and I am struck again by how beautiful this place is.

'What makes a man?' the captain muses, his arms on the rail. Assuming he is about to launch into another discursive speech, I say nothing, until it becomes obvious he is waiting for my reply.

'Achievement?' I suggest. 'Riches? Respect?'

'Intention,' is what the cap says. 'What makes us men is the strength of our desire, Daniel. Our will to do what other men perceive cannot be done. The strength I recognised that first day I saw *you*, as you fought to escape from that criminal gang.'

'But that –'

'That very strength that makes you ready now, I know it, to be trained to wear the suit.'

'The suit?' I say.

'The same,' the cap smiles.

'However … the *suit*?'

'And so it remains,' says Captain Clarke B. 'Do you need to ask me a third time, in order to be convinced?'

'No, sir,' I say, suddenly worried that he will retract his offer.

'Excellent. And in that case: get some sleep. We start tomorrow. Or, in fact, today. And in the meantime I have an appointment with one of those young heiresses.'

And with that he's gone, and I am left at the rail to watch the world coming awake, and to listen to the comings and goings below decks as the day shift starts work in the ship's kitchens, and to contemplate the man I am going to become – as well as to wonder, too, what will happen to the boy I am leaving behind.

The Suit, Then

The first time I try the suit I'm almost consigned to the depths before I've even begun.

It's a glorious morning and a small crowd has gathered to watch my instruction, and I am at the bottom of the river.

There are fish down there, and a greenish light. It's not altogether unpleasant.

'Float, Daniel!' the cap shouts from the ship's deck, where he is holding one end of the rope which is tied under my arms, as he drags me to the surface. 'Let the suit do the work. If you try to swim you will drown.'

We repeat this process a number of times before, having swallowed enough river water to satisfy a whale, my body either surrenders or begins to understand, and allows itself to adapt to the demands of the outfit, and I have it.

Strapped into the suit one proceeds feet first, with the back held straight and ankles locked together ahead by means of a simple stirrup mechanism – which the captain has adapted following my suggestion to include a fitting to secure a raised short sail, when required. Steering and locomotion are achieved by means of the short double paddle, and for the most part one needs to keep one's head lifted to see ahead.

Inside the suit's thick rubber cowl there is an almost complete silence, other than the sound of one's own breathing, and the lapping of the water and paddle. Occasionally I feel a fish or other creature brush against me, or the bump of a rock if I float too close to the shore. The first two or three times that I take the suit out properly I'm happy for the captain to insist that I be secured to the boat with a length of rope tied to my foot, which can be rapidly shortened if I start to drift off course or fall too far behind.

The suit fits me almost perfectly, and I note again how similar my physique has become to the cap's these last couple of months. I lie on my back, watching the clouds above the soaring cliff walls drift across the blue sky, and the birds wheeling high above, who are apparently as interested as I am in trying to work out what type of thing I might be.

With little to do save paddle and occasionally correct my course, I find myself musing on philosophical issues, such as the nature of the soul, and the meaning of the paths of planets and stars, and whether our character is fixed at birth or made by experience – and I start to understand better how and why Captain Clarke B. is the man that he is.

It seems that, wrapped in that strange rubber embrace, one encounters almost an undoing of one's personality, and every vain concern attached to it. My worries, hopes and dreams all seem as if they belong to someone else, and are replaced by what I can best describe as a great feeling of solidarity with the land-scape – a comradeship with every tree and rock and creature in it, with every drop of water and all the rest of nature besides.

I wonder what I have been doing with my life up until now, and how I have managed to waste so much of it.

By the end of that first day I am already happier out on the water than anywhere else. I realise that I could contentedly never return to land, and while I am there I can think only of being back on the water. Having agreed never to take the suit out without his express permission and supervision, I wake each morning and pace the deck until the cap is up. After that he is happy to spend the day sitting in a deckchair at the back of the boat, smoking cigars in the sun and shouting encouraging phrases – 'That's it, boy!' and 'You have it!' and 'Watch that stroke, now!' – as I attempt to keep up.

I practise submarine rolls, and breaching by the use of the paddle to submerge myself, then relying on buoyancy to shoot me almost out of the water, and the negotiation of rapids and fast-moving water, and the launching of flares, and some crowd-pleasing theatrical tricks including pouring drinks and rolling cigarettes while on the water, and I am a fast learner and soon become more than proficient.

The cap starts adding me to his afternoon and early-evening presentations, at which I demonstrate the operation of the suit while he narrates, dressed in formal wear, which we agree brings a more polished and theatrical air to the proceedings, and certainly seems to please our audiences. I also occasionally note, as I daily display myself climbing in and out of the suit, the appreciative gazes being cast on my body by some female members of the crowd, and some male members too.

I am invited to join my mentor and a variety of the other ships' captains for regular late night drinking sessions, and made to feel like a man among men, and listen attentively to their sentimental, teary stories of life on the high seas, and adventures in foreign ports, and loves and limbs lost in wars and other tricky situations. I am made to swear never to pick up arms except in self-defence, to always come to the aid of those in danger at sea, not to use certain unlucky words and phrases aboard any ship, and to start every day with a ration of rum.

And so am I inducted into the noble fraternity of water-going men, and, as the landscape beyond the gorge widens out into endless farmland and forest, I spend these long days mostly as happy as a man can be.

In Which We Are Asked to Fuck Off

Our downfall, when it comes, is swift.

For the last couple of weeks the captain has been spending every evening at the card tables on the ship – 'Think of the difference this money could make to our work, Dan!' – and is often to be found taking bets from the passengers during the day, too, on everything from the time it will take for us to reach a particular bridge or landmark, to whether or not he will be able to successfully guess a married woman's maiden name.

This latter gambit is also the tried and tested opening move in the cap's seduction technique – 'For what woman doesn't want to remember the girl she was before marital responsibility closed down her options?' – and it appears that there is still no shortage of women wishing to recapture their youth in the arms of the accommodating Captain Clarke B., or at least to be provided with a brief distraction from the responsibilities of their daily life. Most of them are willing to pay in some manner for the privilege, too – from which the ship's captain will take ten per cent for his trouble, as per our agreement, to nod and smile and look the other way.

Of course, not all of the captain's clients are unaccompanied, and more than once I end up having to entertain a disenfranchised husband while the cap is giving his wife a personal tour of some ruins, or the romantic windswept ramparts of a fairy-tale castle, or some other more private location, while being told how good it is for her to get out on her own for a while, what with all that she does for others, and her being a veritable saint, and so on.

It's such a husband – possibly a minor English lord, and a military type, whose nervous, highly strung wife Captain Clarke B. has been surreptitiously romancing for a week or so – that the cap has just taken for ten pounds at the end of a very long game, and a very long evening.

'Well played,' says the captain, as he rakes in the cash.

'Oh no,' says the husband, calmly, 'it is you who has played well. And, I think, it is I who have been played. And for quite a while.'

'How about another game?' the cap suggests, very friendly-like. 'So as you might win your money back?'

'And as for the theft of my wife?'

'I think you have me at a disadvantage now,' says the cap.

'Oh, I don't think you've been disadvantaged at all. I'd say you've been doing very well for yourself, by all accounts.'

'Look, if this is about the money –'

'This is about my *wife*, sir!'

And there it is, and there can't be any going back now.

Well, the inevitable result is that the wounded party demands some measure of satisfaction, and, these sorts of things being taken just as seriously here in Germany as they are back in England, before we know what is happening a duel has been arranged for dawn the following morning, and the cap and I are in the cabin with the ship's captain.

'You've overreached yourself this time, Clarke, and no mistake,' the ship's captain is telling us. 'There are rules with these people.'

And here's the cap, whipping the foil back and forth in the confined space to get the weight of it – 'I've not handled one of these in twenty years' – while putting a brave face on things …

'Plus, this doesn't look good for my business,' our host continues. 'I can't have people getting killed in duels for fucking other men's wives on my boat.'

'And if I win?' asks the cap.

'Well that's not exactly an improvement for me, is it, with a dead lord and a grieving widow then on my hands?'

'Ah, but what a woman.'

'That's hardly the point though, is it?' says the irritated ship's captain.

'What do you propose, then?'

'I propose the pair of you fuck off, as quickly as possible. I'll cover for you and hold the boat up for a day or two.'

'And what of *my* reputation?' says the offended cap.

'Well now, I would ponder on that, but presently I seem to have forgotten entirely who you are so would you please *fuck off my boat right now before I throw you off.*'

And surmising that he would, too, we do as he has requested, and fuck off sharpish.

ᏩOREST

At least the river for this part of its length runs through a vast valley, which means a slower current, and so, despite our rude chucking-off from the ship that has lately been our travelling home, we are able to continue upstream the following morning under our own power again, the cap paddling in the suit and I following behind in our little boat once more.

'Well, this is the way it was always supposed to be, eh, Dan?' the cap suggests to me. 'Just you and me and the water below.'

'Yes sir,' I tell him, 'it surely is. And likely just the way you wanted it, all along.'

At this he gives me a look back over his shoulder, unsure whether or not I have taken a sarcastic turn, and if I'm honest I am not entirely clear myself.

'Exactly that!' says the cap, and resumes his paddling with strong, confident strokes, and so we make our way up the river.

And, in fact, with the good summer weather and the gentle meandering of the watercourse, things could altogether be much worse than they are – and will eventually become so whether we like it or not – so we may as well both enjoy this pleasant interlude while we can.

By day we pass through rich farming country, and wave at surprised farmers and milkmaids who watch us from the grassy banks, and at night we camp in low-lying fields and pasture or ancient woodland. We are now on the edge of the famous Black Forest, which, the cap assures me, is a wild land full of boar and bandits, as well as worse things if you want to go looking for them, and so he tells me to keep a sharp eye out. But this pastoral landscape is so calm I find myself doubting that anything could happen to us here.

Which turns out to be a considerable miscalculation, on both counts.

On the day in question, I have woken up in the early hours next to the smouldering white ashes of our campfire, and, discovering an urgent need to piss, have got up and walked some way deeper into the wood in which we have camped, leaving the cap asleep.

I am leaning against a tree in order that nature can take its course, and admiring the soft grey light that fills the dawn wood-land, and the first songs of the birds, when I make out the eyes and shaggy head of the huge tusked beast that is watching me – whether with rage, or curiosity, or hunger I don't know – from the other side of a clearing, and which seems to stand as tall as a man.

I slowly back away from the monstrous pig, silently willing it not to charge at me, but terrified to turn and run in case this somehow activates the instinct to do so in the creature's brain. And I'm still walking slowly backwards when I reach the edge of our camp again, and so I hear the gang of bandits who are holding the now awake captain at gunpoint before I see them.

Still, I have enough smarts about me to stop and conceal myself in the undergrowth before I am spotted, and so watch as the three men, all of them armed with pistols, tie up the confused captain, speaking roughly to him in German, before going through our gear to see what we have that might be worth stealing.

It does occur to me to wonder what I might do if the men decide to kill the cap, and also to entertain the thought of my somehow charging into the camp and mounting a rescue, but as I am unarmed and outnumbered, and a coward besides, I decide against this course of action.

I am also aware that the boar is still roaming about somewhere close by, and don't want to do anything that might attract its attention. And so, trapped between these two threats, I do what I do best, and stay hidden.

It takes the men over an hour to give up waiting for my return, but they eventually do. The sun is coming up, and I suppose bandits, like bats and owls and badgers, prefer not to be caught out and about by day. They take one last look around, and one of them strikes the cap with the butt of his pistol, sending him, still tied up, to the floor, and then they all move off, carrying what they want.

I wait for another ten minutes, and then another five after that, and then burst from the bushes, ready to share with the cap my rehearsed lines about having got lost in the woods, and then having been chased by a giant wild boar that almost gored me to death, while also demonstrating my shock about his situation, and asking what has happened, and where are the bandits now.

When I see the captain's bloody face I am disgusted with myself, although I am aware that there was nothing much I could have done, and that the pair of us being tied up would certainly not have made matters any better, and could have put us in even worse danger, had we been stumbled across by the boar or other animals.

The first thing the cap does when I untie him is complete an inventory of our gear, in order to see what we still have. Thankfully the suit is still ours, as well as the boat, and most of our personal effects.

'And the money?' I ask.

The cap sits down heavily by the remains of the fire.

'It's all gone, Dan.'

We sit there like that for a few minutes, each lost in our thoughts, until eventually I decide that at least one of us should speak, even if there is not much of use to be said.

'Well,' I ask, 'why should the Fearless Frogman be defined by material means, anyhow?'

The captain looks up, sniffs once.

'It's a good point,' he agrees.

'Danger is what motivates him, after all,' I add, 'and the challenge of pitting his will against the elements.'

'True enough,' says the cap.

'Not to mention the importance of saving lives at sea.'

'Indeed there is that, yes.'

'And the scientific possibilities of –'

'All right, Dan, that'll do,' says Captain Clarke B., getting to his feet. 'Let's start packing up what we've still got.'

'Right you are,' I say, and get on with the task, for – thank providence – we still have an appointment with a waterfall, and no choice but to carry on, even if we wanted to give up.

HOLD YOUR HEART, OH WANDERER

And so, eventually, there is the grey morning when we arrive at the border city of B——, where we argue with the border guards in our poor French and the cap's worse German, before paying the appropriate tolls and bribes, and wait as the spiked, thick wooden beam that lies across the river is raised, and we are able to pass into the country of Switzerland.

'The Mighty Helvetic Confederation!' declares the cap, as we enter this new land, the fifth we have now travelled through by my calculation.

But once in it, the landscape quickly takes on a gloomier, more oppressive character – the gorges now threatening, the cliffs casting giant shadows, no longer romantic but dark and unsettling, and the distant mountains now looming with dread. Soon every town we pass is a spa, and every spa is filled with the sick and the lame and the desperate, from the pale sons and daughters of minor aristocratic families to the mountain people themselves, afflicted with goitres and other illnesses, all hoping to find a cure in the mineral waters. In the bars and markets of the towns where we stop to put on shows people mutter in strange languages, and a vague sense of doom seems to cover everything.

Still, I accept every chance I get to take the suit out and practise in the cold, rushing waters, trying to recapture a feeling of accommodation with the landscape.

For his part, the captain maintains a steely calm.

We begin to see flyers advertising the upcoming great event itself in the bars and cafés, with a hand-drawn picture of the captain in his suit, at sea, riding the crest of a giant wave while calmly smoking a cigar, and also a sketch of the falls themselves under the name 'Rheinfall', and more words in French and German and other languages. The flyers are courtesy of the cap's man Mcinerney, who has been travelling ahead of us, his coat likely flapping in the wind all the way, and who we eventually catch up with as agreed at a hotel in P—, where he touches the brim of his bowler hat and looks me up and down, and is clearly more impressed than the last time we met.

While he and the cap talk business, I visit the post office to collect a cache of letters from my brother, which read as follows:

Dear Travelling Dan
How is life on the river? Here is hot, and much the same as ever. I ran away again after accidentally setting fire to Jim Cooper's boat, which was after stealing Jim Cooper's boat, which was no accident. If not for the boat, I would have likely made it but a gang was raised to bring me back so I might pay for the damage and now I am in debt for the rest of my life.
  Send money! (joke)
  Your Will

To my brother Dan
Susan the vicar's daughter is to be sent away! She has been caught doing nothing good with Joseph and Jeremiah Parsons. Joseph and Jeremiah are bereft although they are not the ones being sent away.

She says to say hello and how she remembers your good hands. I do not know what this means.

Your chum, Will

Dear Dan
Giant Pete the innkeeper asks to be remembered to you and Captain Clarke B., as does his wife. I attempted to run away again, taking the pig with me. We had some fine adventures together out in the fens, me and that fellow, and he was good company. Now I am in 'The Dog House'. Also the pig died.

I miss you,
Will

Hello Dan
I am now an apprentice oysterman and it is bad work. I am out from dawn until night six days a week and my hands are a mass of wounds, and stink too. I am allowed to curse as much as I please, however, and drink too, and now I have employment I am considered to be 'A Catch' among the village girls.

How is Europe?
Will

To my Dan
I Am a Wanted Man!
Helen Dunning had a fight with Ada Crook over who would get to marry me and everyone in the village came to watch. Ada Crook now has a broken nose and I am to become a rich man and build Helen Dunning a house and give her six strong boys and girls.

I worry that there are no riches in oysters.
Will
P.S. Did you spot my joke?

To Dan

Well, my arm is broke again, and you can imagine how. I don't know what will happen now. I will try to forbear everything.

I hope the news is better with you, and that I will soon see you again.

Your brother.

In order to recce the location of the Great Stunt, Mcinerney has hired a rowing boat for the three of us, and we approach the falls from downstream. The route is a tortuous one, with numerous bends in the river, and I sit brooding over my brother's letters until we round a last corner, and then there is the terrifying spectacle itself, and everything else is forgotten.

Even through the thick spray, which quickly soaks us to the bone, the power of the falls is horribly apparent, not least in the thunderous noise that echoes off the high walls of the basin in which we sit. Above us the river crashes through a tight gorge, forming a set of awful rapids split in the centre by a gigantic mass of rock. From there the foaming waters cascade over a precipitous edge and into a maelstrom from which, surely, no man could ever come out alive.

In front of the castle that sits atop the cliffs, looking over the river, a single rope has been strung to prevent onlookers throwing themselves as a mass into the waters below during tomorrow's event. I can't imagine that it will be enough. It seems as if the weight of water must be in danger of pulling down the cliffs themselves, and dragging all – the castle, the surrounding trees, the three of us sitting in the rowing boat – away with it.

'Hold your heart, oh wanderer, firmly in mighty hands,' says Mcinerney, taking off his bowler and holding it to his chest, as if in church.

The captain looks at his man, who shrugs, then puts his hat back on.

'What do you make of it, Dan?' asks the cap, and I offer that I am impressed.

'I am not sure how any man could survive it,' I say.

'Not any man, though,' says Captain Clarke B.

I agree that this is true, and then the Cap and Mcinerney share another glance. The cap takes two cigars out of his pocket, trims them both and hands one to me, lighting it for me as I lean forward.

'You, Dan,' he says.

So.

The Falls

At the inn on the far bank of the river, overlooking the roaring waters, the three of us with strong drinks, the following conversation, or near enough, proceeding about as well as you might suspect:

'This is your baptism, Daniel,' says the cap. 'How I envy you! If there were any possibility, I would, of course, prefer to perform the stunt myself. If it weren't for my shoulder injury.'

'You haven't mentioned this injury before,' I reply.

'I didn't want to trouble you. And with all the money invested by our creditors. Not to mention those poor souls lost at sea. They are who I have uppermost in my thoughts. And it's also true that you already have more skills on the water than any man or boy I've known.'

'How many others have there been?'

'Christ, Dan.'

'How many?'

The waitress comes and replaces our empty glasses then, causing us all to fall briefly silent, and avoid each other's glances and hers, until she has gone away again.

'Five,' says Mcinerney, honest at least.

'But they weren't *you*, Dan,' continues our esteemed Captain Clarke B. 'You're the real deal. I'm sure of it.'

'How many of them lived?' I ask the cap's man. There is another pause, and this time not because of the waitress.

'If not for me,' says the captain, 'then consider your brother. If we don't make this stunt, the tour is off. What happens then? Is your father going to take you back?'

I look out of the window at the foaming river below the falls, staring at the churning water, possibly in search of a solution, more likely because I know there is none.

'People have paid to see you,' I say, 'not me.'

'And that's the beauty of it!' Captain Clarke B. tells me. 'In the suit no one will even suspect. And after you've completed the passage you simply proceed around the bend in the river and land out of eyesight, where I'll be waiting to exchange costumes with you.'

'Because we are the same size,' I say, finally catching up.

'It's all thought out,' says Mcinerney.

'It seems it has all been thought out for a long time.'

'I'd advise you not to take that tone,' he says. 'You may find you have fewer options than you think.'

I look to the cap, who opens his hands.

'We are all at the mercy of historical forces,' he says. 'We live in a diminished age.'

'You sound like the Widow Timmermans.'

A short, sharp laugh, then. And for the first time since I've known him, the Captain Clarke B. looks beaten.

'I thought I saw something in you, Dan,' he says, quietly. 'If I was wrong, I blame myself, not you. And I genuinely beg your forgiveness.'

★

91

At dawn the next morning the crowds are already lining the clifftop, and the lower banks of the river besides. Men, women and children of many nationalities, all here to watch me being torn to pieces on the rocks, await the action with some excitement. I am exhausted, having spent the night drinking in the bar of the hotel while trying to gather the courage to run away. Mcinerney is now sticking so close to me that even that option is no longer available, and the two of us watch Captain Clarke B., all dressed up in the suit, shaking hands and signing bills and posing for photographs and being interviewed by the press.

'What's in all of this for you?' I ask my companion, who scratches his face for a moment.

'Don't really know what else I could do, in all honesty,' he says.

We are approached by an English newspaperman to give a representative view from the audience: 'And how do you feel?' I am asked. I reply that I'm finding it very hard to make sense of the whole adventure.

And then it's time to head up to the top of the falls, and some 300 yards beyond, where the cap and I are to make the switch itself under cover of a small wood which skirts the river. I strip off my clothes and hand them over to the captain, who has already removed the rubber outfit. As the two of them help me into the costume, my hands are shaking so much that I am unable to secure any of the straps and buckles.

I hand over a letter to my brother, to be sent only in the event of my death, which the captain takes solemnly, tucking it into his top pocket. Then Mcinerney holds a silver hip flask to my mouth – 'this will help' – and I gulp down something flavoured with herbs and incredibly strong. And so I step out of the wood and wave to the people gathered on the far bank and enter the water.

How can I describe that awful journey?

I could mention the great roaring noise of the falls, how I

remember the sound filling the air even almost to the point of shaking my teeth out of my head – but, in truth, once in the water with the cowl secured, I can hear little other than my own blood pounding in my ears, and more likely *feel* everything else.

I could explain my navigation of the initial rapids, how I use the paddle to take me this way and that, expertly steering between obstacles, submerged and otherwise, with every skill I have learned over the past weeks – whereas I actually remember very little other than feeling utterly at the mercy of gravity and other physical laws.

What I recall most of all is the captain's words about letting the suit do the work, and quickly realising that this is a fight I can never win, and so deciding to stop fighting, and as a result almost nicely riding out the entire length of the rapids, perhaps even feeling briefly that I'm going to survive the whole thing, and come out a hero too. But then there's the looming rock which deals me enough of a glancing blow to send me spinning as I approach the edge itself, and my brother's face somehow before me, and the sensation of his lead soldier pressed against my heart, and then the world suddenly dropping away and everything turning to whiteness.

And a silence that lasts for a very long time.

The Prince and Princess of B—

I wake up with the sun on my face, and it is warm, and I am lying in a wooden bed in a small, stone-walled tower room, lined with books, and from somewhere there is the sound of beautiful music, repeatedly stopping and starting. I realise that I am naked, and wonder if I am dead and this is heaven. I discover that I ache everywhere, and that my right arm is strapped up, and my head bandaged, and I am surprised by the thought that we might carry our injuries with us over to the Other Side.

I struggle out of the bed, finding that I now have a limp to deal with also, and look out of the window and see the day coming up over a huge, misty landscape of farms and forests, which stretches out far below the base of the mountain on which we are perched. Then I wrap the blanket around myself and decide to descend the stone staircase that winds down the centre of the tower in search of clues.

Following the sound of the music, I eventually find myself at the entrance to a great hall, seemingly long disused and in a state of ill repair. Cobwebs cover everything, and here and there are piles of stone, and chests pulled open spilling out fabrics and clothes, and discarded wooden children's toys. Old flags and banners hang from the walls, and through a hole in the roof a single shaft of sunlight reaches the floor, where a deer is drinking from a puddle of water.

The deer and I consider each other for a moment, both likely wondering which of us is the intruder and which has the right to be here, before a movement from the far end of the hall startles the creature, and it dashes away. I'm left with the sight of a young girl, dressed in a white tunic and wearing a silver winged helmet, lowering her bow and arrow, before she too ducks from view and disappears down the echoing corridor in pursuit of her quarry.

Dead, then?

I eventually find the source of the music in another hall, this containing a stage where at least half an orchestra are practising a Very Loud Piece of Music, accompanied by a large, pigtailed singer dressed in the same manner as the mysterious archer.

And here's Captain Clarke B. himself on the sidelines, listening appreciatively to the performance, which is being interrupted, once again, by the cap's companion, a slight, intense man with a moustache and a huge mass of rakishly pomaded hair, who seems determined that everything be repeated in even more expansive a style, and is animatedly explaining this in something that may or may not be German to the orchestra conductor.

Seeing my approach, the captain comes over and, remarkably, embraces me – sincerely, it seems – causing me to wince.

'Broken in two places,' he says, proudly, pointing to my arm. 'How do you feel?'

'I am glad to be alive,' I admit.

'You need to get your strength back,' the captain tells me. 'You were unconscious for almost a week. We thought …' And here there's a pause. 'I do owe you a debt, Dan.'

'But we were successful?'

'It worked perfectly,' he says, sounding almost surprised that we have got away with it, 'all things considered.'

I am about to ask more questions but at this point our pomaded friend notices me, and, forgetting his argument with the conductor, rushes over, exclaiming, 'Our mysterious guest is finally awake!' and also 'Is that one of my blankets?'

'May I present Mr Daniel Bones, Daredevil Assistant,' says the cap to the man and, to me, 'Daniel: this is the Prince of B—, patron and sponsor of the arts and sciences, and our noble host in our hour of greatest need.'

Having never met a prince before, I have just enough sense about me to bow, blanket-wrapped and all.

'Oh, please,' says the prince, 'just call me Otto.'

And before I can answer the band strikes up again.

We spend the rest of that morning, once my clothes have been located, along with a walking stick, and my injuries listed for me – arm, ribs, head, knee, ankle, and so on – being given a tour of the castle by the excitable prince, and I am as surprised as anyone to discover that, being somehow returned from death, and a famous daredevil too, I now mix with royalty, and that we are to be guests here until I am recovered from my injuries.

The prince is proud to tell us that his architects have been working on the construction of his giant folly for more than ten years, prompting me to admit that I had thought the place an ancient ruin, not something new.

'The exact effect!' the prince tells me, as pleased as a child showing off his favourite toy.

We are shown around the zoo, where various animals including apes and wolves are apparently free to roam the castle's cata-combs – 'Enter at your peril!' our guide warns us, delighted – and an indoor maze, and a hall where, through some miracle of stage-craft and magic, it appears to be permanently snowing. We visit a room filled with a giant model of the castle and its surrounding landscape, including the soaring mountains, and the villages that sit on the plain below where farmers and their cattle and other animals are crafted in detail, and it is possible even to look in through the tiny windows of the houses at the intimate scenes of everyday life. In another long hall lined with moth-eaten tapestries showing scenes from the quest for the Holy Grail, we encounter a group of men dressed in the style of medieval knights, apparently drunk, sitting around bonfires made from burning chairs and other furniture. They raise their glasses to us.

'Who are these people?' I ask the cap, quietly, as the prince goes around the men, distributing money and small gifts.

'Actors, mostly,' he replies.

'There was a girl with a bow and arrow,' I say.

'My cousin, the Princess Elisabeth,' says the prince, joining us again. 'I am her guardian, if you can imagine that. She has been with us since' – dropping his voice to a somewhat theatrical whisper here – 'her *illness* began.'

'What illness?'

I learn then that, despite her appearance, the prince's cousin is in fact an adult woman, but that she stopped growing on or around her twelfth birthday, which was either the cause or the consequence of the great sadness from which she now suffers – a deep melancholy which has so far proved incurable, despite treatment from every healer, herbalist and mystic in Europe, and some beyond – 'And as a consequence,' the cap explains, 'can't be married off.'

In fact, that afternoon the young princess herself joins us as we eat in a hall made out to look like a mountain meadow, with grass laid on the floor, and a wooden shepherd's hut, and snowy peaks painted on the walls, and also a girl from the nearby village employed to dress like a shepherdess and keep three sheep, which nose around our feet. The princess makes a show of ignoring us, chewing on a leg of chicken with her eyes fixed on the painted mountain scene, but I notice she and the captain exchanging glances more than once.

Later that evening, unable to sleep, and hunting about the castle for more food, I come across the diminutive Princess Elisabeth again in another of the halls where, despite the mid-summer heat, she is throwing old books into a roaring fire, which sits in a fireplace taller than I am.

'Do you believe a person can make a world in their own image?' she asks, without looking round.

'My friend the captain would say so,' I reply.

'And you?'

'I mostly consider myself a prisoner of circumstance.'

As I say this I wonder if it's still altogether true. But the princess hands me a pile of books, and I join her at her work.

'Although, after all,' she says, 'isn't the mind where we construct our entire reality? What else do we have?'

'Are you speaking from personal experience?'

'Did it hurt?' she asks, ignoring my question. 'When you went over the waterfall?'

'I don't remember,' I say.

'And now?'

'It's not so bad.'

So she throws a book at my broken arm, causing me to yell out in pain.

'Now it hurts, yes,' I say, gritting my teeth.

'And would you say that the pain is entirely in your mind?'

'No.'

'Well there's a lesson in philosophy then,' she says. 'Would you like to see Venus?'

So I follow the tiny royal by various staircases to the top of

98

one of the towers, where a giant brass telescope is set on the battlements – 'My cousin uses it to study the phases of the moon' – and we take turns to peer through the lens at the glory of the heavens, but apparently have already missed the evening star. In the balmy darkness I can feel rather than see the awful weight of the mountain peaks leaning down on us from above. Only their jagged summits are visible as dark silhouettes against the star-filled summer sky.

'He speaks to the dead, you know,' the princess tells me.

'Don't many people have imaginary conversations?' I say, thinking of all the times I wish I could speak to my brother.

'No,' she says. 'The actual dead. He had his favourite uncle dug up and stuffed. He consults with it in one of the libraries. I don't believe he's left this castle in five years.'

'And what about you?' I ask.

But the princess, still on tiptoes to look through the telescope, doesn't answer.

How We Are Lucky to See Such Times

The next day the captain and the Princess Elisabeth and I are required to be up early for the prince's monthly surgery in the great hall, at which our host holds court at a trestle table while various locals, many of whom have been waiting at the castle gates all night, come forward to ask him to facilitate the return of stolen cattle, or solve arguments between neighbours, or cure ailing children, or help with flooded fields and failed crops.

'These people actually expect me to guarantee their harvests,' the prince tells the captain and I, translating, as the latest supplicant waits before the table. 'It's as if they think I'm a god.'

As the cap says nothing, I suggest, 'Is it possible that they're asking for money? In order to buy food?'

'Money, is it, now?' says Prince Otto, exasperated, waving his arm around to indicate the great castle hall itself. 'Don't they see everything that I've built for them?'

When a father and mother bring forward their only son, a skinny boy of 5 or 6 years old with a mangled leg, and the prince turns to us asking, 'You see? What can I do? What can I do?' I think of the value of the golden watch in his pocket which he has been consulting roughly every five minutes since this surgery began, but I say nothing.

After an hour or so the prince declares, 'Enough!' and claps his hands, and the confused villagers are ushered from the hall again, and we are informed that we are to join in a game of hide-and-seek. We are given costumes to wear – Captain Clarke B. the top half of a suit of armour, myself a chainmail pullover, the princess something resembling a giant wedding dress – and are dispatched to find places to conceal ourselves around the castle, the princess shouting over her shoulder, 'This is ridiculous, Otto,' as she departs.

For the next few hours we hunt each other in and out of rooms and up and down staircases and round and about the apparently endless palace. At one point I open a door and find three men in a small room trying to wrestle a live bear into a cage; at another I interrupt a group of actors outside the castle kitchens who are loading mirrors, plates, candelabras and other silverware onto the back of a cart – at my appearance they decide enough is enough and quickly head off down the road with their loot. More than once I catch the distant sight of the captain guiding the princess into some new hiding spot, manoeuvring her behind a heavy set of curtains or through a secret doorway activated by a hidden lever, one of his hands helpfully on her arm or the small of her back, and the two of them always gone before I can catch up.

The prince and I, then, hiding in a cupboard together, our knees pulled up to our chests, the prince excitedly asking me questions such as: 'And was the captain's journey over the falls as terrifying as he describes?'

'My heart was indeed in my mouth,' I say.

'And his triumphant presentation at the University of C—?'

'Unforgettable.'

'And the attack in the Black Forest?'

101

'Exactly as you have heard, more than likely.'

'We are lucky to see such times,' says Prince Otto, 'and to know such a man.'

'As much as anyone can truly know anyone else,' I reply.

Which causes the prince to look at me strangely, before screaming out at the top of his voice, 'Here we are!' to the approaching search party.

Later that afternoon, when the captain is about some business elsewhere in the castle, I am given a tour of the prince's art collection, the princess joining us on our walk-through of the halls full of giant landscapes and statues and portraits of the prince's ancestors and paintings of horses and giant mythological nude figures besides.

'And my cousin is, of course, a great artist in her own right,' says the prince, nodding at the princess.

'Oh,' says the princess, lowering her eyes, and, 'Well.'

So we are shown into a studio which is lined with sketches and photographic prints too, and all of them are studies of naked figures, men and women, posing alone or together or in groups of three or four or more, some with objects, or engaged in various carnal activities with each other, women with men or women with women or men with men, of all shapes and sizes and colours, and in all manner of arrangements, at least a couple of which I don't even entirely understand.

'The princess made all of these,' the prince tells me, proudly.

Somehow it is agreed that I am to model for the princess, what with my excellent bone structure and many interesting injuries too, and a couple of easels are set up and I am ushered onto a raised wooden platform.

'And I should …?' I say, indicating my costume.

'Please,' nods the princess.

'All of it?'

'If you would, yes.'

'Everything?'

She raises an eyebrow impatiently. And so, not wanting to offend my hosts, and not knowing to what extent this is or isn't normal behaviour in this part of the world, I disrobe, and submit myself, naked, to the attentions of the tiny artist.

As I am sketched, the princess hard at work with her charcoal and paper, and apparently not afraid to stare at me as hard as she needs to, I realise I am proud of this new body I've been building for the past few months, the look and the workings and the effectiveness of it, despite its current disrepair. I flex my muscles a couple of times to see what effect it might have, and am pleased to notice parts of the drawing being rubbed out and re-attempted, and wonder what they would make of this back home, and if Susan the vicar's daughter might know what she is missing. I try to read the expression of the Princess Elisabeth, but can make out nothing beyond her furrowed brow, perhaps a slight flush on it, as she concentrates on translating my physique – strong arms, fine legs, good chest and belly and cock and all – onto the paper.

And then the prince, apparently satisfied with the princess's work, or bored of it, declares, 'And now do me! Do me!'

The two of them share a look briefly, and then, with a resigned sigh, and a sharp glance at me as if to say *and this is not even the first time either*, the princess nods to the prince, who is out of his outfit and up on the podium before I've even managed to gather my clothes about me.

As the princess folds her paper over and I get dressed again, I steal a look at her sketch of me, and am proud to see that there's my cock all right, captured in pencil and big as life. Then she starts works on her next picture, and I follow her eyes up to see the prince, naked, hands on his hips, ready to be sketched, with

103

a beaming smile on his face and with his own gigantic cock standing stiffly out at an angle of approximately forty-five degrees, and I quickly finish dressing and leave them to it.

THE APE

'We need to rescue her,' I tell Captain Clarke B., as he is priming and loading the gigantic iron crossbow on the ramparts with another spear-like arrow. This done, he lights the tip, which is coated in tar and rags, and, once the arrow head is aflame, kicks the release to send the flaming projectile flying high over the valley.

'I don't think the prince is a good influence,' I add.

'Interesting,' the captain says, as we watch the arrow fall short of the river, instead landing in a farmer's field where, luckily, there is no one to be hit or incinerated, although it does start a fire which rapidly spreads among the bone-dry wheat, and ends up burning for days.

The cap hands me the next oversized arrow. 'Your turn,' he says.

We've been at the castle for a couple of weeks now, while I have been regaining my strength, and in that time we have become part of the daily life of the place – in as much as there is any regularity to the strange goings-on that surround us.

Among the random events we witness or take part in are hunting parties in which wild animals are released and pursued through halls and corridors, and medieval musical performances, and strange silent oriental plays, and vast banquets, and historically accurate duels, and horse races, and demonstrations by travelling impresarios of water clocks and steam machines and other mechanical devices.

There are competitions of strength, in which men and women from the village wrestle each other for a purse, and prizes for the most beautiful and talented children. There are even lectures and debates featuring visiting experts, which are almost always disrupted – to the cap's considerable entertainment – by the incessant and usually irrelevant questioning from the prince.

And every day the princess requires that I take my clothes off in her studio, so that she can draw me again from a new angle.

She draws me reclining, and standing, and walking around. She draws my broken arm, and my fading bruises, and my weak leg. She draws the scars of cuts on my face. She draws me holding swords and shields and other classical props, or wearing helmets and sandals, or re-enacting biblical scenes. She draws me with stuffed animals, or holding tools, or in front of columns and tapestries and paintings of imagined landscapes. Occasionally, when she requires a group scene, she draws me along with other models, mainly made up of old and young men and women from the village, who are paid for their time, and stand around staring in wonder at the expensive draperies, and then are dismissed immediately once the princess is done with them.

The only constant is that, hats and footwear aside, I am always required to be captured in the nude.

When I, jokingly but not entirely jokingly, ask her how it is acceptable that she is in a position to constantly see me, and indeed her other subjects, naked, but that we are not allowed to have things the other way round, she responds with laughter.

'Do you know what a muse is, Dan?' she asks.

I reply that I don't.

'Well that's what you are,' she tells me, 'all the same.'

I wonder if I am falling in love with the tiny Princess Elisabeth, and she with me.

'Well she is a woman, after all,' says the captain. 'Despite appearances.'

'Exactly,' I say. 'Everything is there, just in miniature. At least that's what I assume to be the case.'

'Indeed,' says the cap, stroking his chin and thinking on the subject.

One afternoon an ape escapes from the catacombs and kidnaps a child who is visiting the castle as part of a group up from the village, and we are required to split into armed search parties to track down the beast and its hostage. Apparently this is not the first time that this has happened.

Eventually we corner the ancient, grey-haired creature on one of the battlements, where it is clinging on to the terrified child, and howling almost like a grieving human at the possibility that it may have to give up its prize. Concerned that the child may be thrown to its death, the prince gently speaks to the animal as he would an old friend, telling her that it is time to put the child down and finish this game.

'She has always had a love for children, this monkey,' the princess whispers to the cap and I, as we watch the negotiations between the prince and the hairy kidnapper. 'The prince has known her since he was a boy.'

Nevertheless, when the ape finally loosens her grip on the child and sadly, almost shamefully, holds it out to be taken from her arms, the princess quickly steps forward, raising her rifle and shooting the monster in the head, killing it instantly.

As the traumatised child is ushered away, the prince throws himself on his dead friend's massive furry chest and weeps inconsolably.

'You can never be too careful,' the princess tells the shocked cap and I, before handing me the gun and heading back down the stairs.

'Well,' says the admiring captain, as we watch her go. 'A formidable woman, that is.'

And I can only agree.

Of Narcissistic Disorders

It is a few days before we plan to be ready to leave, and I am making good progress in my recovery.

Every morning I make my rounds of the castle corridors and ramparts, building up the strength in my leg, and I am no longer walking with a cane. My arm, while still weak, is now out of its sling, and my other cuts and bruises are all healed, although I still have slight double vision at the corner of my left eye, which I will end up carrying for the rest of my life as a reminder of the falls.

The Princess Elisabeth now has an entire portfolio of sketches and paintings of me, and I have even posed for a number of photographic exposures, during which experience I am required to hold a perfectly still pose for minutes at a time while the princess busies herself under the blanket that covers the back of the giant wooden camera, capturing my naked form in the form of chemicals on glass.

I wonder aloud how the subjects of some of the princess's more shocking photographs managed to maintain their poses for the length of time required, surmising that some of them must have had very strong legs, at least.

The princess laughs and replies, 'Perhaps you would like to join the next group session?'

I bashfully decline, but think how willing and happy I would be to hold one of those poses if the princess were involved in it too, and for as long as she required of me.

Towards the end of the afternoon, clouds begin to build across the plain below the castle, and by the early evening the air is so thick that we move up onto the ramparts to try to escape the heat below. The prince orders his orchestra to be brought up to play for us while we eat, and their performance is rendered all the more impressive by the view of the horrible mountains behind us, and the sight of lightning starting to dance along the distant horizon.

At least the rain, when it eventually comes, will put out the fires which have been raging across the wheat fields for the last few days.

Our host and the captain discuss our likely itinerary for the rest of the tour, and the prince's investment in it. There is talk of Italy, and the Adriatic, and Various Planned Exploits, and the minor royals and other distant relatives of the prince who we might look up or call upon for favours.

I notice the princess picking at her food gloomily, and so ask her when and if she might be able to help the rest of us spot the rising of Venus this evening, and for my efforts am rewarded with a withering look.

When three members of the brass section are struck by lightning, it is decided that we should descend below again.

An hour or so later I am lying awake in bed, having left the cap and his patron to their game of drunken indoor golf, when the Princess Elisabeth appears at the door of my room, wearing a nightdress and clearly agitated. The storm has finally broken and rain is roaring down from the heavens. With each crack of thunder echoing back off the sides of the mountains and lighting up the valley below, I am reminded of the Bible story about the Day of Judgement.

Without stopping to explain, the princess invites herself to join me in the bed, then pulls the blankets up to her neck. As I'm not entirely sure what it is that I'm expected to say or do in response, I decide that the best course of action is not to say or do anything at all, and so we both lie there in the dark, side by side, listening to the storm.

'You could come with us,' is what I say, eventually. I have a vision of the three of us, travelling together. A real, live, miniature princess in our show! And what would they make of that back home? I wonder how it would all work, and who would play what role, and what it would mean.

'What makes you think I would want to do that?' she says, in the dark.

'Don't you want to be rescued?'

'I like it here,' says she. 'Look at everything I have.'

'But I'm in love with you,' I say then, because I suddenly feel I can't not say it any longer.

'Oh, Daniel,' she says, sounding disappointed. Then she raises herself on an elbow.

'Trust me,' she says, 'you are not.'

'How do you know?' I ask her.

'Because I am used to it,' she answers. 'You're just fixated as a consequence of my condition. It isn't the first time. Even the prince was obsessed with me when he first bought me.'

'The prince *bought* you?'

'Did you believe I was a real princess?'

I admit that I did, and she laughs.

'My family lives in the village, Dan. Until I was ten years old I lived an almost normal life. Then the prince heard about my condition. I think he hoped I would become one of his pets. But I was too smart for that.'

'So you aren't waiting to be married off?'

111

'I should say not. Good God. And rot in a series of society drawing rooms? No, thank you. Here I have both the freedom to pursue my art and the excuse for being left alone to get on with it.'

'But then the prince and yourself ...'

'He is of a narcissistic disorder.'

'What does that mean?'

'Thankfully, he can love only himself.'

'He and the cap have a lot in common,' I say.

'Indeed they do, in some things,' says she. 'But not all.'

I look at her in the dark.

'What does that mean?'

'The storm is passing,' she says, getting out of bed. 'I should go. Thank you for the company, Dan. And for sitting for me. You were a very fine subject.'

She leans over and kisses me on the forehead.

'It was my pleasure,' I say, quietly, as I feel my heart breaking into dust, and I'm sure it will never be able to love anything ever again.

Loot

It's still half dark when I'm woken by the captain's hand on my mouth. Putting a finger to his lips he motions for me to get up and get dressed.

'What has happened?' I ask him, but he shakes his head to quieten me. He waits until I'm done, which still takes some time on account of my arm, and then I follow him down the stairs. Neither of us makes a sound.

Outside the castle, in the blue half-light, I see the horse and cart, already loaded with our gear, plus an assortment of candlesticks, and plates, and one or two small jewellery chests, and even a couple of paintings. There's a chill on the wind as the cap pulls and secures a tarpaulin over the haul.

'What are we doing?' I ask.

'Get in the cart, Daniel,' says the captain.

It suddenly seems very important that I stand my ground.

'What are we doing?' I repeat.

Captain Clarke B. leans in very close to me, his face against mine, and he says, very quietly, 'Get in the cart. I won't ask you again.'

And so I get in the cart, and the captain does the same, and we make our way down the mountain road as the birds in the surrounding forest begin to noisily welcome the new day.

For the first hour of our clandestine journey I keep looking over my shoulder, expecting to see a light in one of the castle windows, or a rider on a charging horse in thunderous pursuit, or alarms being sounded from the battlements. Finally, when I realise that no one is going to follow us, I say: 'I asked her to come with us.'

'I know,' says the cap. 'She told me.'

'She was too good for you,' I say, and the captain laughs, darkly.

'Everyone is too good for me, Dan,' he says – and then, turning to me – 'and she was no better than anyone else.'

'They could still arrest us with all this at the border,' I say.

'It's 188—, Dan! They don't arrest people at the border any more. Anyway, he won't even notice any of this is missing. He would likely have given it all to us if I had asked him. He's my friend.'

'So why didn't you ask him?'

He doesn't say anything to that. And, when we come to the crossroads at the bottom of the mountain, he pulls a canvas bag from the back of the cart and hands it to me. Inside are a couple of peasant's smocks.

'Put that on,' he says, and I do as I am requested.

'I was in love with her,' I tell him.

'No you weren't,' he says.

'Why does everyone keep saying that?'

'Because you're too young to know what it means. And besides, she was too old for you.'

'But not too young for you?'

'I didn't do anything that I wasn't invited to do, Dan. You might ponder that.'

'Would the prince have seen it that way?'

'The princess is not the prince's property. Nor yours, despite the claim on her that you seem to think being in love gives you.'

'Well aren't you the hero then,' I say, and after that we ride on in silence for most of the rest of the day.

The journey to Lake C— takes the better part of the next three days, and we keep our heads down for most of the way, sleeping like fugitives in haystacks and hedgerows, tying up the horse and cart well away from the road every night. In the back of the cart our equipment and the stolen booty is hidden under the tarp, but at a couple of villages, once we're far enough away from the castle that it's safe to do so, the cap pulls back the covers outside bars and inns to allow potential buyers to examine the odd piece.

At night, by the light of our campfire, I write a letter to my brother, telling him, in truth, that I don't know exactly what is to come next, but assuring him that I have plans to fix both of our situations, and hoping he can find the strength to hang on. I don't tell him about the falls, or about the princess, but I do demand, and receive from the guilty-looking captain, a couple of small banknotes, which I include with the letter when I post it at the first large town we come to.

It occurs to me, watching Captain Clarke B. out of the corner of my eye, how diminished he seems sitting by a fire in his farm-worker's shirt, sucking the meat from a rabbit's roasted leg, and I wonder again how much of what we are is purely a result of the person we decide to present to the world. But I know, too, that he still represents the best chance I have of making a life for myself and my brother, and that I am in it until the end, for better or worse.

So we continue on, mostly in silence, until we finally arrive at the resort town of L—, where we remove our travelling disguises and check in to the finest hotel in town, which has been booked

115

for us in advance and where, at least, we are able to clean ourselves up and spend the night in good beds. The cap makes arrangements by various associates to offload the rest of the stolen loot, and we begin preparations for the next part of our adventure.

A Week of Water-powered Wonders

The next morning the captain and I eat breakfast in the hotel restaurant, which looks out across an expanse of lawn and oriental gardens reaching down to the lakeside, and a long narrow dock, and then across the lake itself to the mountains some five miles or so away on the other side, and all in all the view would probably be wonderful if I weren't so depressed.

Out on the water, huge boats are already going this way and that in the morning sun, and there are floating islands constructed from pontoons supporting tall diving boards and giant arches and signs and posters in at least five languages, all promoting the 'Week of Water-powered Wonders' to which the resort has been given over, and including advertisements for Night-time Lake Tours and Spectacular Fireworks Displays and other adventures aimed at people less appalled at life than myself.

My mood isn't improved when the cap offers a chair at our breakfast table to a Very Tall Young Woman who is apparently unable to find a free seat elsewhere. She thanks the captain and joins us, and we discover that this is Miss Edith Williams, currently travelling from England.

117

'And we are enchanted,' says Captain Clarke B., toasting her with his coffee cup, then pouring one for her.

'And who are you?' says Very Tall Edith Williams, to me. ·

I let the cap make the usual introductions.

'Well that's a fine title, isn't it?' Edith Williams says. 'And how is the daredevil-assisting business, Daniel Bones?'

'It has treated me better, all things considered.'

The captain explains to Edith Williams how we are in town *for the shows*, and briefly regales her with a few choice tales of our adventures, and asks after her plans, and I can see his canny mind at work as we have both already taken in the expensive ensemble of her dress and personality, not to mention her responsiveness to the cap's flirtations, despite the fact that she's likely much nearer my age than his.

'And how do you come to be travelling alone?' I interrupt, sourly.

She leans forward, conspiratorially, glances around the room, then 'I'm a newspaper journalist,' she whispers.

Then she sits back again, smiling proudly, her hand on her chest, as if she can't believe it either. 'I am travelling around Europe in order to take the temperature of the continent, during this time of potential great change,' she announces.

'A noble calling,' says Captain Clarke B.

'Isn't it?'

I notice that even Edith Williams's hair is gigantic. It's as if everything about her has been cast to a slightly bigger scale than the rest of the world.

The cap and she discuss the workings of the London press, and throw a few names that neither recognises at each other, and it's agreed that they'll line up an exclusive interview to be conducted in the next couple of days. They both nod and wink and mug to each other so much at the word 'exclusive' that I almost throw up my breakfast there and then, right on the table, before our guest thankfully, finally, takes her leave of us, with a promise to see us again very soon.

'Well,' says the captain, clearly satisfied with that bit of business.

But then here's our old suited and overcoated friends, the captain's creditors from the demonstration back in G—, a thousand miles or so ago, and apparently the reason we are here in town today, suddenly appearing by our table, all big smiles and expensive cigars.

'Well look at this. If it isn't the prodigal son. Sons, even.'

The cap puts his napkin over his plate and stands up, resigned. He nods at me.

'Take the day off, Dan?' I ask.

'Take the day off, Dan,' says Captain Clarke B.

And so I am left to my own devices.

In the event, it's not even an hour later that I meet the same Edith Williams again, having decided to explore the town on my own, but failing to get more than 500 yards from the hotel before I come across her under some manner of palm tree, leaning against a railing with her back to the beautiful blue lake, still tall, smoking a cigarette, as if this sort of thing happens to her all the time.

'Oh, hello,' she says, nonchalantly.

I nod at her, not intending to stop.

'We met this morning,' she adds, as I pass.

'Please,' I say, just about as politely as I can manage, 'leave me alone.'

'Actually,' she says, putting out her cigarette and hurrying to catch me up, 'I could use your help.'

I keep walking, though with no real sense of where I'm heading in such a hurry, as she explains, at length, how she

119

requires – and who would have thought, in this day and age? – a chaperone, of all things, in order to be allowed to ride on the town's aerial cableway, the first of its kind in the world, which climbs up to the top of the row of hills that line this side of the lake and allows a spectacular view – 'Although, apparently, not one that is to be enjoyed by *unaccompanied young women*, on account of the dangers of altitude or enclosed spaces or something else equally horrifying and ridiculous. But if an accommodating male friend were to pose as, say, a cousin or other relative ...'

'I'm sorry for your inconvenience,' I say, 'but as you can see I have an appointment ...' I wave my hand vaguely, in the hope that she'll fill something in herself.

But then, 'I can pay,' says our Edith, and there it is.

'How much?' I ask.

'Well,' says Edith Williams, in all her tall glory, 'what's the going rate for a daredevil assistant these days, anyway?'

So we buy our tickets and climb into the small cabin, which is then hoisted from the ground by means of a long cable, and carries us up the side of the hill, swaying somewhat alarmingly on the way. The view from the summit is as good as they say, as the pair of us stand looking down on the lake and all the towns along its twenty-mile length, and the great activity of boats on the water which seems to be taking up half the country, and my mood is lifted despite myself, and the money Miss Edith Williams gives me doesn't do any harm either.

'I'd like to make it clear that I'm not in the habit of this sort of thing,' she tells me, as she counts the notes into my hand, the wind ruffling her gigantic hair.

'Of course,' I say, stuffing the cash inside my shirt.

'But I should also mention that there's more where that came from,' she adds. 'And that I'm planning on visiting the lighthouse, the town museum, the public library and a number of other sites of interest before the day is out.'

'In which case,' I say, because I have finally decided, here and now, to Take Control of My Destiny, 'I am at your service.'

'That, Daniel Bones,' says Edith Williams, 'is exactly what I had hoped.'

THE ENDLESSLY TALKATIVE EDITH WILLIAMS

'Mud cures,' Edith Williams tells me, as we sit at a table outside a café on a steep cobbled street overlooking a section of the lake. On the water, Captain Clarke B. is bravely taking part in a miniature naval battle, being fired on by the canons of tiny steam-powered battleships and cruisers, while struggling to bat away the stinging projectiles with his oar, to assorted light-hearted cheers and mild applause which reaches us even up here in the high part of the town.

'Salt cures. Clay cures. Seawater and seaweed cures. Electrical cures.'

'Electrical cures?' I ask.

'You lie in a bath. They run an electrical current through it. Very popular treatment for the headstrong young daughters of very rich men, needing to be cured of their wilfulness. It doesn't work, but it is fun trying. Almost as much fun as the vibrational therapy.'

Drinking my coffee, listening to Edith Williams – the endlessly talkative Edith Williams, the frequently looming Edith Williams – I feel I am having The Most Sophisticated Day of My Entire Life (and I, remember, have spent time with princes and princesses).

'You seem to know a lot about it,' I say.

'I've done my research, Daniel. I have an audience of very eager and interested young women.'

'You and the captain both.'

'He does have quite a following, doesn't he?'

I recognise the sharp knife of jealousy poking me in my side.

'He's not everything he seems,' I reply.

'Are any of us?' She fixes me with a smart look. 'Are you, Dan?'

'I'm not sure who I am,' I say, being honest there, at least. 'Or what we're doing here.'

Edith Williams lights her one thousandth cigarette of the day.

'Well I'd say you're mostly helping out a bunch of gun-runners at the moment' – and then, reacting to my expression – 'Come on, now. The miniature submarines? The "Amazing Torpedo Craft"? The Fearless Frogman outfit? This is the biggest armament fair in Europe.'

'But there's no war on.'

'There's always a war on. There always will be until we can find a better way for businesses to make money.'

And then the black-coated man at the table next to ours – and I'm starting to wonder, where do they all get these coats? – lowers his newspaper.

'You are assuming, of course, that the people will be able to wait while you all make up your minds,' he tells us. 'And also that they will choose to do so.'

Then he gets up, tips his hat and leaves to join another man who is waiting for him by the street corner.

'I didn't know the anarchists were having a convention, too,' shouts Edith after him.

And just for a moment, before they leave, the second man meets my eyes, as if trying and failing to place me.

123

But I place him straight away.

That evening I head back to the hotel to wash my face and rearrange my hair because I have agreed to meet Edith Williams in the oriental gardens in order to watch the Spectacular Fireworks Display together. In the corridor outside our room I find the cap being marched away between the leaning shoulders of a couple of his thuggish friends, and can see through the open door that the room has been turned upside down, and despite my disgust with him I ask what's occurred here and attempt to plant myself between the group and the lift.

'There's no need to involve yourself in this, Dan,' says the cap, as casually as he is able, attempting to straighten his clothes while still trapped between his assailants, who have stopped to consider me and work out whether or not I'm a threat. And so there is a stand-off, of sorts.

'Dan …' says Captain Clarke B. 'Please.'

Unsure whether the captain is trying to protect me, or to avoid being humiliated any further in front of me, I move aside, and the trio carry on down the corridor. I watch until they get in the lift, the cap casting me the briefest of unreadable glances as he disappears from view, and then I continue with my plans for the night.

It is a beautiful, sweet-smelling evening out in the gardens, and because I am early I spend some time smoking a cigarette among the rhododendrons and azaleas and Japanese maples, which are described by helpful plaques. Along the wooden dock people are already queuing for the night-time lake tour, and others are gathering to watch the fireworks from the lawn, with picnic baskets and blankets. Looking across the gardens I am surprised to see the very tall figure of Edith Williams climbing out of one of the hotel's second-floor windows, big dress and all. I watch as she carefully drops to the ground, landing safely in some bushes, then wait until she looks about her, finally spotting me, hiding half in and half out of a hedge, and comes over.

'Why were you climbing out of the window?' I ask.

'Why are you hiding in a hedge?' she says, and it's a fair point. 'But look at this,' she continues, producing a bottle and a couple of glasses that she has somehow concealed about her.

So we sit down under the darkening purple sky and ready ourselves for the show, and Edith Williams leans over and kisses me, and it's a fine old kiss but I still say, 'Ahem,' and hold out my hand.

'Oh, you monster,' says Edith. Nevertheless, she counts another collection of notes into my hand, which I put away into my pocket.

'And now may I?'

I nod, and she takes a giant swig from the bottle, then hands it to me, and I haven't even swallowed before her hands are at their wonderful work about my clothes, and soon she is pushing me backward to the ground and we are both laughing, and by the time the bottle is finished, and the spectacular fireworks too, their echoes booming back at us from across the lake where the oversubscribed paddle steamer *Juliana* has just set off from the dock, I have been marvellously deflowered by Edith Williams among the azaleas, and picked up a few useful tricks besides.

We are happily lying on our backs in the grass, sharing a cigarette and counting the stars, as well as discussing the possibility of a discount being offered for a second go, when the flash from the explosion on board the tour boat lights up the sky and causes us both to sit up suddenly, just in time to feel the heat from the shockwave as it reaches the shore.

WHAT I KNOW I HAVE TO DO

The face that hangs before my eyes, as Edith Williams and I run back, half dressed, towards the hotel, the blazing *Juliana* lit up like Christmas and sinking into the darkness of the lake behind us, is that of the man who tried to threaten the Widow Timmermans in S—. The same man who was paid by the widow's driver later that night. The same man who failed to recognise me outside the café earlier today. The same man who, I'm sure, I saw in the queue for the lake tour earlier in the evening, overcoat and stuffed leather briefcase and all.

In the hotel bar, where there is general panic and people are running around in the confusion, and there are calls for boats to be launched for a rescue operation, and numerous stories being shouted about what may or may not have happened, and more questions than anyone yet has answers to, I find Captain Clarke B., sourly drunk and sitting at the bar, his face bruised and bloodied from his meeting with his creditors, oblivious to everything.

'The suit,' I tell him, breathlessly. 'The passengers. A sinking boat on the lake. A rescue operation.'

The captain turns to look at me, attempting to focus. Takes in the flushed sight of both myself and Edith Williams. Tries to work out what has gone on, and how it might affect him.

'Lives are in danger at sea!' I declare, hoping to cut through the fog of his injuries and alcohol.

And the cap curls his lip in disgust.

'Tell them to send out one of those miniature battleships,' he says, 'see how they like it.'

As he tries to turn back to his drink, I grab him by the front of his shirt and pull him to his feet, not sure what my plan is but suddenly possessed by a fury I've been running away from for a very long time. The captain seems to recognise it in me too, is briefly caught between being outraged and concerned, but decides in his drunken state to go with the former, and gets one of his arms clear enough to slap me hard across the face.

This stuns me enough that I step away from him, causing the cap to stumble forward, his attempted follow-up punch missing me completely and the momentum sending the man himself sprawling to the floor.

And that's where, having briefly considered all the other possible courses of action, I leave him, and head for our room, and the suit, and what I know I have to do.

By the time I reach the first of the survivors, some quarter of a mile offshore, a couple of small pleasure boats are already trying to work their way through the flaming wreckage on the surface, their crew members shouting out names and prodding at floating debris and bodies with long fishing gaffs. The steamer itself is almost completely submerged, with only the prow still visible, where five or six men and women are just about managing to hang on, half in and half out of the burning water.

And then all around me in the flickering dark I start to hear cries of 'Help us!' and 'Over here!' and 'Dear God!'

Paddling my way as close as I can get to the flames, I spot a young boy and girl being held by a badly burned man who is barely keeping all three of them afloat by means of a broken

127

length of wood. He's too far gone to do anything but hand the children over to me before he slips under the water himself, but I manage to get the two of them under my oar, and then carefully propel us all to the nearest rescue boat, shouting out 'Ho!' and 'Look now!' and bundling them aboard, where they are given blankets and hot drinks, as I set off back towards the horror again.

Next there are two young women, half delirious, sharing a leather life-preserver, then four more children, who have been tied to a broken-off section of wooden hull by some smart, doomed soul, now nowhere to be seen, and then more, and more besides, all of whom I deliver to the arriving rescue craft – some struggling, others having already accepted their fate; some horribly injured, others suffering nothing more than shock. It's true that I watch far more die than I can save, some of them in my arms, and that the margins between who is chosen to live and who to die seem impossibly thin and entirely arbitrary.

Thankfully within a couple of hours the waters are full of boats, and besides there's no one left alive to be rescued by then, and only the floating bodies to be counted, and those gone under the water to be accounted for, and I am helped into a small sailing boat and given brandy by the skipper. I try to ask him how many have been rescued and how many lost, but am unable to make myself understood. Instead, the man just claps me on the shoulder repeatedly, shaking his head and smiling and also wiping away tears.

As we sail back towards the shore, the sky coming light now by degrees, I find a couple of the cap's cigars in the waterproof inside pocket of the suit and, offering one to the skipper, light up the other. Looking behind us I can see the gathered ships and the few flames still burning on the surface of the water, and already as the last remaining survivors are ferried to dry land bodies are starting to be dragged from the water and laid on decks.

It's only then I wonder what became of Edith Williams when she disappeared from the bar.

AN AGREEMENT

Captain Clarke B. is fast asleep, passed out face down and snoring among the wreckage of our hotel room when I return, so I strip off the oily, soot-stained suit and leave it by his prone body and go out again walking for a few hours, and watch the town wake up to the aftermath of disaster.

A company of soldiers from the town barracks are already drilling in bright blue uniforms in the town square, though it is not clear what use their canons might be against further bombs. Along the lakefront, sailors and other rescue workers sit drinking spirits outside cafés that have opened early, or never closed, in order to serve them. At the small hospital, off-duty doctors and nurses are arriving to help with the injured, and carts carrying bodies are lined up along the road. I stop counting the shapes under the white sheets when I reach one hundred.

The smell of smoke is everywhere.

When I eventually return to the hotel late in the morning I don't know what to do with myself, and so I go to sit in the empty restaurant and order a coffee. Out on the water the clean-up operation is still ongoing, with a large gaggle of boats crowded around the spot where the steamer went down.

Hundreds of people watch from the gardens and the dock, all other entertainments for the day having been cancelled.

After a few minutes I see the tall figure of Edith Williams, dressed in her outdoor coat, enter the restaurant, and I wave to her. Just for a second, a look of surprise – almost panic – flashes across her face, but then is gone by the time she sits down opposite me.

'You're down late,' she says, sliding the paper she is carrying towards me.

The front-page headline, face up, reads '*Anarchistische Gräueltat*'.

'It was a long night,' I reply.

'Clearly. It says here that the brave Captain Clarke B., "Famed Fearless Frogman", currently on a tour of Europe, saved over twenty-five people.'

'He must be very pleased with himself. Wherever he is.'

'At the moment he's out front giving an announcement to the world's press.'

I feel my shoulders sag.

'It's what he does best,' I say.

Edith Williams considers my face for a moment, and her expression is unreadable.

'Daniel, I –'

And then a middle-aged, rich-looking couple – the man in possession of a giant set of moustaches, the woman, as tall as her husband, with huge hair, both dressed for travel, and probably that's their vast collection of luggage being carried by porters through the lobby right now, amid much noise and management – approach our table. Seeing them, Edith gets up.

I stand too, and am introduced to Mr and Mrs Herbert Williams of Leicester, currently travelling throughout Europe with their daughters, Edith and Aster – 18-year-old Edith I've already met, obviously, and look, here's 12-year-old Aster herself, arriving late as always, narrowing her eyes at her older sister, wondering what she's up to *this time* …

'And this is Daniel Bones,' says Edith, carefully avoiding meeting my eyes. 'Daredevil assistant to the famous Captain Clarke B.'

'Then we have been sharing a hotel with celebrity,' says Big Herbert Williams with a smile, shaking my hand. 'And how is the daredevil-assisting business, Daniel Bones?'

'I still have a lot to learn, it seems,' I reply.

'Terrible story about that boat.'

'Yes, sir.'

'Still, we can thank God for men like the captain.'

'That we can,' I say. And so on.

After a couple of minutes of this it's time for the Williams family to be going, and there are further handshakes, and as she grips my hand Edith leans forward and grazes my cheek with her mouth and says, 'Don't think badly of me,' and I realise that I don't, and not just because of the money. And then their party departs, and Tall Edith Williams, inventor of herself, is gone out of my life as quickly as her heroically long legs delivered her into it, and I'm left alone again.

I sit back down to finish off my coffee, and try to make sense of the dense text of the thin newspaper that Edith Williams left behind, but I can't understand any of it. So I decide instead just to wait for the inevitable, which presently arrives in the shape of the heroic Captain Clarke B. himself, who comes striding through the lobby and into the restaurant wearing, surely not, *the actual suit?* But there it is, still burned and battered, and he's even holding the oar too, his bruised face helpfully adding to his heroic look, as he answers more questions from the reporters and local dignitaries and hangers-on who are surrounding him as he walks.

'And I promise you all this,' the cap is declaring. 'As long as the threat of the terrorist menace remains, men like myself will always be there to put ourselves in harm's way.'

He takes questions then, and gives further details of his bravery, and fearlessness, and sadness that he couldn't save more, and what it was like out there on the water, and also what he plans to do next, including the creation of a charitable fund to assist the victims of this and other disasters on the water.

Finally, his shameless eyes meet mine.

I raise my coffee cup in a toast to him.

'To which end,' says the captain, barely missing a beat, 'my daredevil assistant Daniel Bones, seated over here, will now come among you and begin collecting whatever you feel you are able to spare, in order that some good may come, even now, from these terrible events. Daniel?'

I watch as the reporters immediately start digging into their pockets, and am impressed by this at least. But I don't get up.

'Dan?' says Captain Clarke B.

The journalists, confused, begin to look towards me too. And I do not particularly enjoy being the centre of their attention, and almost weaken then. But I manage to hold my ground long enough for the captain to complete his recalculations of the situation.

'But first,' says the cap to his crowd, 'if you could perhaps excuse the two of us, just for a moment or so, I believe my assistant here would like to briefly step into the garden with me to discuss a private matter.'

And because I am smart, and cynical now, and know how the world works, I agree to that.

Out in the garden, Captain Clarke B. hands me a cigar and lights it for me. On the lake a large portion of the wrecked steamer has been snagged in a net and is being pulled, inch by inch, to the surface.

'Is this the point where I list my demands in return for playing along and keeping my mouth shut?' I say.

'It's what I would do,' says the cap.

'I'll want a regular wage then.'

'Done.'

'And more time off.'

'Of course.'

'And a cut of the profits.'

'Oh, everyone wants a cut of the fucking profits now, do they?' shouts the cap, throwing his hands in the air and walking around in a circle. Nevertheless, I know enough about him now to be able to confidently wait him out, and eventually he says, 'Well you'll have to get in line behind everyone else.'

'Agreed.'

Our business concluded, we both take a moment to savour our cigars.

'Did they hurt you very much?' I ask.

'I've had worse,' he replies, then adds, 'Was it bad out there?'

'It was bad.'

We watch the salvage crews attempting to untangle the length of railing and planks that they have pulled up, listening to their distant shouts until it's time to put out our cigars and go back inside.

And so I don't go back to England.

Book 2

THIS WHOLE, MARVELLOUS COUNTRY

'And, of course,' Captain Clarke B. is explaining to his audience, which as usual is mostly made up of a mix of the local nobility, representatives of business and politics, and a few rich holiday-makers who have managed to score a ticket to this evening's event in the small town hall, 'in such situations there is no time to think of one's own personal safety. A man acts on instinct, honed by years of action, tempered only by his own will to succeed. And there, ladies and gentlemen, is the single element that makes all the difference.'

As the cap's words are translated into Italian by the small man in a grey suit there is another round of applause. The town mayor, who is also the owner of a substantial portion of the local tour-ism business, and who is standing next to me at the side of the stage, clapping enthusiastically, whispers, 'He is an inspiration,' in my ear.

We have been working our way along the shores of Lake M— and Lake O— and Lake L— and Lake I— and Lake C— for the last couple of months, word of the cap's exploits during 'The Miracle of the *Juliana*' having crossed the Alps into Italy ahead of us, and laid the path for our late-summer tour. At each pretty, palm-tree-lined town where we stop for the night there is a dinner held in our honour by the local chamber of commerce, and another medal ceremony for the brave captain, and crowds lining the waterfronts and bridges to get a glimpse of the man himself, and an event such as this one at which the cap relates the story of That Terrible Event, with memorable details which he embellishes further on each telling. Later on in the evening there might even be the chance for the captain to have his choice of rich female sponsors, and perhaps the opportunity for me to pick up a few welcome gratuities here and there too, and show off what Edith Williams taught me back on the other side of the mountains.

'But let us not forget,' the cap continues, 'the reason that I am still here to tell this awful tale to you,' and there's my cue to carry the suit onto the stage and help the cap into it, pulling it on over his evening dress, as he explains the proceedings and points out the various features of note, and strikes a few poses too, and our short friend translates.

These days the practical, on-the-water demonstrations of the suit itself are almost secondary, and mostly left to me, the captain being busy with meetings and social events with our new rich friends, and his endless efforts to raise more money. Even as we have more funds coming in than we have ever seen before, the cash is going out again just as fast, the cap's creditors, or their heavyset local representatives, meeting with us at least once a week to receive their cut, which is set at eighty-five per cent of everything we take in. 'I was a desperate man,' the cap explains to me, when I ask why he ever agreed to such unfavourable terms in the first place. 'At the time eighty-five per cent of nothing at all hardly seemed a terrible price to pay in order to continue my work'.

For my part I make sure that the cap hands over my weekly wages at the same time, in notes which I stuff into a slit I have made in my coat, and which I change up into larger denominations as and when I am able. I write regular letters to my brother detailing our growing fortune and promising that the day is coming when I will be able to send for him, meanwhile checking in at every hotel and post office in every town we pass through on our itinerary in the hope of finding a letter back, not having heard anything from him since I went over the Rh— Falls.

As the captain brings the demonstration to a close we are both already scanning the crowd for the likely big spenders – the minor royals desperate for the chance to prove their usefulness to the world, the businessmen with an eye for a sponsorship opportunity, the wives or widows or women of independent means with a taste for danger and adventure. And all of them with hotel suites overlooking the water, or grand houses on the lakefront, or brightly painted palaces up in the hills, and drinks to be served, and guests to be impressed, and money to be gambled, and cigars to be smoked at card tables or in high-backed leather chairs, where the ever reliable Captain Clarke B. will keep everyone enthralled until dawn with endless entertaining stories, and then promises will be made, and checks signed, or deeds handed over, or wills changed and re-sealed, or items of jewellery and other heirlooms removed from around necks or taken out of drawers and gently slid across tables, or bags full of money proffered, and more besides.

'A new world!' the cap is exclaiming to the eager crowd. 'A safer new century, led by science and progress. Not because of men like me. But because of men and women like *you*.'

And in the morning we'll be on the move again, Captain Clarke B. possibly excusing himself from the bed of another new woman friend – it hasn't escaped my notice that none of the women who occasionally make the most of *my* services ever ask me to stay the night – our gear already loaded up for the short, pleasant carriage ride in the sunshine to the next yellow- and blue- and pink-painted town. There we'll set up and do the whole thing once more, in front of another group of exactly the same people, with the same predictable, welcome outcome, and it seems sometimes as if this whole marvellous country may be entirely made of lakes, and we may never have to stop.

In fact, I am beginning to wonder if summer ever even ends this far south.

A Misdirection

But here comes the first cold breath of the new season, all the same.

We have arrived in the town of G——, where there is no letter from my brother, but there are the usual gangs of likely-looking young boys and girls, probably half of them no younger than me though poverty has stunted their growth, who watch us as we unload the gear in front of the blue hotel, all of them dark-eyed and dressed in not much better than rags, and who gather round again later in the day as I check everything over for my short demonstration down by the water.

As I've done elsewhere I throw the oldest boy, who I assume to be the leader of the pack, a coin, and indicate that there's more where this came from later – '*Molto bene, molto bene*' – if they don't cause us any trouble. Apparently satisfied, the gang move on to cause mischief elsewhere, and that seems to be that.

But it's after the demonstration, as the crowd of a hundred or so people starts to clear from the narrow shingle beach below the promenade, and I'm packing the suit up again, that the same boy reappears, muscling his way through the other bodies and holding up that same coin again to get my attention.

I ask him, 'What?' and he bites into the coin, as if to demon-strate that it's a fake, which we both know it isn't. When that doesn't persuade me, he holds up the coin between two fingers, indicating that I should watch closely, and then passes his other hand quickly in front of it, causing the coin to disappear, before it is apparently snatched again from the empty air in front of my face. This does tickle me, and I reach out to grab for the coin but it's gone again before I know what's happened, and the boy is holding up both his empty palms in front of me with an expres-sion of theatrical surprise on his face. As I watch carefully he slowly begins to rotate his left hand, then quickly darts out with his right, brushing my ear with his fingers and coming back with the coin again, which he hands to me before disappearing into the retreating crowd.

This time it's me who bites the coin to check its credentials, but it's real all right, and warm from the boy's hand.

And then I look down to my feet to find, of course, that the suit is gone.

I shout out for the crowd to stop the boy, and attempt to give chase in the direction I think he has headed, pushing my way up the stairs and onto the front, where people are going this way and that in the afternoon sunshine and the road is full of horse-drawn carriages and omnibuses. I spot what might be the back of the boy's head slipping between two buildings on the other side of the street and only just avoid being run down as I give chase, but by the time I reach the alleyway, and begin to figure that surely he wasn't working alone anyway, he's gone – if it was even him at all.

I spend the rest of the afternoon searching about the town for the boy or any of the other members of his gang who I might recognise, but see no sign of any of them, the whole criminal bunch obviously having gone to ground to wait things out.

Eventually I have to return to the hotel, beaten, to find the captain sitting on a bench on the lakefront with two other men, one short and one tall, as if the three of them are enjoying the view of the lake.

In fact, the cap is in the process of handing over our weekly eighty-five per cent, via a canvas bag, to a couple of representatives of the local criminal syndicate with whom our creditors have made advance contact. The shorter of the two laughs when I announce, breathlessly and near to tears, that the suit is gone, and explain what has transpired.

The captain turns as white as milk, but the man smiles and casually indicates his gigantic associate, who stands fully a foot taller than either the cap or myself and is dressed in a fisherman's coat and cap, despite the hot weather.

'Gio will help you,' he says, and then goes on to explain the situation to his huge colleague, and soon the three of us – the giant, Captain Clarke B., and myself – are setting off to retrieve our property.

Well, the first thing this giant Gio does is to grab a passing street child, lift him off the ground by his ear – the boy forced to hang on to his captor's massive arm to prevent the ear being ripped off – and bark a short sentence at him. In agony, the captive child quickly gives up the name of a street, and so we're off, our new friend pulling the protesting boy along with him.

For the next half an hour or so we are led through a maddening maze of connected squares and alleyways, each with houses leaning so steeply into each other that they seem to meet at their roofs. The streets become steadily narrower at each turning until we are forced to walk in single file, and even then our shoulders are in danger of scraping along the walls, and the stink of the open drains that run beneath our feet is even worse than the most reeking low tides I remember from home.

Finally we come to a ruin of a house, the roof gone and the front door missing, and go inside – the giant having to duck his head – to find the juvenile gang crouched on the floor among the rubble, in fervent discussion over a game of dice. There in the corner, on top of a wooden pallet, is – thank God – the suit.

Our guide throws the little boy to the floor as the surprised gang look up. Momentarily frozen, they all seem to consider their options for a second or two, before deciding to scarper, jumping out of windows and falling over each other in their haste to get out of there, our freed hostage scrambling after them. All except the gang's leader, my pal with the coin tricks, who waits until his associates are gone and then stands up and addresses our friend in his own local dialect.

The giant bursts out laughing, but the boy maintains his composure.

'What is it?' asks the cap. 'What does he want?'

'Money,' explains Gio. 'For finding suit.'

Gio reaches inside his coat and takes out a short club, but the captain looks at the boy and smiles, impressed.

'Ask him if he wants a job,' he says.

Gio looks from me to the cap and back again. I shrug. So he puts the club away and says something to the boy, who laughs darkly then looks at the cap with narrowed eyes, nods, and says in English, 'Yes.'

And none of us needs that to be translated.

Welcome to the Travelling Circus

I can say this for the new boy, whose name turns out, as far as we can tell, to be Andrea: he is a fast learner, and strong too. In fact, it seems the cap has mostly hired him for his strength alone, as his role for the next couple of weeks is largely to follow me about my business and stand around looking surly, in order to scare off any local street children planning the same crime that he and his associates almost got away with. And although I am hurt by the captain's obvious loss of faith in me, and concerned for the future of my position, I'm not unhappy to have the extra muscle around, and help with fetching and carrying besides.

Initially we communicate through pointing and gestures, but soon we are picking up the basics of each other's languages – *buongiorno* and *buonasera* and *sommozzatore* and *quelli persi in mare* – and start to develop an effective, if fractious, working relationship. On the first night our new assistant is invited to join us in our hotel room, and to share my bed, and the pair of us end up spending half the night fighting for space on the mattress until I give up and decide to sleep in a chair instead, but make my point by taking the blanket with me. In the event I get little sleep after that, and neither does he, as every time I crack open my eyes to check on the situation I see him doing the same and staring back, as watchful as a wild animal.

In the morning when we both strip off to wash I see that he is skinny but well muscled, and also that his body is covered in scars, some of which I recognise – having not had an ideal childhood myself – as the result of whippings and stabbings and the marks of hot metal. The consequences, I suppose, of a life spent on and off the streets.

We learn that this Andrea is likely a couple of years older than I am, that he has no idea who his parents were, or whether he has any family – the captain wonders aloud if he might be North African – and that he has spent at least some of his early life in church orphanages but won't be going back. Beyond that he is, as the cap puts it, 'A blank slate – like all the best of us', and so is Andrea Del L— officially welcomed to our travelling circus, Captain Clarke B. mock-knighting him with the oar.

'Can we trust him?' I ask the cap, as we watch Andrea checking over the suit on the lakefront dock at the end of that first day's work, the two of us smoking cigars and considering the view of the mountains.

'We can't trust anyone, Dan,' says the captain. 'I would have thought that was obvious by now.'

Then, perhaps realising the harshness of his words, he lays a hand on my shoulder.

'But at least when you know that someone is actively trying to con you, you know what to look out for, hey?'

And so I do.

It's less than a week later when I'm first truly given cause to wonder exactly what I should be looking out for in the case of young (older than me) Andrea.

The cap is away for the evening hobnobbing with his new rich and famous friends, fundraising as ever to support our *impor-*

tant and potentially life-saving work. Andrea and I, bored, have spent the last hour leaning on the railings on the waterfront of the latest town, sharing a bottle of cheap wine and watching the running lanterns of the odd fishing boat still out on the lake, our backs to the promenading holidaymakers and the busy strip of restaurants and bars. After swigging the last drops from the bottle my companion gestures to ask if we should go buy another, but I turn out my empty pockets by way of reply, not having told him or anyone else about the growing sum of cash that I now carry everywhere with me, worn in a wallet on the inside of my shirt.

Andrea considers me for a second, then nods and holds up both his hands to indicate 'ten', telling me to wait, and disappears into the crowd. And sure enough, after ten minutes or so, during which time I smoke a cigar and think about my brother, and wonder what he would make of this place, the fellow is back. He opens his jacket, smiling, to show me the bunch of notes he now has in his inside pocket.

He also has a cut under his eye, and the beginnings of a dark bruise on the side of his mouth.

'Where did you get the money?' I ask, but he just smiles and shrugs, as if he hasn't understood. Then he puts a friendly arm around my shoulder and guides me across the street and down a couple of side streets to a tiny and very dimly lit fisherman's bar, where he buys a drink for me and one for each of the three other patrons who we can barely make out in the dark fug of pipe smoke, and we proceed to spend the evening getting drunk.

It's only after the third or fourth bottle of wine, by which point our drinking partners have changed four or five times, and everyone is laughing at a joke that I haven't really understood, that I gather the courage to ask again where the money came from. This time Andrea stops and his eyes darken, causing me to

147

think I might need to fight my way out of things before the night is over, but instead he stands up, takes the rest of the money from his inside pocket and throws it in my face, and then, as our new fishermen friends scrabble to grab the notes, he turns and walks out.

But not before I see the handle of the knife that he also apparently carries inside his jacket.

The Same as Everyone Else

It's a couple of days later that Captain Clarke B. announces our tour of the lakes is over, and we are to head south and inland. So we say goodbye to the beautiful country and our gear is stowed once again on the roof of a rented carriage, and we undertake the two-day journey through forested hills and farmland to the city of M—, where we have business.

During the journey little is said, the cap catching up on his correspondence, which includes numerous requests for personal appearances, and signed pictures, and endorsements, and Andrea and I look out of the carriage windows at the cottages and farmhouses and endless trees, wrapped up in our own thoughts about the past and the future.

On the way into the city there are huge camps and workers' rallies on every spare patch of ground, and shops and offices boarded up. The word *sciopero* is chalked on walls everywhere. In the centre of the town the streets and squares are dusty and strangely quiet. Despite the lateness of the year the giant stone buildings still seem to hold the heat of the summer.

The carriage driver takes us to an empty shopping gallery, where the cap buys a new suit of clothes for Andrea – who up until now has still been dressed in the rags he was wearing when we picked him up – with the help of a couple of nervous shop assistants, who close up the shutters of their small shop behind us as we leave, our footsteps echoing under the giant iron and glass roof of the gallery.

The event at which we are to demonstrate the suit is at the docks in the south of the city, and the captain addresses a group of businessmen and military officers as I change into the suit on the dockside, and then narrates as I perform rolls and other stunts on request in the oily water, including swimming around and under obstacles, and retrieving and moving various objects, and being timed by stopwatch as I row measured-out lengths of the dock, all to what end I have no idea. During an interlude I am required to rescue Andrea from a simulated drowning, and both of us are almost pulled under by his eagerness to play act, as it seems to me, the desperation of a dying man. Neither of us have spoken of the night with the money since it happened, but I wonder if he is trying to make a point, all the same.

Afterwards we are invited to the palace of the mayor, and a huge meal is laid on, at which the other guests include politicians and more army and navy officers, as well as a couple of priests who eye Andrea and I suspiciously, and to whom Andrea bares his teeth, as well as a local duke or two, who all noisily make short work of the whole boar that is the centrepiece of the dining table. And here again, too, mixing with the rest of the great and good, are the cap's creditors, changed now into linen suits more appropriate for the southern weather.

Andrea and I are placed at the furthest corner of the table from our host – the cap, of course, sits at the mayor's right hand as guest of honour – and I watch Andrea stuffing his pockets with veal cutlets and potatoes and deep-fried pieces of fish when he thinks no one is looking, and I wonder how long it has been since I stopped doing the same. As Captain Clarke B., heroically

150

haloed by a giant chandelier and utterly in his element, delivers the same speech that I've heard hundreds of times by now, I think about the impossibility of any of us ever truly escaping who we are.

Then we hear the noise from the square outside and are all ushered out onto the balcony to look down on the vast crowd of protestors – hundreds? Thousands? Certainly more people than I have ever seen in one place before – that has gathered in the plaza in front of the palace, carrying all kinds of flags and banners, and who are chanting something in unison.

'What do they want?' I ask the cap, who is smiling and waving at the crowd out of force of habit.

'The same as everyone else,' he says, out of the corner of his mouth. 'Unfortunately.'

I notice the priests and dukes are looking nervous, and keep attempting to move to the back of our little party, as if preferring not to be seen. Then the strutty little mayor joins us on the balcony, apparently intending to address the gathered masses, but the crowd erupts in boos and jeers as soon as he is spotted, and begins throwing fruit and bread and anything else they can find in our direction.

As an orange bounces off the head of a retreating captain of industry I note the mayor nodding to one of the army officers, who then nods to another, who disappears back inside to relay the message on to someone else, while the mayor remains out on the balcony, enduring the hail of projectiles with a fixed smile for all of the thirty seconds or so that it takes until the shooting begins.

The striking workers, surrounded on three sides of the square by at least four companies of rifles, have little chance. I've no idea how many go down in the first fusillade, but before the soldiers have had a chance to reload, the survivors are already running or dragging their wounded comrades – women and children among them, and hundreds more left behind bleeding on the cobbles – towards the steps at the southern end of the square, where a tree-lined park offers the opportunity of escape. And where they are charged by at least fifty cavalry soldiers on horseback, who have been hiding in wait for exactly this moment, sabres drawn.

Watching the chaos gleefully, the smell of gunpowder and blood already reaching our noses and the sounds of screaming and gunfire echoing off the walls of the square, the mayor asks us, in English, 'Have you ever seen such a sight?'

For once, even Captain Clarke B. is lost for words.

Only Andrea, who is taking the opportunity of the chaos to steal as much food from the table as he can fit about his person, plus cutlery and candlesticks and other silverware too, seems entirely unaffected by the horror.

ᴀLONE

It's the following bright, warm morning and we're standing by the side of a canal on the edge of the city, the Cap's now-linen-suited friends waiting by the open door of the carriage which brought us here from the hotel, having just unloaded all our equipment onto the tow path, and told us to get out, when the captain informs us that he is leaving.

'A few days, at most,' he explains. 'Two or three administrative events in the north. Which cannot be avoided. And I can travel faster' – looking at his creditors, unsure – 'alone.'

He shows us the itinerary that he has already planned out for the next few weeks of the trip, and the map of how the canal will take us – myself, Andrea, the suit, and the boat – all the way south to the P— river. From there we will be able to head east with the current, passing through the various places where the cap will meet up with us along the way for demonstrations and other arranged events, in between leaving again to take care of other business, plus things that we should watch out for and potential situations to avoid.

'I believe in you lads,' he says, and I have no way of knowing if he is telling the truth or not, or even if he would know the difference. 'And I know I will see you again at C— in seven days.'

The captain looks at his creditors, who nod their approval, and then he lowers his voice and leans towards us, with something like genuine concern in his eyes.

'And I would strongly advise you both to be there,' he says.

And then, advancing me a small sum of money from my wages for food and other provisions, he leaves us to our journey – or rather is hurriedly bundled into the carriage and driven away, taking one last look at us, and at his livelihood, through the window as they speed off.

None of us slept well last night – the captain up and about in the small hours with comings and goings to and from his room next to ours, and raised voices and slamming of doors, and I seeing over and again the bloody events of the afternoon every time I tried to close my eyes, and trying to understand how it was that I ever ended up as one of the people who would be on that balcony instead of down in the square, and even Andrea eventually pacing our room like a trapped animal in the hours before dawn. Now, I wonder what would happen if I just sat down on the canal towpath and closed my eyes, and let someone else take on my responsibilities, and make the next decision for me.

But then Andrea puts his hand on my shoulder, and nods, and hands me the suit, and that's that.

That first day on the canal, as I lead the way while Andrea follows behind in the collapsible boat, and I get used again to the meditative action of the paddle and the water over a prolonged period of time, and the countryside going by, and the vast sky, I note how strange it is – though not unwelcome – that I have taken on the captain's role. Looking back over my shoulder I shout out encouragement to my assistant, who I've discovered is a poor swimmer and is afraid of the water and even the boat as a result, and I remind him of things to watch out for, and give

154

advice on the position of the sail and the oar and such matters. As I do so, I realise how much I have missed this simple mode of travelling in all the accommodations and back and forth of the last few weeks.

With no current to fight and only the occasional lock in the way of obstacles, we make good progress despite my companion's nervousness. We spend the day passing farms and crafts-men's cottages and ironworks, and meeting barges carrying coal and textiles and livestock and fish and glassware coming from the south, and waving to the surprised people that we pass, and it proves to be the same the next day and the days after that.

The weather is still warm so at night we camp on the canal side or in hedges or abandoned barns, taking it in turns to watch over the gear. And I keep an eye on Andrea too, because I am still the smart boy I always was, and sleep with one hand on my wallet, and the other on the boat knife that I have removed from our equipment bag. Still, I don't complain or ask questions the couple of times he disappears early in the evening to return with pilfered bottles of wine and bread and cheese.

Our conversations around the fire are still somewhat limited by language but we get on well enough, and I tell Andrea stories of the cap's adventures, and what has happened on our journey so far, and also tales from my own life, and about my brother and our life back home. I talk of my hopes for the future, too, although I'm unsure how much of this he understands. When I discover how little education he has actually had, I try to share what I know about science and history and geography and reli-gion and other subjects, and answer his questions about how the world is and what makes it work – some of which I have to guess at, not having had that much of an education myself beyond the age of ten. For his part, Andrea only ventures to tell me that his life has been 'mostly bad'.

When we attempt to discuss what we saw from the balcony in M—, I find I can't even start to make sense of it in my own language, let alone his.

In the mornings we are up and out on the water each day before sunrise, and we paddle thereafter until dusk, and in this way we travel the length of the canal and make the P— river in less than four days, the red dome of the church at W— looming over the flat landscape from five miles off as we approach on the last morning, and then framing the scene behind us as we sit on a sandbank celebrating our achievement with a smoke and an ill-gotten bottle of wine.

And then we launch ourselves onto the wide, fast-flowing river, and head eastwards towards whatever next adventure awaits.

On the River P—

On the River P—, we discover, the sailors row their boats standing up instead of sitting down, and whistle to each other by way of saying 'hello', and the fishermen land giant catfish in nets lowered into the water from huts on stilts. Boats of all sizes work their way up and down the river, and their pilots and crew wave and chat with Andrea as we pass, and ask what we have seen.

The first evening we come across the wreck of a fishing boat run aground on a sandbank, and decide to spend the night in it, and scare ourselves thinking about the ghosts of dead sailors and fishermen. After that we go back to sleeping in the open.

At the small town of R— we pass under the stone bridge and are cheered on by a group of giggling schoolgirls on their way to class, which causes us to wonder if we are already famous, while outside G— we are amazed by a glimpse of the dark back of a huge animal that neither of us can identify, briefly breaking the water not ten yards away from us.

I compose a long letter to my brother, telling him what has happened since we crossed the mountains, and tell him how much I would like to hear from him, and of the likely date of our arrival in V—, to where he should direct any letters. I also share with him some of the obscene words and phrases that Andrea has taught me in Italian.

Meanwhile Andrea is adding new words to his English vocabulary every day, and not all of those inappropriate for polite company.

At B— we share our waterside camp and our dinner with an old woman and the four underfed young children with whom she is travelling along the river. Their transport is a broken-down rowing boat that looks even older than the woman is, with only an old canvas sail slung over a frame for protection from the elements. Sitting by the fire, the woman gathers her skinny troop – three boys and a girl – and treats the various injuries that they all seem to be carrying, from black eyes and sprains to bruises and cuts that she stitches up herself, all while the children complain loudly.

Andrea translates for me as the woman explains.

'They fight,' he says, indicating fists punching, 'for money.'

'Who do they fight?' I ask.

'Other children. Each other. Men, sometimes. Up and down the river.'

'They fight grown men?'

'At shows. For money. She used to do the same.'

The woman proudly shows off her fists, which are, it must be said, gigantic. It makes some sense of her toothless smile.

'And their fathers?'

The woman laughs.

'There are no fathers.'

In the middle of the night after the fire has gone out I wake up to find two of the children sharing my blanket with me for warmth. I put my arms around them and think of my brother and go back to sleep contentedly.

In the morning the strange family is gone before we awake, and I am sad for the rest of the day.

Between the towns of L— and D— we are hailed over to the riverbank by the captain of a small group of soldiers who are marching from some place to another. While the soldiers take the opportunity for a smoke and a chat, the young-looking captain asks to know who we are and what we are about, though apparently more out of personal interest than in his professional capacity, as he doesn't ask to see our credentials but instead requests that I demonstrate the workings of the suit for him, and is genuinely excited when I perform a few stunts on the water, clapping his hands delightedly.

'*Insegnante*,' he tells me, putting his hand on his chest to indicate that he's talking about himself, and, via Andrea, explains that he's a schoolteacher – or was until he joined the army and ended up in charge of these fine lads here, indicating the soldiers, who are now lounging around on the riverbank eating or playing cards, and who wave good-naturedly back at us, clearly used to their captain's enthusiasms.

I realise that this is the first time I've demonstrated the suit without the cap's permission, but do my best to explain to this fine fellow both the mechanics of the thing as well as the wider purpose and context in which they should be considered, including Captain Clarke B.'s ground-breaking scientific work, and the tragedy of lives lost at sea, and other approximations of the captain's usual performance, although I stop short of asking for donations from the happily relaxing soldiers.

'Bravo!' the captain tells me when I have finished, and embraces me like a brother, then encourages his little troop to give us a round of applause.

As we sail away I look back and see the former schoolteacher still waving at us enthusiastically, and wonder if he wouldn't have rather come with us himself, all things being equal.

But it's on the third night that our trip almost comes to disaster.

We are finishing up our evening campfire meal in a small wood a few yards from the river, when we hear shouts approaching us in the dark, and soon enough two drunk local policemen, apparently on their way home from a night in the pub, appear in the light of our fire with rifles over their shoulders.

There commences a threatening conversation in Italian which Andrea doesn't translate but which clearly communicates that these two are of a mind to arrest us for some crime or other – vagrancy will likely do it – until they strike on the bright idea, illustrated with gestures, that we might buy our freedom, and not necessarily with money.

At this Andrea gives me a look and says, in English, 'Get everything ready,' then says something to the two men which includes pointing at me and shaking his head, before leading the pair of them away into the darkness.

While they are gone I quickly get myself into the suit and launch the boat in record time too, and have just got it onto the water in preparation for our escape when I hear the scream and see Andrea come running out of the trees. He jumps into the boat and the two of us paddle away from the bank just as one of the two tormentors comes stumbling out of the undergrowth, holding up his trousers with one hand and with the other clutching at his stomach, which is dark with something I don't want to know about, before toppling forward into the water with a loud splash.

He doesn't get out again.

That night we don't stop, determined to put as much distance between us and the authorities as possible, and instead paddle

until dawn, when we hide out for the day under an empty fishing hut like wanted men, surrounding ourselves with washed-up
branches and driftwood and other debris to make sure we can't
be seen from the river.

'*Criminali*,' says Andrea proudly, thumping me on the chest
before doing the same to himself.

And that, it seems, is indeed what we now are.

A New Look

In the evening we set off again and travel overnight on the river accompanied by owls and bats and other ghostly creatures, until we reach the town of C— in the early hours, by which time we're so tired that we have both been hallucinating visions of haunted ships and their crews on the dark water.

In the absence of any other plan, we fall asleep on a bench in the town square with our gear.

At dawn we are woken again by the workmen who have arrived to set up the stage for the public appearance in the square later that day of none other than Captain Clarke B. himself. After some investigation we soon discover that the captain has already stationed himself in the best hotel in town, where he has a suite, although it turns out that no rooms have been reserved for Andrea and myself.

'You're young and fit,' the captain tells us, when we meet him in the hotel lobby later that morning. 'A couple more nights outside will do a pair of strong boys like you no harm.'

Nevertheless he embraces us both proudly, before brushing himself down again. Appropriate to his expensive surroundings, he is dressed in a new white jacket, trousers and boots. He has also acquired a pomade since we last saw him, and he now has a cape too, which he wears over one shoulder in a theatrical fashion. In contrast, Andrea and myself look exactly like a pair of strong boys who have been adventuring on the river for the past week.

The cap has also apparently acquired an entourage, who we meet when we are invited up to his rooms, which look as if they have been hosting a party for the past twenty-four hours. Laid here and there on couches or on the floor or sitting at tables are rich-looking men and women, in various states of disrepair, smoking opium pipes or drinking and playing endless rounds of cards. Two or three small yapping dogs run around, chasing each other under the furniture, and on the bed a couple appear to have passed out halfway through taking each other's clothes off, the woman naked from the waist up and the man from the waist down.

Hotel staff are rotating in and out of the room, clearing away plates and glasses and bringing more food and drink, and being handed tips from a roll of notes by the cap, as Andrea and I are introduced to the various counts and countesses and barons who make up the captain's new group of friends – 'Just a few fine people who I have picked up along the way' – and who briefly look up from their business to acknowledge us, momentarily interested in the possibility that we may be a new form of entertainment. Andrea, speaking their language, answers a few questions and is rewarded with a couple of laughs and a proud arm around his shoulder from Captain Clarke B.

I tell the cap that all is well with the suit.

'The suit,' he says, as if remembering. 'Yes. Well, of course. I never doubted that, Dan.'

And then he asks if I wouldn't mind getting him a drink while he has a short word with my young associate here, who is steered away into a corner for a brief conversation that I can't hear, but that I can't help but notice includes the captain surreptitiously palming a couple of banknotes to my travelling partner.

The demonstration of the suit itself is due to take place that afternoon following the cap's usual performance and, tired as I am, I entrust Andrea to check and prepare the suit while I recce the location, which is a wide stretch of river a couple of miles' walk outside town, bounded by farmed fields of wheat. When the time comes to put on the show the audience of farmworkers and townspeople gathers along the riverbank and the captain and his new friends arrive in their carriages, from which they don't descend, instead continuing their revelling with bottles of wine and ongoing games of cards.

I put on the suit with Andrea's assistance and then, with a wave to the small crowd, descend into the water and strike out for the middle of the river, from where I intend to undertake the usual set of rolls, turns and other tricks. However, it soon becomes clear that the suit's floatation chambers haven't been correctly inflated, and I am starting to sink. I attempt to tread water, while blowing into the manual inflation tubes, but as fast as I can get air into the chambers it is leaking out again, and I am starting to be dragged under by the waterlogged suit. I raise a hand to signal my distress to the shore, while trying to keep my head above water by paddling with the other arm, but the audience, assuming this is part of the – so far underwhelming – show, merely wave back weakly. Meanwhile, the only people who might spot that something is wrong, in other words Andrea and Captain Clarke B., are otherwise wholly engaged in drinking champagne with the cap's new chums, and not likely to look in my direction again until it's much too late.

As it turns out I am only saved by the intervention of a couple of field hands who, eventually realising that I am in trouble as I go under for the fourth or fifth time and then fail to come up again, dive into the water and drag me to the bank, from where I am lifted out and laid on the grass, gasping like a landed fish.

It's only then that the captain and his new friends notice what has happened, and are not impressed.

The Day After That, and the Next, and the Next

Of course, the possibility of sabotage occurs to me. I know that our new assistant has everything to gain – not least my wage – and likely very little to lose by taking my place in our crew. When I inspect the suit by firelight that night, while Andrea joins the cap, cape and all, plus the rest of his gang, for another night of cards at the hotel, I find that the seals around the internal floatation bladders have entirely come away – or have been picked away – and have to be repaired with catgut and by heating the surrounding rubber to make a watertight finish once more, a job that takes me until the early hours to complete.

I determine that from now on I will check the suit thoroughly myself before every performance, and keep an even closer eye on my work mate.

The following day we are on the move again, and the captain announces that his new friends will all be travelling with us for a couple of weeks – 'And I have plans, Dan my boy,' he tells me, 'big, big plans!' – and so we set out in a convoy of six or seven carriages to make our way to the next town on the itinerary, and the next hotel, and the next performance.

As will come to be their preferred manner, the revellers spend the journey leaning out of carriage windows shouting to each other and the people we pass on the road, or handing messages or bets or bottles of champagne up and down the line, or sometimes climbing onto the carriage roofs to chat and enjoy the passing countryside, or collapsing exhausted from the previous night's entertainment and sleeping for hours. Whenever we stop to water the horses everyone staggers, blinking, down from the carriages and stumbles around like they have been at sea for weeks, much to the interest of the locals, who take the opportunity to sell these dizzy strangers all manner of useless odds and ends.

Meanwhile, the confused travellers keep bumping into me and asking, in various languages, 'And who are you, again?'

And it will prove to be the same the day after that, and the next, and the next, and each one that follows besides.

At W— we stop in the grounds of an old monastery, where I perform rolls and dives and quick turns in the fishing lake, while the cap's rich friends shout at the locals and throw money around.

At B—, as part of the captain's ambitious new plans, I am pulled through – or rather, *across* the surface of – the water by a team of racing horses that run along the riverbank, as I balance on a pair of polished wooden Tyrolean skis that the cap has acquired, and his gang gamble on how long it will take me to fall.

At F—, I am required to tow a boat filled with dancing girls and a four-piece band the length of a man-made lake, as everyone else lights fireworks and throws them in my direction.

At G—, I find myself strapped to a rotating water wheel and almost drown while demonstrating the suit's underwater capabilities.

At P—, I am launched fully thirty feet into the air after sliding down a repurposed hay chute, before executing a perfect tuck-and-dive into a reservoir.

167

'The only thing left,' I tell the cap, 'is to be fired from a canon' – which doesn't get the laugh I was hoping for, but instead leads my employer to make a series of genuine enquiries as to the availability of army surplus artillery (which proves, thankfully, beyond our budget).

And every day I find myself sitting, again, in the front carriage of our ridiculous caravan, mostly in silence, jammed up against the door, as the be-caped Captain Clarke B. holds forth on various subjects to his new court, seven or eight of whom are always crowded into the carriage to hear his opinions and win money from him, making me wonder whether he recognises himself as the king or the jester in this situation. And all the while I am forced to try to ignore whichever couple is next to me as they spend most of the journey engaged in various acts of furtive lovemaking – my being so irrelevant to their pursuits that I doubt they even notice I'm there.

Still, the cap seems happy enough with his new place in the order of things, if perhaps not as respected for his scientific achievements as he might feel he deserves, and the weather is warm, and no one is being shot at, and even if my value has apparently fallen in the eyes of my employer I nevertheless continue to be paid. So for the next couple of weeks I attempt to keep my head down and carry on with my duties as we follow the course of the river eastward, putting on our travelling show in market squares or at harvest festivals or on the estates of rich landowners, where I demonstrate the suit, and perform increasingly spectacular and pointless stunts, and the captain works the crowds with Andrea acting as translator, and his entourage behave like idiots, and the celebrations go on long into the night while I sleep, most of the time alone, under the stars.

The Boys Who Had Been Before Me

But of course the day soon comes around when the cap tells me that he'd like me to train Andrea in the use of the suit – 'And you'll always be our go-to man, Dan, that goes without saying, but there's no harm in having a back-up, is there?' – and I realise then what the plan has been all along, and that sooner or later, I am likely to be replaced.

In the meantime, however, what choice do I have but to carry on?

The morning of our first lesson there's a mist on the river, and the day is not unlike the one on which the captain first trained me. I get Andrea up early, and he is not happy, having been hanging around with the cap and his entourage until the small hours, but he is smart enough to be aware of the potential possibilities that may present themselves as a result of learning this new skill, so he doesn't argue too much.

As I help him into the heavy rubber suit, I can't help but note the similarity in our bodies and builds – and then realise that this is why the cap chose him, after all, just as he chose me. I remember Mcinerney talking about the boys who had been before me, and wonder how many there have been altogether over the years, and how many might yet come after us. I wonder, too, how many of them quit on their own terms, and how many were fired, and how many died or were invalided out after suffering serious injuries, or were simply abandoned on the edge of strange towns in foreign countries like this one after outliving their usefulness to the captain or having learned too many of his tricks, and whether and how they managed to ever make it home again, and what stories they told about their adventures thereafter.

Not for the first time I ponder the man who I might be when all this is over, if I am to make it to the end.

Despite Andrea's game attitude, his fear of the water makes this first lesson very difficult, as his natural instincts make him fight against me. Once in the shallow river I have to support him in my arms in order to get him to take up the correct position and hold him firmly there, which almost leads us to come to blows a number of times, as we are both suspicious of the other, and I have not entirely discounted the idea of letting him drown in order to reclaim my spot in the captain's favour.

'Keep your back straight,' I tell him, as the cap once told me, 'and your head up. Let the suit do the work. Let the water support you.'

The ducks and geese, paddling past, watch us curiously.

Eventually, after going under and almost squaring up to me a number of times, Andrea begins to adapt to the situation, and I am able to let him float from my arms, and feel a rush of pride despite myself when he finally gains the confidence to move away from me and strike out across the water on his own.

'That's it,' I tell him, and, 'You've got it,' and I understand how a parent must feel the first time they realise that their child will eventually outstrip them.

From then on we are up and about early most mornings to practise, and have the river to ourselves and the time to chat about the cap's strange new crew, with whom Andrea is apparently no more impressed than I am, referring to them by a series of Italian nicknames which he translates for me as 'Mean Man', 'Stupid Man', 'Stupid, Mean Man', 'Mean Woman', 'Laughing Woman', 'Mean, Stupid, Laughing Woman', 'Mr Fat Arse', and 'Cock Face', as well as a few choice others.

He also reveals that he has been making a sideline in tips from them, as well as skimming off the profits of the bets he collects on their behalf – a practice that I find reason to celebrate when I have my own run-in with the captain's friends.

At the town of C—, where I beat the local swimming champion in a race over a weir, the cap and his companions spend the evening celebrating in their usual wild manner at the hotel we are all checked in to. All night, errand boys and working women and other kinds of entertainers have been coming and going from the room in which the evening's party activity has been taking place, but in the early hours things take a darker turn.

I am on my way to my bed when I come across a line of six or seven tired and nervous-looking young children, the oldest of them no bigger than my 10-year-old brother, waiting in the corridor outside the room. In my broken Italian I ask the children what they are doing there, but can't get a sensible answer out of any of them. However, given the lateness of the hour and what I know of the crowd inside the room, I fear the worst. And so I give each of the children a few coins and tell them to go home.

I have just seen the last of them off when the door opens and one of the room's occupants – let's call this one 'Angry Man' – sticks his head out. Not seeing what he has been expecting, he looks up and down the corridor in confusion, and then, spotting me, narrows his eyes.

I open my arms and shrug, giving the man my most obsequious smile.

In return I see only murderous anger, and the promise of a spoiled rich man's vengeance, which will make its way to me sooner rather than later.

ROPE

The last day before Captain Clarke B. is due to leave us for another couple of weeks and head off back up north again for some further business with his creditors, we arrive on the giant estate of one of the richest families in the region, where a huge party is being thrown with the cap as guest of honour.

As our convoy travels up the mile-long drive to the big house I notice the workers in the fields being guarded by men on horseback with whips and rifles, and point this out to my companions, but as everyone else is otherwise engaged in gambling or drinking or attempting to pleasure each other, my words are mostly ignored, and I don't remark on it any further.

That evening I demonstrate the suit on the estate's small ornamental lake before an audience of quiet farmworkers, who mostly keep their heads bowed and avoid eye contact with each other or anyone else, while the men on horseback patrol up and down the water's edge. The captain then delivers the standard speech recounting his personal heroism on That Famous and Terrible Evening, which is translated by the now well-practised Andrea, who I have to admit has developed a fine voice for public speaking these past few days, before the cap adds some words about the personal qualities of the estate owners, including the history of their family in the region, and the many fine things they do for the people of the area. Our hosts – husband, wife, and five well-dressed children – look on proudly.

'And as we stand on the edge of this new century,' the cap tells them, 'it is to people of vision and will such as yourselves that we look for guidance and leadership,' and so on, and so on.

The announcements completed, the captain and his assorted hangers-on plus personal translator are then ushered into the house, where entertainments including dancing girls and acro-bats have been laid on, as well as a grand game of cards, while I prepare to bed down in the stables.

But it's not long after that I am disturbed by the sound of whistles, and shooting, and the barking of dogs, and the arrival in the stable yard of a party of four or five men on horseback, who are half dragging a young man and a young woman on ropes behind them. At all this noise the doors of the house are opened again, and our host re-emerges, followed by the rest of his laughing guests including the cap and Andrea, in time to see the pair of escaped farmworkers who have just been recaptured thrown to the cobbles and, at a nod from the master of the house, whipped twenty times each.

When the entertainment is finished – and by the end no one is laughing any more – the unfortunate farmworkers are taken away and the revellers turn and troop back into the house to see what thing will be put in front of them next, and what after that, and what after that besides.

Andrea, whose black eyes have returned my gaze throughout the whole event, nods at me once and then follows everyone else inside. And as I lie back down to sleep, my hand on my money, I wonder how much we are bought and paid for just like every-one else.

It is still dark when they drag me out of my straw bed again a couple of hours later, five or six of them holding me down and tying my hands behind my back and pulling a gag tight around my mouth, despite my struggles. All the same, I manage to blacken a couple of eyes and break at least one nose with my boot before they have subdued me enough to do what they are planning.

I am dragged, thankfully not behind a horse, across the cobbles and out onto the lawn at the front of the house, as the group of counts and baronesses and other minor royals and professional hangers-on screech and howl and wave flaming torches as if this were all a great game. And I suppose it is.

The captain, either by accident or otherwise, is nowhere to be seen, but the angry man from the incident in the hotel corridor a few days back is there all right, and leans into my face and tells me, in English, 'You need to be reminded of your place.' And then a rope is looped around my neck and the other end thrown over a tree branch, and I am hauled to my feet.

Up at the house I see that the lights are all still on, and from the windows more people are watching the show, including what looks like the landowner and his whole family, and I briefly think about what the children must be making of this, and then I am on the tips of my toes and struggling to breathe and thinking how this is a ridiculous way to go out when I hear the gunshot.

And then here's Andrea, with a rifle in his hands which he reloads as he walks into the centre of the small crowd, and then points, almost casually, towards each member of the group one after the other, asking them what they think about this fine turn of events, and what they'd like to do about it.

Thankfully for us, and despite their fury, each decides that they're better off doing nothing, and so we have a stand-off until

Captain Clarke B. himself arrives, asking 'What's going on here?' but deliberately not meeting either mine or Andrea's eyes, and the group sullenly breaks up and troops back to the house, and the party is over. As the captain unties my hands Andrea keeps the shotgun trained on him, and I wonder whether this is because he fears the return of the cap's friends, or whether he is sending a message to the cap himself.

The next morning the three of us are out on the road again before anyone else is up, and with no polite send-off from the master of the house or the cap's friends either. After travelling the five miles to the nearest town in silence our gear is brought down from the carriage, and Andrea and I prepare the suit and the collapsible boat ready for getting back on the river for the next leg of the journey. Captain Clarke B. seems to become his old self again; he lights a cigar, shakes our hands and claps us both on the shoulder, saying, 'Godspeed, boys,' before climbing back into the carriage and heading off on his own part of the journey.

But even before he is gone I am aware that something has changed in the geography between the three of us, and I find that it makes me more uncomfortable than I can account for.

The Marshes

We have been travelling on the marshes, Andrea and I, for what may be less than a week, or might well be over a year. Out here there are no seasons, and the days each begin and end with the same watery red sunrise or sunset, the whole world floating, and faded, somewhere between the sky and the endless inland sea.

And the two of us floating, ridiculous, somewhere out in the middle of it all, long past understanding why we are here, or where we are going, or much else other than the tides and the sound of water, and the mud, and the reeds.

It's as close as I have felt to home on this whole journey.

In the last few days we have come across eel farms and abandoned fisherman's huts and secret smugglers' hideouts, and camps of runaway indentured farmworkers and political criminals who will never be found, and no one has asked us who we are or where we're going or why we are here, and we haven't asked those questions of anyone else. At night we've slept on the reed beds, and every day resumed our paddling towards our destination, where we are due to meet the captain either today or tomorrow, depending on how long the rest of the journey takes. And every evening we've lit fires to keep away the disease-ridden airs that roll over the marsh after sunset, and which cause the tertian fevers and sickness that seem to afflict everyone who lives along the edge of the great lagoon.

'Malaria' is what Andrea says to me when we first notice the ghost ship, which we spot drifting in and out of the mist behind us, seemingly carried on the current, and crewless too. We have encountered these boats already, their crewmen all struck down by the disease, either dead or too exhausted to do much more than let the wind and the water take them wherever they will until the recurring fever has passed. But after the three-sailed fishing boat reappears a further three times over the next hour, and still on the same course that we are following, we begin to suspect we may be being actively pursued by the spirits.

A cold wind is moving across the marsh and ruffles the reeds and the water as we slow and wait for the drifting ship to catch us, determined to find out one way or another exactly what's afoot.

Our question is answered as the patched-up, creaking, half-rotten boat pulls alongside, and the old man who is its captain stands up from his hiding place and points an ancient shotgun with a flared barrel at us, at the same time whistling to his two-man crew, or one young man and one boy anyway, to come out of their own concealed spots and train their weapons on us – which turn out to be, of all things, bows and sharpened wooden arrows.

So we tie the collapsible boat to theirs, as ordered, and both climb aboard. We stand on the deck while the crew keep us covered with their makeshift armaments and the old man, still holding the gun, interrogates Andrea as to who we are and what we could be worth.

My guess is that the old man is the father, and the others his sons, and I can just about see the resemblance in the three of them, never mind that they are all equally dressed in little more than rags. The older son is shifty and nervous while the younger boy looks scared, though determined, and I find myself thinking about the relationships between all three and musing on whether the boys love the old man, or respect him, or have spent their lives just waiting for him to show a moment of weakness.

The man is clearly fascinated by the rubber suit and muses aloud in Italian on how much he might get for it, while I am more concerned with the money I have hidden inside it, and I assume Andrea is equally worried about his own stashed cash. I don't mind our chances against the bows and arrows, but don't fancy much going up against the shotgun, which, while it would more than likely explode rather than fire if the trigger were pulled, would still probably do all of us a great deal of damage. Still, my irritation at myself for being held up by bandits for the second time in a year – and by such a barely held-together family of them as these are – is even greater than my fear, and so I decide to act.

'Hey,' I say to the old man, 'look at this,' suddenly hefting my paddle and then, as he turns the barrel of the shotgun towards me, swinging it with both hands and knocking the gun, thank God, from his grip, sending it flying against one of the masts where it discharges itself harmlessly with a loud bang. It's my return swing that does the damage though, as I connect with the fellow's head with enough force to almost take it off, and certainly to remove the last of his teeth, before he crumples to the deck. Where, I am ashamed to say, I commence to rain further blows down on him, and don't stop even when he is no longer moving.

The ship's captain taken out of action, Andrea leaps at the bigger of the two sons, pulling out his knife and sticking him twice in the arm and once in the thigh, and chasing the lad around the ship before he manages to get away by throwing himself overboard. Then Andrea comes back and gently takes hold of my arm to prevent me from striking my prone victim any further, and lowers the paddle for me, nodding towards where the youngest son stands watching, horrified, his unloosed arrow still pointing at me.

Panting, I hold out the paddle, which is tipped with his father's gore, to the boy. On the deck the bloodied old man's breath is coming out with a rattle.

The boy shakes his head.

But then he turns and shoots his arrow into the old man's leg.

ᏞIKE ᏗNIMALS

It's early evening when Andrea and I finally arrive at the rotting city of V— after another half-day of travelling, to discover that Captain Clarke B. is not in town yet, but that there is a room reserved for us at the small, crumbling hotel where we have arranged to meet. The manager looks us up and down like we are a pair of pirates fresh from the marsh, and he isn't far wrong at that, but the room is paid for in advance and here the two of us are, as large as life, and there is, finally, a letter for me from my brother at the reception.

We go up to our damp room which overlooks one of the city's many stinking canals, and from where there is a view of the sunset which is currently painting the entire room red, and I read the letter while Andrea takes a bath in the tin tub in the corner of the room, singing some Italian tune to himself. Far out at sea huge pink clouds are climbing the edge of the sky.

Dear Dan

Our father has died. It was an accident in his boat. We have held a
funeral and I have taken on the business, what there is of it. I am
glad to hear you are well and alive.

I will write again soon,
Your Will

I read the letter three or four times, not sure how I should feel
about it, before getting up and walking around the room. I look
out of the window and at the mouth of the canal; the boats are
coming in for the night from the lagoon, and the sun is going
down behind the spires and rooftops of the town, and all the
world is on fire.

I wonder what my father's last thoughts were, and whether he
pictured my brother's face, or my own, in his final moments, or
if he was even aware of what was happening to him. I wonder if
he felt fear, or guilt, or relief that his own suffering was finally
over. I wonder if he died still blaming everyone else for his own
monstrous selfishness.

I hope that he suffered.

Andrea gets out of the tub and is drying himself, singing that
same Italian tune, softly, and I tell him to shut up. He laughs, and
then sees my face.

And then he starts to sing louder.

I tell him to shut up again, and of course he doesn't,
instead walking towards me with the towel around his shoulders,
singing at the top of his voice now, his black eyes not leaving
mine, his naked, stringy body half in shadow and half lit up
like bronze by the setting sun. When he stops, right in front
of me, still singing, I offer him one last chance to save himself,
and because he is as stupid and doomed as I am, he doesn't take
it.

The first blow surprises him enough that he staggers backwards, knocking over a table and putting him in a poor position to counter when I follow up with the second. By the third punch he is already halfway to being on the floor, but having been in this game a lot longer than me he knows a few tricks that I don't, and manages to kick out with a foot, winding me and gaining himself enough distance that he can get back to his feet, and then clatter me on the side of the head with a metal water jug.

We are now both bleeding, and consider each other for a second before launching into battle again, I by now having abandoned any pretence of fighting skill and instead relying on pure rage, and Andrea realising that he may well be fighting for his life here. I charge into him, send us both bouncing off the wall, a glass picture frame coming away with us too, and the pair of us then tumble over the back of the ottoman, me trying to get an arm around Andrea's throat to choke him.

As we hit the floor he gets the heel of his hand up under my chin and forces my head up, attempting to break my neck. I feel the pressure of his thighs wrapping around one of my legs as he tries to squirm out from under me, and I put all of my weight into the elbow that I am driving into his chest in an attempt to force him to stay where he is, but he manages to get his other arm free and, grabbing my hair, pulls my head back even further. I have time to wonder, with my eyes full of blood and the stink of my own sweat or his in my nose, which part of which one of us will break, or snap, or be pulled or torn from its socket first, and what will happen after that.

And then suddenly his mouth is on mine, of course it is, or mine is on his, and we are biting each other or kissing each other or possibly there's no difference between the two. And our arms and legs and hands are all over each other as if they belong to other men entirely, and I am still on top of him and I can feel him hard against my stomach and he is tearing at my clothes, and then there's my cock in his hand too, and then it seems that neither of us has any choice in the matter any more.

And so we fall on each other like animals.

RICH

In the morning we are given word that Captain Clarke B. has been delayed by matters of business, and we are to wait for him, and should hopefully expect his arrival in the next few days, and in the meantime are to be at liberty about the town. And because everything is paid for we eat a huge breakfast while the hotel manager looks sourly on, and then smoke a pair of celebratory cigars, and then set out to explore the town like a couple of newlyweds who have spent their first night together without sleeping a wink, which is not at all far from what we actually are.

As we wander the alleys and squares of the sinking town, pretending to appreciate the famous buildings and works of sculpture, and counting the minutes until it is reasonable for us to return to our room, and go back to bed, and to each other, I am constantly surprised that no one comes running up either to congratulate or arrest us. But it seems we appear no different to anyone else, and can blend naturally in with all the other tourists, even if I feel as though my entire being is radiating heat and light.

All the same, I feel myself blushing when we stand before the nude male statues outside the Doge's Palace, and hurry my companion along before we are spotted.

In the afternoon we lie in bed and I follow Andrea's scars with my fingers, trying to learn the geography of his body – wanting, I think, to understand where all of him came from. I am amazed by how different and how much the same we are.

'This one?'

'Knife fight.'

'And this?'

'Other knife fight.'

'And this?'

He thinks for a moment.

'Poker. From a fire.'

'And this?'

'Belt. Priest. Dead now.'

He rolls over and does the same to me, walking his fingers across my body, resting his fingertips on each mark and weal and discolouration he finds, looking at me with raised eyebrows.

'Lit cigar,' I say. 'Father. Oyster knife. Father. Earthenware pot. Father. Fishing rope –'

He puts his mouth against the long red scar, blows on it as if he could soothe away years of pain, just like that.

'A bad father,' he says.

'My brother had it worse.'

'But still.'

'A bad father,' I agree.

'Dead?'

'Yes,' I say, even though I haven't told him about my brother's letter.

Then his hand moves further down my stomach, reaches its destination.

'And this?'

And we are off again.

★

That night we go out and get drunk in the town's most famous square, at one point charming a group of American painters, who are at the end of their summer tour, into buying dinner for us, and telling them stories of our adventures. They are excited to meet some genuine friends of their compatriot, the famous Captain Clarke B., and to hear first-hand tales of his many exploits, but are not amused when I attempt to tell them the true story of the *Juliana* disaster, considering my joke to be in very poor taste, and change their minds about inviting us back to their hotel for more drinks.

At the end of the evening Andrea and I are almost accosted by a very young pair of working women after taking a wrong turn on the way back to the hotel, and then, unable to wait any longer, we end up making love on a set of narrow stone steps running between a couple of tall buildings, before I throw up most of a bottle of red wine.

When we get back to our room Andrea takes a small cloth bag from his coat pocket. He empties a pile of jewellery onto the bed, including rings, necklaces, brooches and bracelets, of which he is clearly proud.

'What are these?' I ask.

'From the captain's rich friends,' he explains.

'You stole them?'

He is momentarily offended.

'Some I was given,' he says.

'What for?'

He looks at me like I'm an idiot. And I realise that I am.

'The same as with me?'

He laughs, takes my left hand and kisses it, and I feel his rough beard against my palm.

'Not the same as with you,' he says, and then slips one of the rings onto my finger, a simple gold band. 'You are not rich.'

I close my fist, admire the way the ring looks, want to give Andrea something in return. I think about my brother's lead soldier, but decide against it.

'Not yet,' I tell him.

ℒove and Wild Ambition

For the rest of that week and into the next, as we wait for further word of the captain, we continue to celebrate our weird honeymoon, revelling in each other and our situation, toasting our luck alongside unknowing strangers in bars all over town. Neither of us asks what might happen next, nor wants to consider it.

We rent a small boat on Captain Clarke B.'s account and take it out to explore the lagoon and I tell Andrea how my brother and I used to spend afternoons like this, dreaming of the possible worlds we could escape to. We moor the boat on the edge of a reed bed and slip into the water, at first with the intention of swimming, but then things take a different, though not unwelcome, turn. As we are in the middle of it a dolphin or porpoise chasing a school of fish breaches the water and catches sight of us about our romantic business, and I don't know who is the more surprised.

On the way back to the city the rain that has been threatening for the last few days finally arrives, and with such force that we have to bail out our boat, and we almost get lost in the maze of channels that lead across the marsh because we can no longer see more than ten yards in any direction.

By the time we return to the hotel the ground floors of businesses and apartment buildings and palaces alike are already being bailed out, and duckboards are being laid across plazas. Our hotel manager, in rubber galoshes, is attempting without much success to sweep the rising, slimy tide back down to his basement, which is already completely underwater.

And so as the city floods we spend our days at the hotel or getting drunk at whichever local bars are still open for business. In the early mornings as Andrea sleeps I compose numerous letters to my brother asking about practicalities, and his situation, and the details of our father's death, all trying to make some sense of how I feel about everything, and I don't send any of them. Instead I throw each one into the fire in turn.

Across the town there is an epidemic of coughs and colds as the damp settles in, taking up residence in chests and noses and creeping along alleys and up staircases. Black mould grows in the corners of rooms and climbs the walls, and the smell of rotten wood is everywhere. At night we dream we are underwater, and wake up gasping for breath. Every day at breakfast there are fewer and fewer people in the dining room, and the shutters on the hotel windows are opened later and closed earlier, until the morning when the manager doesn't bother to unlatch them at all.

That afternoon we run into one of the American painters in a small bar not far from the hotel. He is a handsome man in his mid-twenties, alone this time, who I remember from his melancholy air and blue eyes, and who introduces himself properly as William T. Baker and explains that he is planning to spend the day drinking himself into insensibility before taking the last train out of town that evening, and that we are welcome to join him.

'And where will you go next?' I ask William T. Baker, as the three of us toast the city with glasses of wine.

'To France!' he declares, standing up and putting his hand on his chest. Then he sits down again and explains: 'Too cold and wet to winter here.'

'Are you rich?' asks Andrea, getting to the heart of it.

'Obscenely,' says our new friend, nodding.

'I thought all artists were poor,' I say.

'Only the very good ones. The rest of us have to rely on the family fortune to keep us afloat. Is there food here?' – waving at the patron – 'I say, do you have food here?'

We are brought a tray of bread and cheese and meat which our companion immediately ignores in favour of more drinking, and so Andrea and I eat while we are told the story of a life of vast riches and early promise and family tragedy and squandered talent; also world travel and adventures in exotic lands, and affairs with beautiful but unbalanced artist's models, and wasting diseases and heartbreak; and a late-flowering, entirely unexpected romance, and wedding plans, and a terrible accident, and a dead fiancée; and through it all, nevertheless, the appalling requirement to keep existing, and furthermore to continue serving the muse, in the face of the vast and uncomprehending universe, and so on, and so on.

'To love and wild ambition, gentlemen!' shouts our rich, tragic pal, struggling to his feet again, and we all drink to that before he falls over.

When it's time for us to leave, William T. Baker hands me his card, which I put in my inside pocket, and makes us promise that we'll look him up if we're ever on the Riviera.

When we get back to the hotel we are told that our friend has arrived, and find Captain Clarke B. sitting in the empty dining room in the half-darkness. He is wearing a muddy greatcoat around his shoulders and looks as though he has been travelling for days.

191

He has an eye patch over his right eye.

At first he seems not to recognise us, and struggles to answer any of our questions, including where he has been, and what happened there and why it took so long, and the most pressing issue of what became of his eye. It's not until we get a brandy inside him, and I ask, 'What happened to your former travelling companions?' that some of the fog seems to clear, and he focuses on me.

'They moved on, Dan,' he says.

'To where?'

'To the next person.'

Andrea suggests that we should get the captain to bed, and I agree. I ask the manager where his luggage is but am told that this was how he arrived. As we help the cap up the stairs his foot goes through one of the wooden steps which has been almost completely rotted away by the damp.

'Why is everything falling apart?' he mumbles.

We put him down onto his bed, and by the time we take off his boots he is already asleep. We pull a blanket over his shoulders and leave him to it.

Outside the room Andrea asks me the question that has been at the forefront of my own mind.

'What about the money?' he says.

I've Never Been to America

The cap sleeps solidly for the next twenty-four hours, and then for the three days following that does little more than sit in his room and stare at the walls – or, when we get him out of his room, stare at whatever other walls are closest.

Sitting at breakfast or lunch or dinner in the hotel, or in the bar across the road when it finally reopens after the floodwaters have receded, he looks like a man who has been hollowed out. He refuses to give us any more information on what happened to him while he was up north, and what led to the loss of his eye, other than to tell me, 'I made a mistake, Dan, and I have paid the price for it.'

He is unable to engage in any discussions of our upcoming plans, or tell us what might happen next in the absence of them. At the demonstration that we have been scheduled to perform on the Grand Canal, I perform a few stunts and let off a number of rockets, but without the introductory patter from the Captain Clarke B. – and he simply stares at us when we ask if he'll be taking part – the show feels flat, and not just to me.

Lying in bed that night, Andrea and I try to decide what to do about him.

'How do we get the old captain back?' I say.

'Do we want him back?' asks Andrea. 'Do you trust the old captain?'

'No,' I admit, 'but at least I knew where I stood with him. Now I don't even know who he is.'

Neither of us asks the question that we don't want answered, which is what will happen to the two of us if and when we do get him back. But it feels suddenly strange to be lying in each other's arms with the famous Captain Clarke B. sleeping just on the other side of the wall, in a way that it hasn't felt strange before.

Still, we do our best to help the cap out of his funk, and take him for trips on the water, and to look at the beautiful buildings and works of art around the town, and to stand on the famous bridges, and so on. One evening we even hire a woman to provide him with some company, thinking this might encourage him back into his old ways, but the only result is that we are admonished by her at the end of the evening for torturing this poor and obviously ill man.

'Maybe he needs a boy,' Andrea suggests, but neither of us seriously think this likely to help.

It's only during our boat trips on the lagoon that the captain seems to recapture something of his old self, and relax, and enjoy the wind on his face as Andrea and I take it in turns at the oars.

'Did you ever see the Mississippi, Dan?' the cap asks me one day, as he trails his hand in the water.

'No sir,' I tell him. 'I've never been to America.'

'No, of course not. Fine river, though. All the same.'

'So I've heard.'

'Maybe he is homesick,' Andrea suggests that night, and so the following evening we take the captain to see a Wild West show that was recommended by one of the friends of William T. Baker. Unfortunately, we have to leave halfway through when the cap stands up from his seat and begins shouting, 'Liars! These men are liars!' at the performers, who are all dressed in cowboy and Indian outfits.

The next day the captain seems to have recovered something more of his old self, and even takes a trip on a gondola alone after breakfast, before returning to ask Andrea if he has ever visited the south of the country.

Andrea tells him that he hasn't, and the cap replies that it is particularly beautiful at this time of year.

'And besides,' I say, trying to encourage the captain, 'we can't just stay here like this forever.'

'But why not?' Andrea asks.

Later that day we get our answer, when we are joined for afternoon drinks in the otherwise empty hotel bar by two familiar-looking men in overcoats and bowler hats.

'What is this?' I ask, knowing exactly what it is.

The cap rubs his good eye.

'There is to be an event at N—, in the south of the country,' he says. 'A very well-paid event. For all of us. And these gentlemen here have … offered, would you say?'

One of the overcoated men nods.

'… offered to take us at least part of the way there, in return for a very small favour. Although, as always, the choice of whether or not to join me is entirely yours.'

Andrea and I look at each other.

'Have we ever had a choice in any of this?' I ask the cap, and he sighs.

'Well, all the same you are a fine pair of lads,' he says, 'and I am proud to know the both of you.'

So we are taken up to our room to pack our bags, and then we are all led down to the canal, where a small rowing boat is waiting to take the three of us out to the edge of the city, where

195

we are transferred to a two-masted merchant ship which is anchored in the lagoon. On board we are shown to our tiny cabin and required to make ourselves comfortable as best we can while the crew get us underway, the door being locked from the outside just in case we get any other ideas.

'Probably for our own safety,' the cap tells Andrea and myself, fooling exactly no one.

It's not until we have passed the sandbanks at the mouth of the lagoon and are out on the open sea that the cabin door is unlocked and we are allowed up on deck, where the wind is up and there is a fine evening's moon out, and we are already making good speed.

The cap briefly speaks to the ship's captain, while Andrea and I lean over the side to watch the ship's wake, and look for dolphins. When I ask the cap again where we're going, 'South,' is all that he says.

But we don't head south. Not at first.

Either Passengers
or Prisoners

In fact, as we bed down in our cabin that night, it's clear to me that we are heading east, just as we have been since we left the lagoon, following the pale blue line of the coast, and never drifting more than half a mile away from the edge of the marsh, and it's the same when we rise in the morning, and for the next day besides. At the port of T—, where we stop late in the afternoon, we are once again locked into our cabin, but watch from the porthole as we take on an unidentified cargo sealed in numerous wooden crates.

Then that evening we are off again, following the increasingly rocky coastline as it bends towards rougher seas.

Out on the water we do our best to keep ourselves entertained, and adjust to our new situation as well as we can. As passengers, or prisoners — it being not always easy to tell the difference at sea, even at the best of times — there is little for us to do other than keep out of the way of the running of the ship. There's a small amount of food to eat, and letters to avoid writing to my brother, and I spend some time teaching Andrea how to tie a few different knots, as well as instructing him in the names of the sails and various parts of the boat, and other aspects of basic seamanship. As always, he learns quickly, and I find myself proud of both my teaching and my pupil.

If the recovering cap suspects anything of what has passed between the two of us while he was away, he doesn't show it, and we do little to give him or anyone else reason to ask questions, making sure that we keep at least a foot's distance between us when in public, and even doing our best to avoid meeting each other's eyes unless we are sure we are alone. During the night we lie in our narrow bunks as chaste as nuns – and I attempt, as the captain himself once recommended, to think only noble and edifying thoughts.

As for the man himself, it's enough for me that he has regained some amount of self-assurance and, in our eyes at least, a little authority. He spends his days up on deck, watching the horizon, and we decide that the eye patch quite suits him, all things considered.

And for the most part the three of us are ignored by the crew, who don't converse much with each other either, beyond sharing the occasional sharp joke in a language that none of us recognise. When not on duty they play cards silently, or eat, or sleep. Despite their shared rank, even the ship's captain seems uninterested in our heroic employer, beyond his value as cargo, and the cap's occasional attempts to engage him in conversation.

On the fourth day the weather takes a turn for the worse and Andrea, no sailor yet, becomes seasick and is forced to take to his bunk, where I check up on him every few hours, and mop his brow with a cold cloth.

'I wish I was dead,' he tells me, groaning.

'It passes,' I tell him, 'eventually.'

'How long?'

'A few days.'

'I hate you.'

I wipe his mouth and plant a kiss on his cracked lips.

'No you don't.'

That night we make the first of a number of stops, laying anchor off one of the hundreds of small, rocky islands that line the Dalmatian coast, while two crew members lower a boat and row three or four wooden crates ashore under cover of darkness as Andrea and I watch from our cabin porthole. By dawn we have repeated the exercise at three other islands, and the following night the story is the same.

'Are we smugglers now?' I ask the cap, as we drink our morning coffee on deck, enjoying the first sunshine we've seen in over a week.

'We're the same men we've always been, Dan,' he says. Then he adds, more kindly it seems, 'and we're not being paid to ask questions.'

I don't ask him what, exactly, it is that we are being paid for, or who is currently paying for it, but I'll find out soon enough, all the same.

After a couple more days sailing around the islands, and divesting ourselves in the same suspicious manner of another twenty or thirty crates, one evening we abruptly start heading due west and out towards the open sea. We sail overnight and all through the next day too, before arriving at our destination, which seems to be the precise middle of nowhere, shortly before sunset.

Having finally got his sailor's legs, Andrea accompanies me onto the deck to investigate why we have stopped, and we find the cap at the bow of the ship, observing the horizon through a telescope that he has borrowed from the ship's captain. I am unable to identify any landmark other than the endless sea itself in every direction, but the cap hands me the glass and tells me where to point it and there, sure enough, lit up by the setting sun, I find the tiny speck of an island – in fact not much more than a rock – some four or five miles distant.

199

'That's it,' he tells me.

'That's what?' I ask.

He leads us back below decks, where the ship's captain has rolled out a nautical map on the mess table. It doesn't escape my notice that he has laid his revolver on the table too.

Captain Clarke B. shows us the rock on the map, confirming that it lies at the easterly end of an entire chain of islands, some big enough to be inhabited, others even smaller than the subject of our discussion – which is also, apparently, our target.

'There's no way to get a boat in or out without being spotted, even in the dark,' explains the cap. 'Which is why we need to use the suit.'

'Use the suit to do what?' I ask.

He ignores my question and puts his finger on a small inlet, asking the ship's captain, 'Here?'

The man nods, and the cap turns back to me.

'This is where you make the pick-up,' he says. 'You can get in and out in a couple of hours.'

'Pick up what?' I ask.

'As long you make it back to the boat before dawn we can be gone before they even know what's happened.'

'Pick up what?'

Andrea looks closely at the map, reads what it says there in Italian, then looks at Captain Clarke B., and then at me.

'Not what,' he says. 'Who.'

'Exactly,' says the cap, and then proceeds to fill us in on the whole plan.

A Night with Some New Friends

Out on the water I cover the mile or so between the drop-off point and my destination as quickly as I can, eager not to hang around in the midnight black sea any longer than I have to. There is no moon, but the cloudless sky allows me to identify the islands on the horizon by the shapes they make against the stars, and it occurs to me that we may have been waiting this whole time for a night with exactly these conditions. In the dark water I am perfectly invisible from the shore, and indeed can hardly see my own arms as they paddle me towards my target.

Before I left, the cap had warned me about sharks, and told me how a sharp strike on the snout with a paddle would dissuade all but the most determined among them.

'And what about those ones who *are* the most determined?' I had asked, as Andrea checked me over diligently, tightening straps and testing seams before patting me on my cowled head to demonstrate that he was happy with things.

'Those we can't account for, I'm afraid,' Captain Clarke B. had said.

Those and so much more besides, I had thought then.

But soon enough here's the rock I'm looking for, which I recognise by the dark mass of its sheer cliffs and, above those, the looming walls of the only structure that clings to it – the prison.

As I swim around the tiny island towards the place that Captain Clarke B. showed me on the map, I also soon spot a problem: the sides of the island, as I've already been told, are steep enough that there's only one way on or off. This is advantageous for the authorities in charge of the gaol, but now presents an issue for me, since between myself and the narrow natural stone step that I am trying to reach, a small rowing boat, crewed by two soldiers lighting their way with a lantern on a pole, is now patrolling the sea, and heading my way too. In fact, they're close enough that I can hear their voices and smell the dark tobacco that they're smoking in their pipes, as well as see the rifles they carry over their shoulders.

Realising that if I stay in the water for much longer I am in very great danger of being discovered, I decide to immediately try to land at the base of the cliffs. The waves are high enough that it takes me a number of attempts to achieve my aim, as I am alternately thrown against the sharp, slippery rocks as the sea rushes in, and then pulled back out again with the retreating waters, but eventually I'm able to gain purchase and claw myself up above the waterline.

As I slither over the seaweed-covered rocks, keeping as low as possible to avoid showing my silhouette against the sky, I quickly become aware of the terrible stink, but it's not until the eruption of angry barking all around me, and the flurry of movement at my feet, and the sudden clamping of teeth around my ankle, that I realise I am sharing my intended hiding place with a mass of seals.

Without a realistic option of retreat, I strike my attacker – no shark, but still – on the nose with the end of the paddle, and it yelps and shuffles away in the dark.

'Sorry, seals,' I whisper, attempting to find a spot among them to lie down and disguise myself, while they alternately either try to bite me or flounder angrily out of the way, 'but we're going to have to be friends.'

Eventually, perhaps convinced by the strange texture and smell of the rubber suit that I might be something like them after all, the creatures settle down again and allow me to join them, and I watch from my vantage point as the boat makes its patrol up and down the shore, not thirty feet away but oblivious to my presence, though I spend the next couple of hours being reminded of my companions' displeasure with occasional barks and nips, not to mention having to endure the regular belching, pissing and shitting of the awful animals.

I am also aware of the fact that we are running out of time.

It's less than an hour before dawn and the sky is already start-ing to turn from black to blue when I finally hear the single, high-pitched peep of the whistle – so brief as to likely be imper-ceptible unless you were listening out for it, as I have been – which tells me that the coast is clear; or, at least, that this is our last chance. I quickly say goodbye to my stinking chums, although my promises to write to them are largely unappreciated, and launch myself into the water again, following the edge of the island until I see the light of the candle that indicates the pick-up point, and make out the dark shape of a man, in what might just be a prisoner's uniform.

He has clearly been instructed well as he doesn't wait to be asked but launches himself into the water on the first outgoing wave, which carries him straight to my arms. I slip a loop of thin fisherman's rope over his shoulders and under his arms, give him the thumbs up, and then we're off again, with me paddling as fast as I can to get us clear before daybreak.

We're 200 yards out when we spot the patrol boat again, coming around the headland, now quite visible against the rapidly lightening sky, and all I can do is hope there's enough darkness left on the surface of the water to hide us. For a moment it does seem as though the boat turns towards us, but I don't stop to wonder about their plans, and never even hear the lucky shot, if that's what it was, that passes through the shoulder of the suit, only discovering the hole in the rubber when we check things over back on the ship later that day.

By the time we reach the rowing boat the sun is only minutes below the horizon. We are pulled aboard by Andrea and the cap, who row the four of us back to the ship, while our mysterious new passenger, a handsome man with a perfect pair of duelling scars on either cheek, sits wrapped in a blanket, considering us silently all the way.

When we get back on board, the object of our rescue mission is quickly taken to the captain's cabin, while the three of us are left to our own devices until that evening, when we are put ashore on the Italian mainland at B—, and advised that we will never see the ship, or its crew, or the man I rescued, ever again.

And that's almost how things work out.

ACROSS THE HIGH COUNTRY
BY HORSE AND CART

It takes almost a week for the three of us – Andrea, the cap, and me – to make the journey from B— to N—, travelling across the country from one coast to the other in the back of an open horse-drawn cart that the captain buys from a farmer at the first town we come to, 'almost for peanuts'.

Around the ports along the coast everyone is on the move, with queues of families loading their entire possessions onto passenger boats heading north, or bound for the Mediterranean and beyond, but once inland we find that the country this far south is strangely quiet. We go for hours without meeting another soul on the roads, and pass through empty, abandoned villages, and others where the only inhabitants left to tend the fields are old men and women.

'Where is everyone?' I ask.

'No money. No food,' says Andrea. 'Gone to America.'

'Where they will doubtless make their fortunes,' says the cap, proudly. 'Like so many before them.'

'You didn't,' Andrea replies.

The cap gives him a look halfway between hurt and resigned, says, 'Not yet, Andrea, not yet,' and goes back to watching the road ahead.

Outside the town of L—, where the land starts to rise towards the hills that separate one half of the country from the other, we come across a village destroyed by a flood. Hardened mud covers everything to a height of four or five feet, with chair legs and bedsteads and picture frames still sticking out here and there. None of us mention what might still be under the mud, as we stop to look around. A few scavenging pigs seem to be all that are left of the former population, and they come to investigate us, and tolerate my attention and let me scratch them behind the ears and chat to them about the pig I used to own, and make me sick with longing to see my brother Will.

On the road out of the village we come across the oldest man I have ever seen in my life. He is sitting on a stool and leaning on a cane, seemingly watching the world go by, though by his complete lack of reaction to us he could well be blind and deaf too, if not halfway to death.

Nevertheless, Andrea hops down from the cart to talk in Italian with this old gent, and ask him how things are and whether he needs anything – not that we're in a position to give much – and the two of them seem to have quite an animated conversation, with much smiling from both parties, despite the fact that the man never takes his eyes off the far horizon and Andrea has to almost shout into his ear to make himself heard.

When he gets back into the cart, having given the old fellow a squeeze on the arm as he left, Andrea tells us, 'Dam collapsed.' He rubs his fingers together to indicate 'money'. 'Not looked after. Everyone died, except him. He's still waiting to join them.'

He looks back and watches the old man recede into the distance, until we round a corner and he's hidden from view. For the rest of the day we don't talk much.

As we ascend into the high country we begin to feel the cold, and travel with blankets wrapped around our shoulders and across our knees. At night we sleep in ruined farm buildings, lighting fires in the disused hearths to keep us warm, as well as to dissuade scavenging wolves or wild dogs, which we are convinced we can hear howling out in the far darkness. Nevertheless, on a couple of occasions when we're sure the captain is asleep I persuade Andrea to venture outside and into the night with me, although we never manage to get much further than the yard before I pull him into my arms, sick and desperate as I am with desire, and we go at one another under the frozen stars.

On the whole journey we only come close to getting caught once, when we are disturbed one afternoon in a forest of cork trees by a young girl leading a herd of goats, and are forced to flee laughing and frustrated back to the road, where Captain Clarke B. is still smoking a cigar thoughtfully while waiting for our horse to finish refreshing itself at a stream, and asks us if we have sufficiently stretched our legs, what with that there energetic run that we have just undertaken, and we have to agree that we have.

We're still a couple of days away from our destination when we get the first view of the giant smoking mountain which sits outside the city, and which looms over us, piling great poisonous black clouds high into the sky, as we come down from the hills and cross the plains.

'Is it dangerous?' I ask the cap.

'Oh, quite deadly, by all accounts,' he tells us. 'The last eruption killed over a hundred people. They say nothing was able to stop the rivers of lava.'

He pulls up the horse and lights another cigar, and we all consider the horrible sight.

'And yet one can't help but wonder, if a man, properly equipped and outfitted, and sufficiently determined, might perhaps not one day *swim* across the crater –'

'But we are not ...' Andrea asks, '... I mean, this is not the plan?'

Captain Clarke B. laughs.

'The volcano? No. Not this time.'

He hands us both a cigar, lights them for us.

'We're going to meet the King, lads,' he says.

THE KING OF ITALY HAS A MAGNIFICENT MOUSTACHE

The King of Italy has a magnificent moustache. This is the first thing that I notice when we are ushered into his presence at his equally magnificent palace – one of his many magnificent palaces, I imagine – in the centre of the town. It's a moustache that soars and swoops across half his face, before rising to a pair of lacquered peaks that project out approximately six inches from either side of his head. It's a moustache that, based just on the hours that must daily go into its maintenance and upkeep, immediately inspires respect. It's the style of moustache that I wouldn't altogether be unhappy to own myself, one day, if I am being entirely truthful.

But the King is not telling us about his moustache, despite my preoccupation with it. Instead he's explaining to us about the ceremonial sabre that he is wearing at the side of his tight-trou-sered leg, and how it is, in fact, more than merely ceremonial, having been very effectively used by the King himself to ward off an attack by a knife-wielding anarchist which took place shortly after His Highness's ascension to the throne just a couple of years back, and which happened, coincidentally, in this very city.

'And do you know where this man is now?' the King asks the three of us as we stand in line for his inspection, along with all the other royal visitors who have been invited to an audience with His Highness this morning, nervously watching as our host decides to unsheathe the sabre and slice the air with it three or four times, while considering the way the blade catches the light just so …

'I hope you will tell us, Your Highness,' Captain Clarke B. requests.

'Ha!' says the King, putting the sabre away again, satisfied. 'He is in chains, as he will be for the rest of his life, in a cell too low for him to even stand up in!'

'Bravo!' says the cap, on behalf of us all.

And then the King, with his magnificent moustache, and trusty sabre, and terrible vengeance – or terrible mercy, depending on how you look at these things – moves on to the next person in the line, and shortly afterwards we are released to go about the business of preparing for our public appearance later in the day.

We have been in town since last night, when we arrived to find a city apparently under military occupation, with a ban on public demonstrations and political meetings, and further public demonstrations against the ban resulting in running battles in the streets between protestors and the police. We also discovered that the hotel we had planned to stay at was closed for repairs as the result of a recent firebombing. It took us three hours of trawling the streets with our gear in the cart before we found another place to take us in, the captain having to point out his own likeness on the poster advertising his presence at the public celebrations for the King's birthday weekend, in order to convince the hotel manager that we were not an anarchist terror group, what with all our suspicious-looking equipment and foreign accents and manner of transport.

'Do we *look* like revolutionaries?' the cap had said loudly the next morning at breakfast, clearly still fuming at this slight, and Andrea and I had looked at each other and wondered.

That afternoon we attend the reception at which the cap is to be guest of honour, and which is held on the royal yacht moored in the middle of the bay, and I wonder if any of the other esteemed guests arrived in town yesterday by horse and cart. There is more food and drink than we have seen in a few weeks and, after I have done my bit for the cause by performing a brief demonstration of the suit out on the water, Andrea and I gorge ourselves, and this time neither of us fills our pockets with leftovers.

As the party progresses, the guests are invited to ride in the King's new cast-iron diving bell, which descends to the bottom of the bay on a winch operated from a scaffold on the dock, and gives views of the sandy seabed and the many wrecks and other sites of archaeological interest down there. When it's time for Andrea and I to take our turn we sit in the strange, echoing structure as it sinks through the water, piloted by an excitable young Frenchman who turns wheels and opens dripping valves while narrating the experience for us in three languages, although we can hardly hear him over the sound of the air pump.

A narrow, flexible pipe runs between our feet and into the seawater through the opening at the bottom of the bell. Through the thick portholes we can see that the other end of the hose is attached to what could be a giant metal crab or other armoured sea creature, but is in fact a man in a heavy iron suit, who is moving about the floor of the bay and investigating what he uncovers there with huge clawed hands, while fish swim around and investigate him.

'The future of undersea exploration!' our guide tells us, and who can say that he isn't right?

Back on board the yacht we watch the King – for here he is

211

again, with his magnificent moustache, but no sabre this time – introducing the Famous Captain Clarke B. to his subjects and describing the two of them as lifelong friends, despite the fact that they only met for the first time today. 'A man of destiny!' is how the King refers to our captain, before the cap himself delivers his usual patter to the crowd, though with a more dignified, melancholy air than we've previously been used to, and only partly on account of the eye patch, with its intimations of war and tragedy and loss.

'He looks old,' says Andrea, and he does.

Then the King announces his intention to fund the captain's work for the next five years, as part of his grand plan to make sure that the country will continue to be the foremost military power in the Mediterranean *and perhaps beyond*, which is somewhat at odds with the cap's stated life-saving mission but no one seems to mind, and the two men embrace to general applause.

Loosened up by wine, I invite Andrea to take a walk with me out on deck, to watch the evening stars coming out. I am in the middle of weighing up the excitement of a romantic coupling carried out not yards away from an actual king, against the probability of – and potential punishments for – getting caught in the act, when I realise we are not alone.

It's the cap's man, Mcinerney, emerging from the shadows with a finger to his lips.

'If you value your lives, you'll want to hear what I have to say,' he says.

Andrea and I look at each other, wondering if this is a joke, or a test, or something else new, and then, saying nothing, we both nod at Mcinerney.

After looking about to make sure we are not being watched, Mcinerney hands me an illustrated flyer, which advertises the funicular railway that climbs to the summit of the volcano outside town. When we look up, sure enough there's the actual mountain itself, looming against the darkening sky across the bay, the clouds above its peak lit by the glow from its fiery heart.

'Eight sharp tomorrow morning,' Mcinerney says. 'Come alone. And tell no one.'

Then, with a last look around him, he turns and hurries away.

MCINERNEY'S CONFESSION

The next morning, in order to avoid any complicated questions, we're out and about before the captain – who has been up until the early hours celebrating with the royal party – is even awake. We take a tram across town, and then another out to the funicular station at the foot of the volcano. On the way we examine the flyer that Mcinerney gave me, comparing it to the view from the tram window.

In the illustration the funicular train line appears to run straight up the side of the volcano and directly into the crater at the top, from where fire and smoke are belching into a bright orange sky. In reality the mountain doesn't appear to currently have fire coming out of it, which is a relief, although the summit is mostly wreathed in cloud, so it's hard to be sure.

'Amazing sights,' Andrea translates. 'Eighth wonder of the world. Thrill your family. Excite your wife. All for a fair price.'

'I suppose no one can argue with that,' I say.

When we get to the station there's Mcinerney waiting for us, a copy of the day's newspaper under his arm to identify him, as if anybody wouldn't already know him by that bowler hat and overcoat. He already has tickets for the three of us to ride up to the summit, and so we all get into the little open carriage where three or four other tourists are seated, nervously waiting for the ascent, and at a signal from the station master we're off.

The journey up the mountain takes a half-hour or so, during which time we stare out of the train in horror. The barren, tree-less slopes, covered all over with drifting clouds of poisonous yellow smoke that sting our eyes as we climb, are like a vision of hell. Here and there towards the summit the figures of other visitors come in and out of view, holding handkerchiefs over their mouths in order to breathe. Everywhere there's the acrid stink of something like rotten eggs, or the smoke of a hundred tanning factories.

I catch Andrea crossing himself – 'Habit,' says he, and smiles ruefully – as he looks out across the awful, shattered landscape to the glittering bay below us, no doubt wondering, as I am, how on earth we've come to be up here and not down there where people properly belong.

At the summit station we disembark and follow Mcinerney through the noxious mist along a narrow track, until the vapour briefly clears and we're all of a sudden standing above a drop of a hundred feet or more into the gaping mouth of the volcano itself.

'Dear God,' I say.

'Or the other fellow,' replies our man.

'What's this all about, Mcinerney?' I say then, trying to sound grown-up and business-like, and more in command of myself and my surroundings than I currently feel, what with the tendrils of black smoke curling up towards us from the crater, and the heat we can feel even through our shoes.

Mcinerney looks at me for a moment, as if trying to match me with the boy he first met at the train station in London, then takes off his hat, runs a hand through his hair, and nods.

'They mean to kill you,' he says. 'And likely your friend too.'

'Why?' I look at Andrea, who shrugs. 'And also, who?'

'You know too much,' says Mcinerney. 'Or you soon will.'

'But we don't know anything.'

'Well that's just as dangerous, isn't it?'

'Is it?'

Mcinerney sighs, puts his hat back on and puts his hands into his pockets.

'Tomorrow night you're going to swim out into the harbour under cover of darkness and plant a clockwork bomb under the royal yacht, which will be timed to go off and assassinate the King during the flotilla the following day.'

'So we *are anarchici*!' declares Andrea triumphantly.

'The anarchists are amateurs,' says Mcinerney, disgusted.

'Then which side are we on?' I say.

'You're on the side of money, Dan,' says Mcinerney. 'The same side you've always been on. And at the moment money has decided that the best way of making more money is by getting rid of this particular monarch, and never mind why.'

'But the anarchists will get the blame anyway,' I say, catching on. 'As long as there's no one left around to explain what really happened.'

'Exactly.'

'Why are you telling us all this?'

'Call it a change of heart.'

'And what about the cap?'

'I'm not responsible for the captain any more. Or for anyone else. I'm my own man now. I wish I could say the same for him.'

And with that he looks around himself, as if trying to spot someone else among the choking fog, then holds out his hand for each of us to shake hurriedly and, telling us, 'Good luck, boys,' sets off back along the track in the direction of the station, where he quickly disappears into the mist.

Andrea and I look at each other. 'What do we do?' he says.

I am saved from having to answer by the sound of the woman's scream.

Halfway back down the narrow track there is already a crowd gathered, and by the time we get there the woman is being comforted, and fanned with handkerchiefs, and people are pointing down into the crater, although there is nothing left to see or to do about it by now.

'She is saying she saw the man fall,' Andrea tells me. 'He just went right down … there.'

And, of course, there on the narrow path, at the very spot from which he was sent tumbling over the edge, is Mcinerney's bowler hat.

As we stand there, as powerless as everyone else to change what has happened, or know what we should do next, we spot, through a brief clearing in the drifting clouds of smoke, the man in the black overcoat climbing onto the train that is about to begin its descent of the mountain. He is looking back at us too, as if to make sure his murderous action has made the intended impression.

When the train pulls away he briefly tips his hat to us, then puts his finger to his lips, and is gone.

The Monstrous Future

Of course, when we finally accept that we won't be able to stay on the summit of the volcano forever, and ride the train back down the mountain, they're waiting to meet us at the station at the bottom, three of them altogether, and there is a gun too. And in the carriage on the way back to town the plan is explained, and my role in it, and the obvious and terrible consequences if I refuse or try to escape before playing out my part, and everything is pretty much as poor old Mcinerney said it would be.

When I point out to our captors that it seems as if the consequences for us are just as obvious and terrible whether we play along or not, I am reminded that everyone has a family, somewhere, and so agree to shut up, and that's about it for polite chat and sparkling conversation for the rest of the journey.

'You could leave, you know,' I tell Andrea, as the two of us lie on the floor of our room in a mess of bedclothes, exhausted by the horror of the day and by everything we have just done to each other in our efforts to forget it – which has resulted, among other things, in what feels like the start of a black eye for me, and a bloodied lip for him.

'I know.'

'No one would blame you for it.'

'I know.'

'I have money you could take.'

'I know.'

I roll over and look at him.

'How do you know about the money?' I say.

'Because you are smart, but not that smart,' he says, and then smiles sadly and puts his hand on the side of my face.

In the early evening I find Captain Clarke B. down at the docks, where he is watching the continuing archaeological exploration of the bay. The day's finds, which are being laid out on the dock for examination before being crated up and shipped off to various museums, include rusting ship's bells and broken vases and other unidentifiable pieces of scrap metal that I can't see much point in going to all this trouble for.

'Did you know that they found a 2,000-year-old ship down there,' the cap asks me, 'and that the wine on board was still drinkable?'

I tell the captain that I wasn't aware of the fact.

'Ah, but what would the men who made that wine think of all this?' he says, indicating the mass of activity around us.

From the wooden scaffold the diving bell is being lowered into the water for the day's final trip, and men swarm around it, turning one set of wheels that operate the crane, and another that power the bellows to supply the air. The tank-like iron diving suit stands on the side of the dock, where it has been left to dry after being scrubbed clean of algae. The round helmet piece is covered in glass portholes, in order, I suppose, for the pilot to be able to turn his head and see in all directions, but which give the thing the strange appearance of a gigantic insect.

'This is the future, Dan,' says the captain, striking his knuckles on the chest of the monster, which causes it to ring with a dull clang. 'In ten years we'll have mapped the bottom of every ocean, and then there will be nothing left to know.'

'Surely that's the aim of all scientific endeavours,' I say.

'Is it?'

'You have the King's sponsorship now,' I tell him. 'You'll be able to complete your work. You got everything you wanted.'

At this the captain laughs, sharply.

'Sadly, the King is not the final authority,' he says.

The two of us stand there for a while, both pretending to examine the diving suit.

'Are we going to play this game right up to the end?' I ask.

'What do you want from me, Dan?' says the cap.

'I hoped you might have some last words of advice.'

'I don't think I have any words left for anyone,' he says, turning away to look out across the bay.

And then there's that old feeling rising in me, which might be murderous rage or my heart breaking all over again.

'Do you even have any concept of what's really going on?' I ask him.

'We are not paid to ask questions.'

'Yes, you've said that before.'

'If you live long enough, Dan,' Captain Clarke B. says, 'you'll find that most of life consists of just repeating yourself again and again and again, and hoping that eventually by some miracle it might make a difference.'

When I walk away he is still staring across the water, where the waves, I suppose, have been repeating themselves for the past few thousands of years, and will go on doing so long after we're all forgotten.

220

Not Everyone Has
a Family

In the morning the cap is gone, and he remains gone in the afternoon. By then I have discovered that most of the money I've been hiding in the bottom of my bag – it having got too much to keep carrying around in my shirt – has gone with him, too.

So that's that.

With the permission of my captors I arrange for the hotel manager to send what's left of the cash to my brother. I don't include a note. Then Andrea and I go out and get drunk at the smartest café in town, and behave quite disgracefully, and are eventually asked to leave, and are escorted back to the hotel by our new bodyguards who have been waiting outside the whole time.

The plan is unchanged, and shortly before midnight they come for us.

We are loaded into a carriage, with the suit too, and driven the mile or so to the waterfront with me sandwiched between two giants, and Andrea sitting opposite guarded by the third, and a gun stuck into my side the whole way just to make sure.

During the journey Andrea plays with a coin nervously, moving it between his fingers, as if trying to come to a decision. As our guards watch, amused, he begins making the coin jump invisibly from one hand to the other, then disappear altogether, only to reappear behind the ear of one of our captors.

It's at this point that the guard upon whom the trick is being performed grabs Andrea's wrist with one hand, while taking the coin away and pocketing it with the other.

When the grip is released Andrea looks at the man and smiles. 'Not everyone has a family,' he says.

Then he throws open the door and jumps from the moving carriage, and within a moment is gone from sight and into the maze of dark streets.

The carriage stops after a few yards, and the guard who lost him makes to get out and chase after Andrea, but the lead giant shakes his head and bangs on the roof, and we're soon on the move again.

When we arrive at the dock I change into the suit and then climb down into the water, where the bomb, which looks roughly like a miniature torpedo with a timing mechanism attached to it, is lowered to me. Then, after nodding to the guards, I set out to paddle across the bay and out to the yacht.

The water is warm, and I wonder if this is as a result of some geological process having to do with the volcano, or just sewage from the city being pumped straight out into the bay. I make good time, and within half an hour I am approaching the royal ship, paddling as quietly as I can in case anyone is up on deck and paying attention. When I come up against the hull I secure the bomb against a pair of rivets by means of a screw mechanism, and then attend to the clockwork timer, which I have been instructed to set to go off in six hours, giving my employers ample time to get out of the city, and dispose of me in whatever manner they see fit.

Instead I set the timer for five minutes, and then start paddling away from the yacht as fast as I can, hoping that Andrea has managed to keep up his end of the deal, and will be waiting on the water with a boat to get us out of the bay, and away.

But out in the middle of the bay there is no rescue boat in sight, and I quickly realise that even if he now reaches me in time, we will have a hell of a job to get safely clear, even as the time continues to tick away, and I desperately scan the dark water for any hopeful sign.

And then, just as I assume I am done for, and will either be blown up or recaptured, and likely follow Mcinerney into the crater of the volcano, my salvation appears from below in the form of the monstrous iron diving suit breaching the surface of the water like some prehistoric sea creature. I have barely enough time to wonder at the mechanism behind this, assuming the employment of some form of inflated air tanks, when I am grabbed by the creature's claws and pulled under the water as, right on cue, the bomb goes off.

To France, Again

It occurs to me, as I stand at the prow of the passenger steamer, that the Mediterranean Sea, once you're out in the middle of it, as we currently are, is as impossibly blue as they say. Also, that it is so far removed from the cold and miserable body of water that I grew up next to that it might be a different species of thing altogether, and further that the English language doesn't have nearly enough words to explain all the ways in which they couldn't possibly be the same sort of object.

And while I am thinking this I am watching dolphins leaping from the water as they ride our bow wave, in a way no dolphin ever did alongside any boat I travelled on as a boy, and I am wondering about how those creatures experience the world, and what they make of it all, and what it might be like to join them.

And then Andrea comes up and slips his arms around me from behind, and puts his face into my neck in a way that sends a wonderful shiver of desire through me, mixed with the undeniable thrill of being caught embracing in this way.

'How does it feel to be dead?' he says into my ear.

'I've been dead before,' I say. 'It's a lot less painful than I remember. Look at the dolphins.'

'I saw them already.'

'But did you really *see* them?' I ask.

'I saw them,' he says, and then, thrillingly, kisses me fully on the mouth, out there on the deck, and possibly in view of anyone who might want to see. And I kiss him back, too.

The journey to France takes four days, via the islands of Sardinia and Corsica, and at each stop we pick up the latest French and Italian newspapers in order to follow the continuing story of the failed assassination attempt by anarchist terrorists on the Italian king, including eyewitness testimony of the terrible events from our very good friends the Carmagnolle brothers of Marseille, inventors, who are pictured next to their patented atmospheric deep-sea diving suit and diving bell, the inside of which I now know very well. There are also defiant quotes from the King himself, who has offered a public challenge to any of his would-be murderers to meet him in single combat, at a time and place of their choosing.

There is no mention of the actual conspiracy, or the conspir-ators, but there's a sketch of the heroic Captain Clarke B. himself, missing and presumed dead, and as far as we know our captors must now be operating under the assumption that I was killed in the explosion. All the same we keep looking over our shoul-ders, half expecting to see that the ship is being followed, and we pull our hats down over our faces every time the boat takes on new passengers.

For the rest of the time we hide out in our cabin and make happy love for hours, unable to believe our luck, or take walks on the deck with scarves around our faces, or sit in canvas chairs with winter blankets pulled up to our mouths, pretending to enjoy the sun like an elderly married couple, and thinking that there are much worse things that we could be.

It's a bright, cold morning when we pull into the harbour at the famous French town of N— and disembark with our luggage, which consists of nothing more than two satchels and the frogman suit. The collapsible boat is probably still in the stables of the hotel in N—, Italy, to this day.

At the customs desk I show one of the letters of introduction I still carry, and the suit as evidence too, and apparently we are not considered much of a threat to the well-being of the Republic, as we are nodded through and so proceed to the cab rank. There we secure a lift up into the hills above the port, where the beautiful tree-lined roads are all filled with grand houses, and we soon find ourselves on the doorstep of a pink mansion, hoping that we have the right address.

After some discussion at the door, and the relaying of messages into the house and back again, and the production of evidence that we are indeed who we say we are, we're shown through to the terrace where our would-be host – failed American painter, traveller of the world, spender of the family's fortune and carri-er-on in the face of the vast and uncomprehending etc. etc. – is having breakfast in his expensive pyjamas.

'Well I didn't expect to see you so soon, boys,' says William T. Baker, looking up from emptying a glass of brandy into his coffee. 'But come on in.'

The Sort of People Who Follow Those Sorts of People

Welcome, then, to our new life. Or our new life for the next few weeks at least, as we are installed into the world of our fabulously rich friend, and his equally fabulously rich acquaintances, and all that is entailed by that.

Each day starts in the late morning, with a hung-over breakfast for Andrea and I on the previously mentioned terrace, at which we may or may not be joined by the master of the house, depending on whether he is still drinking off the tail end of another all-night party, and so hasn't gone to bed yet – or is making one of his regular doomed attempts to rise before noon and spend the day in his painting studio.

That first day, during our tour of the house, the studio is the room that our host is proudest to show us, introducing us to each of his unfinished paintings – 'tonally atmospheric, but not necessarily impressionist' – as if they were old friends. Because I am not an idiot, I don't tell him that I have been in an artist's studio before, and one filled with much better work than this one, including two or three modestly spectacular nude drawings of your narrator himself.

Andrea, at least, is genuinely impressed to be in the presence of an actual artist, even one for whom the act of painting seems mostly to be a preamble to, and justification for, getting drunk every afternoon.

At breakfast, as we pass each other the toast, or the butter, or the marmalade, or the milk, and nurse our sore heads, we might consider the view of the beautiful town and the glittering blue sea beyond, and notice the mild air that has persisted past the change of the season, and the birds in the garden, and we will find ourselves filled with a strange hope for our future. Despite the number of empty guest rooms in the house, there has never been a question about Andrea and I spending our nights together. Instead, the day that we arrived a grand double room was made up for us before we even asked, with one solitary, giant bed, and like that we realised that we have been accepted for who and what we are, whatever that is, without the issue ever even being raised.

And on the table in front of us will be the daily newspapers, which we're happy to see have all now moved on to new scandals and outrages and forgotten any of the events in which we played our part. There is no news of any kind of the whereabouts or further adventures of Captain Clarke B. Instead we can find out who is in town, and what they are up to, and what is being said about that, as well as read a forecast of the day's weather, which is invariably a positive one. Perhaps we'll think about a trip to the winter gardens, or I'll try to write a letter to my brother, until our host appears and announces, 'I am defeated by the muse again, lads!' and so bottles will be opened and wine decanted, and we'll set off together on the fabulous adventure of another day and evening filled with wonderful and interesting events and people, including poets and painters and writers and their sponsors, as well as the sort of people who follow those sorts of people – which, somehow, now includes Andrea and myself.

For while there are no shows on the water for me to perform at, and no demonstrations required, and the Fearless Frogman's suit itself is left draped over a life-sized artist's dummy in the studio, instead Andrea and I are earning our keep by being ourselves. By being something new and interesting for everyone to look at, and by recounting thrilling and authentic tales of our adventures and tragic childhoods for our new friends, and by embellishing the stories a little more with each retelling, and by making ourselves available for conversation, and company, and perhaps the promise of more if the situation arises, and by staying up until dawn as and when necessary, or not staying up, and then being ready to get up the next day and do it all over again, all the same, and no matter how we feel about it.

And because, as Andrea and I both know, there are far, far worse ways to make a living, we agree that we are both, all things considered, very happy for the time being.

The Incident of the Watch

And then there's the day that a trip is arranged to visit a ruined castle somewhere in the woods that cover the hills above the town.

On the afternoon in question our party – consisting of Andrea, myself, our host and perhaps fifteen other assorted guests, most of them rich Englishmen and women, as well as a couple of Frenchmen too – is loaded into a series of open carriages and driven through the pine forests to a spot a mile or so below the ruins, where numerous other carriages are already parked up.

As everyone makes their way up through the trees, following the trail made by the hundreds of tourists who have gone before us, carrying various wicker baskets full of food and drink, I notice that Andrea is getting on just fine with one of the rich Englishwomen – who I recognise as having been a regular at our host's parties – or she is getting on just fine with him, anyway.

Meanwhile the other guests are excitedly discussing the current wave of political assassinations that is sweeping the world, to which conversational subject I decide it wise not to contribute.

'And they say that the exact same man was involved in the murders of both the Russian tsar *and* the American president –'

'But never apprehended –'

'Not to mention the attempt on Queen Victoria's life –'

'Oh, surely not!'

'It's true! A count! With the duelling scars to prove it …'

Outside the castle, which stands in a clearing in the forest, a gang of local children are hanging around in the hope of picking up tips from tourists in need of directions, or help with carrying things, or entertainment, and they're still there when we emerge again from our brief tour of the ruins to enjoy our picnic in the warm late-autumn sun.

Watching them begging for scraps, I wonder if any of them would even believe that Andrea and I could just as easily have been in their place as ours, or that we may yet still end up back there.

At some point in the afternoon's eating and drinking and idle conversation I go into the woods to relieve myself and have just finished buttoning up when I hear a noise behind me, and turn to find the woman who has been talking to Andrea for most of the day watching me curiously, while swigging from a bottle of wine.

'I don't think your friend likes women,' she says.

'He's old-fashioned like that,' I say.

'And what about you?'

'How long have you been standing there?' I ask her. I remember now a late-night, drunken conversation between the two of us about the emancipation of women, which mostly consisted of me listening and nodding my head. If she is married to the man who I think she is married to, then she's a good twenty years younger than him – which still makes her at least fifteen years older than me, and no less beautiful for that.

'Long enough to have earned a moment or two of your attention, I should think,' she replies.

'And now you have it.'

231

She steps forward and offers me the bottle and I take a drink, because what else would I do?

'I possibly had something else in mind,' she says.

We are interrupted, thankfully or not, by the noise and shouting coming from the direction of the castle.

When we emerge from the trees we find that one of the Englishmen, who I recognise in fact as this woman's husband, is attempting to grab hold of one of the street boys, who is running around and dodging this way and that while Andrea is trying to intervene, and everyone else – our party, the other children, assorted castle visitors – looks on with amusement.

'My watch!' the man is shouting. 'This little fucker has robbed me!'

Eventually Andrea gets the two of them apart, and, holding up a finger to calm the rampaging Englishman, turns to the boy, who is now bravely standing his ground.

'Did you take his watch?' Andrea asks the boy in English.

The boy shakes his head.

'He's obviously going to lie,' says the man. 'Beat it out of him!'

Then Andrea says something to the boy in French or Italian and the boy narrows his eyes but shakes his head again.

'Are you sure you didn't lose it?' Andrea asks the Englishman.

'You do have hundreds of watches, Harry,' says the woman with whom I have just emerged from the woods – Mrs Henry Colbert, I now remember – and then turns to everyone else and adds, 'He really does.'

'I'll *buy* you a new watch, Harry,' our host shouts, laughing.

'I didn't lose the bloody watch,' says the injured party, furious. 'Are you all going to take this' – indicating Andrea – 'this … *peasant's* word over mine?'

There's an uncomfortable silence then, and I watch Andrea weighing up his options. He mouths something to the boy, who frowns before looking at Andrea's hand, which is held in front of him at an odd angle.

Then the boy nods, understanding, and Andrea smacks him once, sharply, around the head, briefly stunning him, which causes our English chum to shout, 'Bravo!' with some satisfaction.

The boy clutches the side of his face, in pain but still defiantly staring back at Andrea, who then reaches forward and, *as if by magic*, produces a coin from the boy's ear and gives it to him, to delighted and relieved laughter from the rest of the crowd.

'No watch,' says Andrea to Henry Colbert, with finality, and then walks away, leaving him to decide for himself whether or not justice has been served.

That evening everyone returns to the house, with the intention of drinking until the booze runs out or the sun comes up. In the event Henry Colbert is still sour over his lost timepiece, and after moping around for a couple of hours goes home early, taking his young wife with him, and saving me from the continuation of whatever it was that occurred between the two of us in the woods. Besides, there are new people to meet, and stories to tell and to hear, and fascinating moments to observe or take part in, including the filling of an entire ornamental pond with naked frolicking nymphs of all ages, sizes and genders, and a whole bunch of startled carp besides.

Eventually, Andrea and I get to bed around dawn, hardly having shared a word all day, and too drunk and exhausted to do much about it now, despite a brief and half-hearted attempt.

It's not until the next morning at breakfast that he slides the watch across the table to me.

'It would suit you better than him anyway,' he says.

The Next Thing

The first time it happens, Andrea is less surprised than I am, knowing better how these people think and work from his time with the cap's friends, and more than likely his life before that too.

We are at the far end of another long night, a party of ten of us, including Mrs Henry Colbert but not her husband, all having been to the casino and lost more money than anyone has kept track of. Back at the house, for some reason I am called on to show off my physique, and strike a series of half-naked athletic poses in the middle of the living room for the appreciation of the other guests, and end up standing on a coffee table, shirtless, flexing my muscles to general applause, and then everyone is waiting to see what the next thing will be.

Well, what the next thing turns out to be is a mixture of opium and some other mysterious oriental root, which is solemnly passed around in a silver pipe, and which, when combined with the wine and the whisky and everything else, makes the far side of the room suddenly start moving very far away as I am watching, taking the rest of the world with it.

And then everything including me is lost in a fog for a while, although I am aware of people undressing each other, and someone removes the rest of my clothes too, and we are moving to another room ridiculously decorated like something from the Arabian Nights, and then there's nothing until I come to my senses to find that I am in the act with a dark-eyed Mrs Henry Colbert, and we are clinging on to each other as if we are shipwrecked, and there are possibly a couple of other people with us besides, it being hard to tell who is doing what to whom, exactly. I know that at one moment one of the nymphs from the ornamental pond becomes involved, and is either underneath or on top of me, as well as a man who I have never seen before who does something to me that makes my stomach lurch and causes me to lose my breath, before I finally lose consciousness altogether.

But when I wake up in the morning there's only Mrs Henry Colbert left there next to me, naked, propped up on one arm, considering my body and telling me, 'Well, you're a fine distraction, aren't you?'

'Am I?'

'I've been waiting for you to wake up for the last hour.'

'And your husband ...?'

'Let's say he's away on business.'

'Is he?'

However, Mrs Henry Colbert is suddenly too occupied to answer any more questions.

After we are done, again, and Mrs Henry Colbert is satisfied, I excuse myself and tiptoe, filled with guilt and dread, back to our room, where I am greeted by a laughing Andrea who throws me joyfully onto the bed and, pinning me down, tells me, 'Just make sure you get paid next time, idiot,' before he, too, has his fill of me.

And, oh, I am everyone's fool now.

In fact, there are any number of 'next times', and not just with Mrs Henry Colbert. Over the days that follow I am requested to take part in similar situations involving a range of our host's friends, including seemingly upright English wives and husbands, wild French poets and poetesses, Irish painter's models, and even a couple of American stage actors, all temporarily using the excuse of the silver pipe to allow themselves this excess – though not Mr Henry Colbert, who always leaves before the festivities begin, and not our host either, who we soon establish is happier to sit in a chair and watch things from a distance, drink in hand, content that his guests are enjoying themselves but not, apparently, aroused or excited by any of it ('Oh,' he tells me, melancholically, 'it's been a long time since I've actually been *excited* by much of anything at all ...').

Once or twice Andrea is there too, but we realise that this is confusing for both of us, and so decide to keep this strange part of our already strange lives separate, and not ask too many questions of each other, except to compare our weekly haul of gifted bracelets, rings, necklaces and other jewellery. And even the occasional pocket watch.

No matter how many of William T. Baker's close or distant acquaintances that I find myself involved with, however, I soon notice that it does always seem to be Mrs Henry Colbert in whose arms I wake in the morning. And it is Mrs Henry Colbert, too, who I begin having occasional lunches with, down in the old town, that for some reason I don't tell Andrea about.

'And your husband ...?'

'My husband and I,' says Mrs Henry Colbert, sipping her coffee, 'have come to an accommodation.'

'And does he know this?' I ask.

'We have an understanding. Although it's not one I'm always sure he understands. Do you know what a trophy wife is?'

I nod.

236

'Well then. I'm the prize for a lifetime of success. Moulded in that exact image.'

'And what's your reward?'

'This,' she laughs, gesturing at the café, the blue sea beyond, before her dark eyes come to rest on me, causing me to blush like a schoolboy.

'My background isn't any different from yours, Dan,' she says. 'It's just further away. And consequently I can see it more clearly.'

'Do you think I don't see my background clearly?'

Mrs Henry Colbert wrinkles her nose.

'I think you'd need to stop running away from it first,' she says.

That night I accidentally win 500 francs at the casino, and blow it all buying drinks for everyone there, before finding myself back at the house in the room with the ridiculous Arabian Nights décor, in the middle of a squirming mass of people who I don't even recognise.

The next morning even our host suggests that I might want to start taking things a little more gently for a while.

But I don't.

A Poor Swimmer

If winter ever touches this town we have yet to see it, despite the lateness of the year. It's another gloriously bright and blue day when William T. Baker invites us, and half the foreign population of the town besides, to a grand picnic on the beach, and the sun is dancing on the surface of the water in a manner that we would all likely be able to appreciate if we weren't so sick from the previous night's drinking.

Sweating, I sit in a deckchair under a blanket while Andrea attempts to make himself useful helping the staff unload drinks and bread and cheese and so on, so that at least one of us will appear worth our keep.

And here, too, are Mr and Mrs Henry Colbert, he dressed as if for Sunday lunch and she spotless under a white umbrella. Mrs Henry Colbert and I have lately been expanding our surreptitious lunch dates into visits to museums and art galleries and such places, although neither of us has much appreciation or understanding of what we see there. We have also been expanding our adventures with the silver-pipe crowd, to include all manner of strange people and increasingly frightening practices. And while I don't know what I would call what has been going on between us, exactly, I do know that it is not nothing, and that

238

some sort of reckoning will have to be made for it, at some point or another.

We nod our hellos and, pointing to the local families who are enjoying their Sunday off work by paddling down by the water-line, Henry Colbert says, 'Late in the year for a swim, I think.'

'Indeed,' I reply, raising the wine bottle from which I have been swigging to toast him, which causes him to give me a strange look.

As the day progresses and the celebrations are joined by more and more people until the entire beach is a vision of little England – and I have more and more to drink – I find myself taking increasing risks in my public flirtation with Mrs Henry Colbert, including laughing too often at her jokes, and inter-rupting polite conversations she is having with others, and being increasingly rude to her husband besides, to the point that Andrea takes me to one side and asks me quietly to cool things off.

Somehow or other I end up with a blanket tied around my shoulders like a cape, holding court, delighting anyone who is willing to listen with tales of my waterborne adventures, includ-ing the time I thwarted an attempt on the life of the King of Italy, and so on, and in the middle of some anecdote about my own daring I find myself climbing onto one of the wooden picnic tables which have been carried down to the beach and striking a heroic pose, cape blowing in the breeze.

And then the table collapses and I fall.

As I lie on the pebbles I hear someone saying, 'Look at that.' Assuming they're talking about me I ignore them, but then I hear them say, 'Look,' again, and I sit up and look.

Down at the waterline there is a commotion of people point-ing and shouting in French, with some of the men wading out into the waves in their trousers, but none of them are seemingly capable enough swimmers to get out past the breakers, where a couple of children have been swept out by a fast-moving tide and are struggling to keep their heads above the cold water, in very real danger of drowning.

It occurs to me that someone should do something.

And then I see that Andrea, with his shirt off, is already sprinting into the sea. As the crowd watches he fights his way through the heavy waves to try to get to the children, is beaten back and fights on, and eventually manages to reach them, gathering the pair in his arms.

Too late I remember how poor a swimmer he is, and watch as he tries to keep the three of them afloat, and then goes under.

Thankfully there are enough people in the water now that they can form a sort of human chain, and in this way, holding each other by the hand, the local men get close enough to Andrea and the two children that someone is able to grab his collar when he surfaces, gasping, for what would otherwise probably have been the last time, and so the three of them are slowly pulled back to the shore.

When I push my way through the crowd of people Andrea is lying on his back on the pebbles, his eyes closed. I kneel down to check that he is breathing, am relieved to find that he is, and whisper, 'I'm sorry,' into his ear.

He opens his eyes and looks up at me, sees the blanket cape around my shoulders.

'You look like him,' he says.

It's later on, when we have all moved on to someone or other's house up in the hills, and kept on drinking too, that Henry Colbert finally asks me, angrily, if I haven't spent enough time making love to his wife this evening, and I make the foolish mistake of trying to shame him in public by suggesting that he might consider trying it himself.

Clearly humiliated, he briefly storms out of the room, but just as I turn to continue my conversation with his wife, who herself has grown tired of my behaviour and has, it appears, walked out too, he is back, and with some serious purpose, and people are drawing away having seen what he has in his hand, and then there are surprised gasps as he brings up a service revolver and points it at my face from a distance of less than three inches.

'No?' he asks me. 'Nothing at all to say?'

I shake my head as calmly and slowly as I can manage.

'And now?' says Henry Colbert, pressing the barrel of the gun against my nose.

From within the crowd that has quickly gathered around us – and I'm not sure whether they are there out of a genuine concern for my welfare or because they're excited and intrigued to see what might happen next – Mrs Henry Colbert emerges again.

'Put it down, Henry,' she says, sounding more tired than anything else.

'I won't be taken for a fool by you any more, Clare,' says Henry Colbert over his outstretched arm, then, waving the gun around at the rest of the crowd, to a general sharp intake of breath and a sudden widening of the circle around us – 'nor by any of the rest of you vipers, despite what you may think' – before he comes to rest again, this time pointing the weapon dramatically at his exasperated wife.

Which is when the gun goes off, and Mrs Henry Colbert goes down clutching her throat, where her high-collared dress is rapidly changing colour, and a couple of women faint, and, horrified, Henry Colbert cries, 'What have I done?' and then tries to put the gun into his own month – but is saved, again, by Andrea, who grabs hold of him and with the help of a couple of the other guests, wrestles him to the floor.

The sun is coming up when we finally get back from the hospital where Mrs Henry Colbert, seriously but not critically injured, will remain checked in under an assumed name for the next two weeks, before she and her husband will escape from a potentially complicated legal situation by returning to England for good. As Andrea and I undress in our room I notice the parcel that I've had made up for my brother – ready for posting, with a set of new lead soldiers inside – sitting on the bureau, and realise what day it is.

'Merry Christmas,' I say, and try to embrace Andrea, but he pushes me away, and then when I try to kiss him again, he punches me hard in the stomach, causing me to double over.

When I look up Andrea is holding the gun in two hands – is, in fact, aiming it at me – and I just have time to think *so that's where it went,* before the vase behind me explodes, and I realise that a bullet has just gone past my ear, and that another one may follow soon, and maybe this one won't pass me so easily.

'Why does everyone keep pointing guns at me?' I shout.

And then William T. Baker appears at the door and takes in the chaos, and the gun in Andrea's hand. We all look at each other, as if only now realising that we each have no idea who the other people in this little scene may actually be, or what they have been doing, or what they want.

'I'll give you half an hour before I send someone for the police,' says our host.

So, Christmas Day or not, Andrea and I gather our things, including the old frogman's suit, and our bag of stolen or borrowed or gifted jewellery, and William T. Baker allows us to make a couple of sandwiches to take with us, and then we say goodbye to the old place.

And as we walk down the street, back towards the old town and from there towards who knows where, past the mansions that we will never again see the inside of, including the vast blue palace formerly rented by Mr and Mrs Henry Colbert, I realise that we don't have any money.

And so we are cast out of paradise.

BOOK 3

The Only Surviving Sons

There's a cold wind and the threat of snow in the air – although the rust-coloured, rocky ground is still bare – as we descend the goat track above the walled town of St S—, looking for a place to stay for the night and something warm to eat. Although it's still early we can see lamps already being lit in the windows of the yellowed plaster houses, and as we come closer we can smell food cooking. On the edge of town, we ask a couple of boys who are out and about on some errand or other in the cold evening to point us towards a decent inn, and they send us in the right direction, despite looking at us as if we are a couple of wandering madmen who have only just staggered out of the hills, which is not far from what we are.

We have been walking across the hard, empty country for almost a month now.

The rough plan – so rough, in fact, that we haven't discussed it more than once – is to eventually make our way to the channel, and, in the absence of anywhere else to go, likely return to England. But the snow falling on the mountains when we left N— forced us to spend the first couple of weeks heading west rather than north, or risk freezing to death on some inaccessible pass, and we've been travelling mostly in that direction ever since, following the dirt roads and cattle paths and, sometimes, our own noses, as we try to avoid the worst of the winter weather. We've been caught in snowstorms more than once when our path has drifted too far up into the hills, and I have consequently developed an almost neurotic fixation on various methods of meteorological divination, including paying particular attention to the colour of morning ice on village ponds, and the pitch of the calls of crows out in the frozen fields, and the ache in my arm where it was broken, and the sound made by twigs when they snap.

So west it is, for the time being at least.

Stars are starting to come out in the evening sky and somewhere a single church bell is ringing when we reach the empty town square, and find the inn on the edge of it, and head inside to negotiate with the landlord and explain our situation, and see if we can't come to an agreement for the night.

For the last few weeks we've been paying for our food and lodging at hotels and private houses by selling off the contents of the bag of jewellery bit by bit (I have kept hold of Mr Henry Colbert's pocket watch for sentimental reasons), or sometimes by trading the smaller pieces directly for rooms and hot meals. At each hamlet or village or town that we pass through we lay out our wares in the market square, or along the bar of the local inn, or on doorsteps and window ledges, and we describe their beautiful detailing, or exotic provenance, or the effect they might have on members of the opposite sex.

We have invented a story that we are the only surviving sons of a rich family, now utterly destroyed by the habits of a drunken patriarch, a monstrous father who fled after lighting the fire that gutted the family mansion and killed the rest of our brothers and sisters, and who we have tracked across half the continent, funded by selling these few precious family heirlooms, with the sole aim of avenging the deaths of little Yvette, and Isabelle, and Clothilde, and Claude, and poor, tiny Paul.

'*Et notre chère, chère maman,*' Andrea adds solemnly, and we both bow our heads.

We have become practised in our French patter by now, and can roll off words like *montre de poche* and *collier en argent* and *bon prix* and *tempête de feu* and *perte de vie catastrophique* with hardly a pause for breath. And while our performances are not up to the standards of Captain Clarke B. – although I admit I have picked up a couple of his rhetorical flourishes – they are enough to keep us intermittently fed and sheltered.

On this occasion the landlord agrees to accept a particularly fine couple of rings which once graced the lovely fingers of a very rich but only moderately successful English poet, in exchange for a bed for the night, which represents a very good deal for him on account of how his inn seems completely empty this evening. Also included in the deal are a couple of bowls of thin soup with beans and some kind of stringy meat floating in it, and a bottle of wine, and the chance to sit by the fire for a few hours and warm our fingers and toes. But not, it turns out, breakfast in the morning, which we have to negotiate for afresh, and which costs us another ring, in return for some stale cheese and bread and water, and which doesn't do much to set us up for another day out on the cold road, especially after a night spent on a hard, thin mattress under a single lice-ridden blanket.

But with no choice but to keep moving, and a black cat on a windowsill licking its paws as we pass and so presaging another drop in temperature, and dark clouds at our back too, we get on our way. By noon we are another good six or seven miles along, with the scrubby hills covered with stunted trees kept to our right, and rows of vineyards rolling away on our left, and what looks like another potentially more welcoming town five miles distant along the road.

In other words: we are surviving.

Even if our old life seems like a very long time ago.

A Variety of Happy and Unhappy Endings

With little else to do but look out on the endless cold country-side as we walk across it, day after day, we find ourselves talking at length of all kinds of things.

We try to remember the names of countries of the world, and the towns we've passed through, and characters from fairy stories and the Bible, and everyone we've ever met. We share stories from our childhoods, and describe the things we saw there, and how we became the people that we are. I tell Andrea about shipwrecks and smuggling and strange creatures being washed up on the shore, and the winter of 186— when half the village was wiped out in the space of a week. Also various tales of my brother Will's misadventures, with a variety of happy and unhappy endings, including things burned down or sunk or otherwise accidentally destroyed, and a few things I make up on the spot that didn't happen but could or should have, and which make my brother seem even more of a gigantic character than he already is. And, in turn, Andrea tells me of growing up in and out of a series of criminal gangs and church orphanages, and makes it clear which he preferred, and of earthquakes, and seeing friends die, and stealing for a living, and a cat he once owned that he won't tell me the name of because it would be bad luck.

'What happened to the cat?' I say.

'Somebody killed it,' he says, and then doesn't want to talk about it any more, and broods for the rest of the day.

I tell him how we'll likely be welcomed at Dover as heroes for our actions in saving the King of Italy, and be awarded the freedom of my village, and how I'll probably marry Susan the vicar's daughter, and the three of us, she, Andrea and I, will live together as two husbands and a wife in a house I'll build with a yard full of pigs – if she hasn't already shacked up with Jeremiah and Joseph Parsons, that is.

Andrea pulls a face.

'Maybe I'll find a wife for you, too,' I say, and he laughs at that.

The only time either of us mentions anything related to our weeks with William T. Baker and friends is the day we spend two hours trying to catch a stray, injured pheasant which we find flapping around a frozen field, and which looks as if it would make a perfect meal for two cold and weary travellers to roast over a fire. When we eventually give up the fruitless, circular chase, and leave the poor confused beast to the mercy of the local foxes or wolves and sit, panting, against the fence in the cold sunshine, Andrea says, more to himself than anyone else, 'I wish I'd kept that gun.'

One morning on the road outside the town of V—, where we have spent the night in the house of an elderly woman in return for a necklace which may or may not have belonged to a countess, we come across a party of nuns who are walking in procession towards the town, their breath turning to clouds of vapour in the cold air, as they whip themselves alternately over each shoulder with short leather flails that seem to flash in the bright early sun.

'What are they doing?' I ask.

'They think they are paying for their sins,' says Andrea. 'And for ours. And the rest of the world's, too.'

252

'Will it work?' I say.

'I have already paid for my sins,' Andrea replies with some finality.

When one of the nuns slips and stumbles on the icy road and falls to the ground, the others stop what they are doing to help their fallen sister back to her feet, and check her over for injuries, and brush the frost from her robes, and reassure her. And then all recommence their walking and their private, self-inflicted torture, whether on behalf of themselves or the rest of us.

'What about my sins?' I ask.

But Andrea has already walked on ahead, and I am forced to hurry after him.

Eventually there comes the day when we sell the last piece of our jewellery, and, finding ourselves still in the middle of this vast and terrible country, and with no sign of an end to winter, we have to change our tactics.

At first we try to earn our shelter at farms and inns and houses by offering ourselves as odd-job men, and lifters and carriers of things, and rounders-up of animals. But with the harvest finished months ago, and the sheep and cows all down from the hills and safely penned, and the possibility of spring repairs still a long way off too, most people have pared their lives down for the winter and shut up shop, and we find little success.

We consider stealing, but quickly realise that there is very little worth taking out here that wouldn't also be impossible to get away with, what with the two of us often being the only people on the road, and usually visible from miles away.

And so we are forced to offer ourselves in other ways instead.

The first time is with a travelling Bible salesman, of all people. A man who is, or so he tells Andrea and myself as he buys us both drinks at the bar of a small and otherwise empty inn, simply lonely from all these days out on the road so far away from his home and his loving wife and his many loving children, and in the dead of winter too, and, after all, isn't it right that a man should have company on as cold a night as this, and share a bed with friends to keep warm, and that's all there is to it, and it's only right that he should pay for everything, including our time, and if something else *should* naturally follow on from the close proximity of three likely lads such as us in a bed together, well then it's no different from what young men do together in the years before they get married anyway, and perfectly natural, and no harm has ever come of that, wouldn't you agree?

And of course we do agree with him, and in three different languages besides.

ᗞHE ᗞOWN OF THE ᗞEAD

One afternoon the narrow road that we have been travelling on for the last few days brings us into an empty town, where all the houses are shuttered up and quiet, and only a few stray dogs skulk about the street.

When we come to the deserted town square we see the printed posters pasted onto the walls of all the buildings. We are just about to have a closer look at one of them when the door of the church on the other side of the square opens and a monk in brown robes comes out onto the steps and, spotting the two of us, waves for us to come with him, before heading off up a steep, narrow lane.

And because we are tired and hungry and cold, and curious too, we follow him up the hill.

The monk has a head start on us, and we struggle to keep him in sight as he turns this way and that between the tightly packed houses, not slowing until he eventually reaches his destination, where he waits for us to join him outside a large whitewashed building with metal doors. When we arrive, he points to a wooden stretcher that lies against the building, indicating that we should put down our packs and pick it up and accompany him, and before we can say anything he has hurried inside. So we do as we've been asked and, each grabbing an end of the stretcher, nervously enter the building and follow the man down the long corridor.

Even before we go through the double doors at the end of the corridor we can already smell the horror that awaits us inside the makeshift hospital ward. It's in the stink of vinegar and lime, and burning incense too, and roasted herbs and spices, and something sweet and terrible and utterly unmistakeable behind all of that.

And then there's the bare, lime-washed room, with a single drain in the middle of the floor, and the rows of beds down either wall filled with the bodies of the dead or dying, some of them being tended to by the fellows of the man who brought us here, while other members of their order swill the floor down with buckets of water and long, stiff brooms. Two of the monks are lifting one of the bodies, wrapped tightly in its white sheet, onto the stretcher that we are holding, conducting a brief blessing, and then we are thankfully directed outside again with our horrible cargo.

There we are able to briefly catch our breaths for a moment before we follow another monk back down the hill to where a cart filled with more wrapped bodies is waiting, and we are allowed to gratefully tip our own consignment onto the pile, before all is driven away.

And then we are left to sit, stunned, on a bench under another one of the printed posters, which we turn to read and which, of course, warns of the cholera outbreak that has devastated the town.

But we do, eventually, get fed, and are offered a bed for the night, and the next few nights too, at the monastery which is built halfway into the cliffs above the town.

We are each given a small cell with a single bed – we haven't slept apart in weeks until now – and are invited to eat with the rest of the order, but otherwise we are left to fit in where and how we wish. The monks are up and about before dawn each morning, and in bed not long after nightfall, and spend most of their days in the monastery either praying or reading, or, when occupied with more practical tasks such as eating and working in the frozen earth of the garden, listening to others reading or praying on their behalf.

We make ourselves useful chopping and carrying wood and serving food and I help out with some repairs about the place, levelling shelves in the kitchens and re-hanging doors and fixing stools and repairing the wheels on carts and other such stuff – because I am still my father's son, in spite of myself, and in spite of him too.

The first time we are called on to help at the pits, where the bodies of the town's dead are piled into shallow ditches before being covered in pitch and set alight, we spend the rest of the day throwing up, unable to rid ourselves of the stench of oily soot no matter how hard we try. The pall of black, greasy smoke hangs over the edge of town in the still air for hours, looking like a sign from the end of the world.

'The happy news is that our isolation will likely mean that this outbreak is contained,' says Brother Stephen – the elderly monk who has been put in charge of Andrea and I – as the three of us discuss philosophy and religion by candlelight in the monastery library.

'Praise the Lord,' says Andrea, ironically.

'Well,' says the monk, 'he delivered you two in our hour of need, did he not?'

'Him, and our four good feet.'

'In that case,' our friend says, raising his cup of water, 'a toast to your feet.'

And even Andrea can't not drink to that.

257

'And what about you?' I ask.

'He's here to wait for the end of the world,' says Andrea, pointing at the monk. 'As they all are.'

'I might not put it quite like that,' says Brother Stephen. 'Let's say I was called.'

'Like some of sort of quest?' I say.

'I'm not sure if –'

'What if *we're* on a quest?' I say, suddenly thinking of it. 'Andrea and I?'

'Are you?'

'Or perhaps a pilgrimage.'

'Well, which is it?'

'What's the difference?'

'Let's see,' says Brother Stephen, and then takes out and lights a cigar – the first time I have seen him do so – and blows a couple of smoke rings, and seems charmed by them. 'Broadly, when one is on a quest one knows exactly what it is that one is looking for, but not necessarily where one is going' – more smoke rings here, considering the cigar – 'whereas when one is on a pilgrimage, one knows exactly where one is going, but not what one will find on the way. Does that make sense?'

I nod, and wish I had a cigar of my own.

'Quests are concerned with the achievement of a goal,' he continues. 'Whereas pilgrimages should be considered more in the context of the journey and the experience – hardships and suffering and humbling yourself before God, that sort of thing. To put it in the clearest possible terms, you might say that for the most part quests are self-indulgent nonsense. Which is why they're usually embarked upon by young men.'

'But could one perhaps transform into the other?' I ask. 'Might a person set out on a quest only for it to turn into a pilgrimage after all?'

'It is a possibility,' he agrees.

'So which,' says Andrea, taking the cigar from the monk's mouth and blowing a couple of fine smoke rings himself, right into the man's face, 'was it with you?'

And our friend has no answer to that.

That night Andrea and I stay up and argue into the small hours in his cell. I try to convince him to let me share his bed, on account of it having been a couple of months since we've lain down together – or stood up against a wall together, or bent one another over a table etc. – without someone else having been involved too, and money or a roof over our heads at stake besides. But when I attempt to wrestle him, charmingly, into submission he puts his knee into me and sends me sprawling to the floor.

'Never in this place,' he says. 'Do you understand?'

Sulking, I agree that I do, and go miserably back to my own bed, where I lie awake until dawn wondering what has become of my brother, and what will happen to the rest of us, in this world and the next.

A Questionable Life

Still, there are days when I find a sort of peace.

It seems the simple life of fetching and carrying and fixing things suits me, though why that should even come as a surprise I don't know. Each morning I break the ice on the water bucket to wash my face, and then walk out into the garden to watch the watery sunrise. I even pay attention to the prayers and the readings, which make me feel as if I am back at school under the instruction of the vicar's wife. And while there is no pig to tell my troubles to, there are a couple of old egg-laying chickens who live in the garden that I make friends with, so as to be reminded of home. I get into the habit of inviting them into my cell to keep warm in the evenings, which they seem happy enough about, and even don't mind sleeping alongside me in the bed, which is more than can be said for some of my other supposed friends.

As the cholera outbreak burns itself out our work in the town becomes a clean-up operation. Government officials arrive to write reports and interview witnesses, including the few survivors, and relatives turn up to stake claims on abandoned houses and their contents. The business of trade starts up again, and the inn on the town square is reopened to cater for the traffic.

I accompany Brother Stephen on his rounds as we offer spiritual support to survivors and investigators alike, as well as arbitrating between rival heirs and other claimants of empty properties as and when required.

'It seems that one of the younger brothers has taken a shine to your friend,' Brother Stephen tells me, as we are going about the business of tearing down the pasted posters from the town square.

'He's right popular,' I say.

'All the same, we have taken a vow of celibacy. As you would need to do if you joined us here.'

I am silent then.

'Is it something you have considered?' he asks.

'I have lived a questionable life so far,' I say, carrying on with my work.

'Does who you were before matter?'

'Who I was, or what I did?'

'Perhaps they're the same thing.'

'Actions can be excused,' I say. 'A person's character is harder to forgive.'

'I'm not sure that's how He works,' says Brother Stephen, thumbing towards the heavens.

'I wasn't thinking about him,' I say. 'And besides, I have responsibilities elsewhere.'

'And yet here you are.'

'And yet here I am.'

'So what conclusions,' says the monk, 'are we to draw from that?'

That evening it is Andrea who comes to my cell as I am getting ready to turn in, and sits on the end of my bed, much to the irritation of my two friends the chickens, and I can tell that he hasn't come because of a change of mind.

'There's no life for us here,' says he, eventually.

'And what if there isn't a life for me anywhere else?' I say.

He considers this.

'You can have a life with me,' he says.

'And what kind of life would that be?' I ask him. 'In which we are constantly running from ourselves?'

'You are the only one running, Dan,' he says. 'I know who I am.'

'And what is it that you think you are?' I reply, with a cruel edge to my voice, though I don't know whether I am asking him or myself.

When he gets up to leave he stops at the door and looks back at me.

'All those people dying in the village,' he says, 'remember that God did that, too.'

It's still dark when Andrea shakes me awake again, from a dream about the cap, of all people, and for a moment I wonder if he has changed his mind about the romantic possibilities of this place, until I notice the sour smell of blood on him and then I'm wide awake and sitting up.

'What did you do?' I say, and he puts his finger against my lips to silence me.

'If you trust me,' he says, 'you need to get dressed.'

'What did you do?'

He shows me the knife then, and even in the darkness I can see that it is stained black, and half his sleeve is the same.

'I warned him,' he whispers. 'But he wouldn't stop.'

'Is he dead?'

'Not yet.'

I pull on my clothes in the dark, as quietly as I can, and gather my pack, and then the two of us head out into the dark stone

262

corridor. In the gloom of the courtyard we check that there are no lights in any of the windows. I put the pack down.

'We should go back and help,' I say.

'No,' says Andrea, picking the pack up himself.

'But what if they can still save him?'

'Then God will help them,' he tells me. 'But they will still put me in prison. Or worse.'

Quietly, Andrea lifts the wooden latch from the door. I scan the dark windows again, hoping, in my coward's heart, for the sudden warm flare of a candle being lit, or a desperate shout, or the sound of a ringing alarm bell, or anything else that might stop us.

But there is nothing.

'Are you coming or staying?' Andrea asks me.

The Scientific Properties of Frozen Air

The blizzard that has been following us for the last forty-eight hours finally catches up just as we think we have left the threat of the mountains and the mountain weather behind us for good.

We have come down into the wide valley of the River R— after five long, silent days of walking across country, avoiding roads and villages and anywhere else that might lead to the possibility of arrest. We have been sleeping in woods and crumbling, abandoned farm buildings, and have hardly said a word to each other, or eaten, since we left the monastery. The temperature has dropped so low that birds are falling from the trees.

We are not more than four or five miles from the town of G—, where we plan to detour up the other side of the valley, when the storm falls upon us – Andrea has just enough time to say, 'Look at that' – and within less than a minute the world is lost.

Caught in the middle of the swirling immensity we are unable to see more than a few feet in any direction, and soon enough the road is gone too, covered in thick snow, with only our rapidly filling footprints briefly allowing us to guess at which way we're facing. By the time we realise what has happened we've already drifted far off our course, and are stumbling, lost, through what could be a field or a paddock or even a stretch of open wood-land, with drifting snow almost up to our knees, and settling on our arms and shoulders besides, and no clue as to what the right direction might be, but only the knowledge that if we stop moving we are finished.

Eventually – minutes or hours later, it's hard even now to estimate – we see what looks like the looming shape of a vast and ghostly cathedral slowly resolving itself out of the storm and offering us shelter. As we struggle closer we realise that some trick of reflection or refraction or other scientific property of the frozen air is playing havoc with our ability to judge distances, and the apparition is, in fact, nothing more than a small stand of trees. But even this feels like a relief after the howling white emptiness that surrounds us, and so we stop to rest and lean against the tree trunks. Among the trees we find a small wooden shrine, which causes Andrea to laugh bitterly.

'We're likely not a mile away from a decent-sized town and safety,' I tell him. 'If we could only see it.'

He isn't comforted by this revelation.

'I can't feel my toes,' he says, and tries to sit down in the snow. I notice that his lips are blue, too.

'We have to keep moving,' I say, attempting to grab him by the arm, but he shakes off my hand.

'Where is there to go?'

I angrily remind him that he's the reason we had to leave the monastery, and a part of me almost immediately regrets saying this, and another part of me doesn't, and I wait for him to reply in turn that I'm the reason that we had to leave William T. Baker's house, and so am far more responsible for our present troubles than he is, without even taking into account my part in all our previous misadventures. But he doesn't.

'We'll die if we stay out here,' I say.

'And what if that's been the plan all along?' Andrea replies.

'Then I have a better one.'

'You sound like him.'

'I could do worse. He would never have let this happen to himself.'

'He was willing to let them kill you, Dan. And me.'

Suddenly furious, I throw a punch at him which barely connects with his jaw but sends me falling to the snow, where, humiliated, I briefly consider remaining face down. When I get back to my feet I see the knife in Andrea's hand, and like the fool I am I think I understand things better than I do, and welcome what is going to happen next because it is so familiar.

But instead, Andrea hands me the knife, and I wonder whether the fear he saw in my eyes is what has finally broken his patient heart.

He pulls my arm forward so the tip of the blade rests against his belly.

'I would have died for you,' he says.

'I'm sorry,' I say, and let the knife fall on the ground.

And then Andrea begins to laugh.

'What are you laughing at?' I shout at him, realising that in all this time I've learned nothing at all.

'Everything,' is his gentle reply. 'Look.'

And I do look, and see that the air has cleared, and the evening sun has lit up the valley, and we are not half a mile from where we were before the storm came down on us, and there's the town.

'I'm going home, Dan,' says Andrea, then.

I laugh at him through my tears, and he laughs and then starts crying too.

'Let me go,' he says, and then puts his arms around me and kisses me on the forehead.

And then he walks away from me, in the direction of the town, and doesn't look back.

I'm still standing there when I realise that it is getting dark, and stars are starting to come out.

A Dancing Bear

And so, with nothing else to do but keep moving or face the prospect of freezing to death in the snow, I go on alone – heading north, despite the threat of worse conditions to come, with head bent and feet wrapped in cloth to prevent the loss of my toes.

I walk through snow and sleet and freezing fog, as well as beautiful still days when it seems as if the world has stopped and I am the only person left on it. I walk until the weather finally breaks, and the snow is replaced with days of cold rain, which turns the roads to mud and the fields to bogs, and the rivers swell and carry away their banks. One morning I come across a herd of twenty or thirty cows swimming, apparently unperturbed, down a broad creek. About 200 yards upstream I encounter the farmer angrily heading after them in a patched-up rowing boat.

At night I sleep in barns or under bushes on as high ground as possible so as not to wake up in the river myself. Nevertheless, one evening I down two bottles of stolen red wine and foolishly fall asleep under a bridge while sheltering from the rain, and when I wake in the morning I am in the river and being carried away downstream, and am only saved from drowning by the fact that I have fallen asleep with the pack containing the rolled-up frogman suit on my back, and it has retained enough trapped air in its folds to keep me afloat.

I struggle to the bank and slither up through the mud in the rain, my already half-disintegrated clothes finally coming apart and falling off me, until I come to rest in the woods, half-naked and shivering. After catching my breath in the wet leaf litter for a few moments I realise my condition and likely fate if I don't act, and so, having no other alternative, I unpack and unroll the suit, and climb inside it, and there, finally warm and dry, fall asleep again.

From then on I wear the suit like a second skin, sleeping out in the open like an animal, and trudging slowly along the roads and pathways of the country, aware of the strange looks directed my way, but too exhausted to think much beyond the fact that I am dry, at least.

At a village called B— I am persuaded by a group of drunken farmers to perform a demonstration of the suit outside a bar in the pouring rain in exchange for a franc, as if I am a dancing bear, before my audience gets bored and decides to beat me up and leave me in the mud.

Still, I get to keep the money.

At G—, drunk myself, I demonstrate the working of the suit, lecturing in slurred English on the importance of saving sailors at sea, to a group of market traders, who reward me with a small amount of money and some bruised vegetables to ensure that I'll go away when I've finished.

At the hamlet of Le D—, I work in the mud for an hour to free the stuck wheel of a cart driven by two spinsters, who pay me with a leg of lamb and the promise to include me in their prayers, but don't offer me a lift.

And then on the edge of the town of F—, where a group of schoolchildren throw stones at me as I pass, and then run away screaming when I stagger after them, arms outstretched, mud-caked like the Prague Golem, the suit and I are called on to rescue a prize pig which has fallen into a twenty-foot-deep cesspool, and my degradation is complete.

Under my instruction the locals tie a rope around my waist and lower me down into the stinking pit, where I swim around in the thick slurry trying to catch hold of the panicked animal for twenty minutes, unable to avoid both breathing in and swallowing mouthfuls of the foul waste, until I manage to get a loop of rope around the creature's belly. Then I hold the beast in my arms and say soothing chatty things into its ear as the two of us are hauled back up to the world, and we are rolled, covered in shit and happy to be alive, onto the muddy ground, where I lie staring up into the cascading heavens while the pig licks my face.

Then I am rewarded with a couple of coins and the pleasure of being run out of town, with a hail of rocks and rotten vegetables following after to safely see me off.

A state of grace, indeed.

WHAT I REMEMBER

But because I still have one smart trick up my sleeve, or more accurately one last bit of luck, I have finally come, after all this walking, to pass out of the part of the country where the rivers all run south towards the Mediterranean Sea, and have arrived at the point where instead they begin to head north, which I realise the day I accidentally fall down a muddy riverbank and into the water and, surrendering to the current at last, notice the direction in which I am pulled along.

The result is that, even in my weakened state, I am soon able to start travelling on the water again, using the current to take me in the direction of my distant home – and the place that I dimly remember lies between me and it, and where I have decided to head – with little intervention required on my part other than occasionally correcting my course with the paddle.

And so I float downstream, drifting through towns and villages, half starved and often not knowing whether I am asleep or awake, now and then being taken for the corpse of an animal or a man, and being disturbed by the poles of boatmen who prod me to make sure one way or the other, and other times waking up bumping against the foundations of bridges or riverbanks, with fish nibbling at the seams in my suit.

I float for days and nights, sometimes little noticing the transition from one to the other, and even less aware of the changing landscape as I move slowly north. And as I float on I feel as if I am becoming part of the river, and my mind drifts this way and that, and I let it go wherever it wants to wander, and find it roaming about my past, remembering things long put away or lost.

I remember the day when I was left with my 2-year-old brother Will in my care, and lost him while I was playing an experimental, exploratory game with Susan the vicar's daughter that neither of us should have been playing, and searched for him for hours but eventually ended up hiding myself in the house that my father had built for the pig, sure that my brother had drowned. In the event we found the infant boy asleep in one of the beds at the vicarage, where he had been all afternoon, but I was beaten for my trouble anyway, and accepted the punishment happily, so relieved was I to have my brother back.

And I remember the night that the old inn on the spit burned down, which couldn't have been long after my brother was born, and the whole village turned out to try to stop the fire, carrying buckets in a chain up from the shore, but then one by one, as people realised that they were likely fighting a losing battle, instead began running *into* the flames to at least rescue as much booze as could be saved from the conflagration, with the result that for the next week the whole town was drunk, including the inn's former owner, Handsome George Cooper, who would then challenge his business rival Giant Pete to a fight over the latter's suspected role in the fire, which would be gleefully attended by every last inhabitant of the village, and ended with Handsome George Cooper rendered handsome no more.

And I remember the fight between Joseph and Jeremiah Parsons' father Thomas, and Irish Jack Callaghan from two villages over, which went on for an entire day, up and down the main street, and involved knives and lengths of wood and ropes and fishing nets and, at one point, even their own thrown shoes.

And I remember the fight between Susan's father the Reverend Pritchard and his best friend the Reverend Green, up from London for the weekend, over some point of biblical contention, which was conducted according to strict rules of engagement but nevertheless led to seven separate broken bones.

And I remember the fight between Giant Pete's wife Mrs Giant Pete and her cousin Iris after the death of their mother over who would get to keep the old lady's bed, and the fight between Little Pete and Davey Cooper, which took place even though neither of them wanted it but because it was demanded by the crowd, and both of them cried when Davey Cooper won, and then swore that they would never fight again, and never did.

And I remember each of the fifty-five different fights that I can recall having, with boys and girls and grown men too.

And I remember my father fighting, at one time or another, just about every other man in the village, and most of the other villages for ten miles around, and myself, and my brother too, and us laughing along with the other children in the village as we compared injuries over the years.

And I find myself thinking, then, of why my father was who he was, and realise all over again that he is dead, and grieve in my own strange way, remembering the prickle of his chin, and his rare laugh, and how he kept us fed, at least, and the fine work that his hands did fixing everything that came to them, and how his own childhood must have been just as bad as ours was, if not much worse.

And so I travel the hundred or so miles to the small town of F—, which is not far to the south of the French capital, in something like a dream, and when I finally reach my destination and climb from the water, covered from head to foot in waterweed and algae and slime, I am truly more amphibian than man, and as I stagger through the streets of the town women swoon and small children run screaming from the sight of me.

Reports of a Madman on the Loose

In the event the house is smaller than I expected, and sits on an ordinary road behind a high stone wall and an iron gate, to which I am directed after asking a few surprised people out and about in the town for directions.

Having announced myself I wait at the gate for my message to be relayed, and am then shown inside by a watchful house-keeper, who takes in my strange appearance and leads me into a modest waiting room, where I am left to stand, dripping onto the wooden floorboards, the door carefully locked again from the outside to prevent me, I suppose, rampaging about the house.

I look around at the simple wooden furniture, and the dusty paintings of distant countries on the walls, and wonder if I have made another mistake.

And then the door is unlocked again and the Widow Timmermans, dressed in a severe black outfit, comes into the room, and stops at the sight of me.

'Clarke?' she says.

Eager not to disappoint her, I push out my chest and put on a big, beaming smile.

'Oh, Daniel ...' she says.

And then she comes forward and embraces me, dripping, slime-covered suit and all.

That evening, after I have soaked in the tub for almost two hours while my hostess attends to various matters of business, and a set of clothes that once belonged to the late Mr Timmermans have been found for me, and the frogman suit taken away to be washed, I tell the widow a sanitised version of my adventures of the last few months, over dinner in the modest dining room.

I don't tell her about my relationship with Andrea, or the island prison break, or much about our time as guests of William T. Baker, or our involvement in the attempt on the King of Italy's life, or what happened to Mcinerney, or even a great deal about our stay in the monastery. We both ask each other about the cap, but I discover that she knows even less about his whereabouts than I, not having heard anything from him since our eventful stay on Lake C— and the night of the *Juliana* sinking – 'and that was via the newspapers' – which I find comes as a relief.

'I thought by your outfit … that you might be –'

'No,' the widow says. 'This isn't for Clarke. Despite the money he has cost me.'

'I didn't know that you would be here,' I say, feeling almost as if I need to apologise on the captain's behalf, 'at this house. I remembered you talking of a number of properties.'

'Well, they are fewer now,' she says, 'as it turns out.'

Then the housekeeper's daughter comes in to quietly inform the widow of something, whispering into her ear, and after a hurried conversation in French my host throws up her hands and says, 'Well just bring him in, then.'

And so, after apologising to me for the interruption, the widow welcomes this new guest, who goes by the name of

Monsieur Arnaud Something-or-other, local police chief, and is a friendly-enough-looking middle-aged man. He enters the room with his hat in his hands, and notes with regret the lateness of the hour, and asks after the widow's health, and then shakes me by the hand.

I am only able to follow parts of the ensuing conversation, though the widow translates the important points for me. These include the policeman's sworn duty to investigate reports of a madman on the loose about town who was seen asking for directions to the widow's house – 'I think he is referring to you, Daniel,' – as well as his general responsibility for the well-being of every member of his community, whether French or foreign – 'And here he is referring to me,' – and this, it must be stressed, is irrespective of whatever financial straits that any of those community members may, temporarily he is sure, have recently found themselves in – 'And at this point I think it's fairly safe to say that he is being ironic.'

When it's my turn to account for myself, I confirm everything that the widow tells the chief about me, which has the advantage of being mostly, if somewhat selectively, true: I am the assistant of the famous Captain Clarke B., and I was indeed there the night of the famous *Juliana* miracle, and I am English ('Oh, a shame,'), and I have met the King of Italy and the Prince of B—, and so on. The widow adds that I'll be a guest in her house for a few days, to which I nod, and so will more than likely be seen about town, although not, as I am made to solemnly promise, in the frogman outfit, which I agree will not be seen in public again without the advance approval of the local police, and specifically the say-so of our crime-busting friend here.

At the end of the interview, or polite warning, or social visit, or whatever it is that has just occurred, the chief excuses himself, bowing to the widow and kissing her hand, then shaking my hand again and kissing me on both cheeks, and promising to remain at our service. And then he is gone, and the widow tells me that she'll be turning in herself, on account of a headache from all this talking, but thanks me for my company and says that she looks forward to continuing our catch-up tomorrow.

So I find myself once again getting ready to sleep under the roof, and the wing, of the Widow Timmermans.

In the room that I have been given I take out my brother's lead soldier and put it on the shelf, and put Mr Henry Colbert's pocket watch next to it, and the ring Andrea once gave me next to that, and I wonder how far I have come, and who I am, and what might yet be next.

Within minutes of climbing into bed I am fast asleep, and do not dream.

MORE OR LESS RUINED

The following day there is a bright blue sky and the feel of spring in the air, and so after breakfast we walk into town in order to buy me a better-fitting set of clothes than those worn by the – both shorter and stouter – former Mr Timmermans. Word of my arrival yesterday, and the manner of it, has clearly got around, as a number of people stop and not so surreptitiously point in the street, while others stare as we pass by.

In the town department store there is a brief argument with a shop girl – from what I can gather with the rough French I have it seems to be about the quality of the widow's credit – before a manager is called, and things are smoothed over, and the girl is sent home in tears, causing me to consider, again, exactly whose side it is that I am now on.

When we get back to the house there is a cart in the road out front being loaded with pieces of furniture, and chests full of clothes, and framed works of art, and men are coming in and out of the house with more.

Suddenly the widow cries, 'Not that one!' and runs to stop a painting I recognise – the one of a Japanese wave – from being added to the cart. There follows a short stand-off before the removal men agree to give up the picture, which the widow carries inside, clutching it to herself.

In the house there is more activity, with chairs and tables and sideboards and couches being priced up by a pair of well-dressed men who mark each desired piece with bits of chalk. I follow the widow into her upstairs office where she locks the door and then quickly strips the Japanese canvas from its frame, rolls the picture up, and locks it in a small safe.

Then she sits down at the desk, puts on a pair of spectacles and starts searching desperately through a pile of letters.

'But what if they take the safe itself?' I ask, and she stops and laughs sharply, and then lets out a single sob before taking a deep breath.

'What's all this about?' I ask.

The widow takes the spectacles off again and thinks for a second, her hand on her forehead. Then she goes to a bureau and takes out a small framed picture, which she hands to me. It's a picture of a young man, not much older than me, who I immediately recognise, not least from the newspaper reports.

'But this is –'

'Someone I tried to help,' the widow says.

'Is this your son?' I say, and she looks at me, impressed by my reasoning.

'Not mine. Not by birth, anyway. My late husband's by his first marriage.'

'But I was there,' I say. 'On the lake that night. It was him.'

'Yes.'

'Did you know what he was involved in? What they were planning?'

'Of course I didn't know, Daniel!' she shouts suddenly, before composing herself again. 'I knew what he believed in, obviously.

And had sympathy with it. But he'd been … we lost him a long time ago.'

'He was still taking your money. I saw your driver pay him.'

'I couldn't very well abandon my husband's child, could I?'

I remember what Mcinerney told me on the volcano, and of the plotting behind the attempt on the King of Italy's life.

'Was he in the pay of someone else?' I ask.

She looks at me strangely then.

'As far as I know he was sincere,' she says. 'Whether he was working for less sincere people …' She waves a hand in the air.

'His sincerity killed a lot of people,' I say, and am cast back to that night, and the flames on the water, and the people. 'His sincerity and your money.'

'My money has paid for a lot of things, Daniel,' she says. 'You among them.'

And I am rightly stung by that.

'Does the policeman know?'

'He suspects that there's something fishy about my situation, I think. I don't know how much he actually *knows* about any of it. I spent a great deal of money keeping my name out of the papers. And myself out of prison. But as you can see, that had consequences of its own.'

Downstairs we can hear the removal men shouting to each other.

'How bad is it?' I ask.

'Well, I am more or less ruined,' the widow answers. 'And rather more than less. I have been outmanoeuvred by people who are better at this than me, and who know exactly how to exploit this kind of situation. Which is likely no more than I deserve, I know. In the short term I can still extend a couple more lines of credit against what's left, including this place. But my future doesn't look particularly …' – and here she is casting

281

around for the right word just as we hear the crash of something large and expensive being dropped somewhere in the house – '… inspiring.'

It takes a couple more hours for the bailiffs to complete their work, by which time the house has been greatly reduced in both character and usefulness, a number of rooms being completely emptied of furniture, and others containing not much more now than the odd chair or side table. The widow placates her housekeeper by paying her and her daughter's next two months' wages upfront, and is rewarded with the loan of a kitchen table and a couple of chairs, the rental fee on those being paid in advance too.

Our friend the police chief stops by on his rounds to see what has been going on, and walks around the now half-empty house tutting sadly, before putting the entire local police force at the widow's service, if there is any assistance at all that they can provide at this difficult time. Then the lawyers arrive, and the lady of the house has to get back to work, and the chief and I are left alone to go out into the garden, where he offers me a cigar and lights it for me.

'A formidable woman,' he says, and I can only agree.

'Still, these things are all tests, aren't they?'

I nod at that too.

Then he says something that I don't understand, before pointing two fingers towards his eyes, and then pointing at my chest, which needs no translation. And then he shakes my hand, and doesn't kiss me on either cheek, and goes on his way.

A Stand-in

That night, after the widow and I have eaten a subdued dinner at the borrowed table in the kitchen, and the housekeeper and her daughter have gone home, I light a fire in the drawing room and we sit on the floor together and share a bottle of good red wine from the cellar. All around us are piles of books that were formerly housed in glass-fronted bookcases, as well as framed prints and paintings leaning against them that were rejected by the bailiffs.

'Well,' says the widow, toasting me. 'This is the very life, isn't it? I hope it was worth your trip.'

'It's still beyond anything I could have dreamed of even a year ago,' I tell her, truthfully.

'Then you may need to teach me a thing or two about living within my means.'

'I think the cap would be horrified to hear that,' I say.

'Clarke would recommend that I find someone else's means to live within. Or more likely beyond.'

'To the captain, then,' I say, raising my glass again, and then finishing my drink and getting to my feet.

'Where are you going?' says the widow.

'You said your money had paid for me,' I say, then throwing my arms wide theatrically, add: 'Well, then, here I am.'

'What are you doing, Daniel?'

'Use me,' I say.

'I don't –' she says, then, 'Oh.'

For I've already begun undressing, taking off my shirt, which she has paid for, and my boots, which she has paid for too, and my trousers the same, and my underwear also, until I am standing there in the drawing room naked, in order that she can get a decent look at my good chest and arms, and my fine legs, and my firm arse, and my serviceable cock besides.

'I can more or less guarantee good service,' I say. 'And although I may not have Captain Clarke B.'s years of experience and knowledge of esoteric Eastern practices, I nevertheless come recommended by several members of the English upper classes, all of whom were satisfied with what I provided.'

I can see that she is now taking me seriously. She considers the situation for a long time, and looks me up and down without embarrassment, and I can tell that she is not unimpressed. Then she gets up too and stands in front of me.

'Was this your plan, all along?' she asks, raising an eyebrow.

'There's not so much difference in our ages,' I tell her.

'Ha! And thank you for that, at least.'

'I am at your service,' I say, and, taking her hand, put it flat on my chest. 'Don't you deserve this?'

She doesn't take her hand away. In fact, she looks at it, and moves it gently on my chest, as if testing to see if we are both real.

'Perhaps this *is* what I deserve,' she says. She turns her hand around and strokes my chest with the back of it, and I close my eyes.

And then she laughs, gently, and says to me, 'Put your clothes back on, Dan.'

I open my eyes again and, seeing my disappointed expression, the widow puts her hand on my face.

'Please believe me when I say I do appreciate the offer,' she tells me, 'and may well come to regret refusing it on some long cold night. But I think I can find a better use for you than this.'

I sit back down by the fire, sulking and embarrassed.

'Clothes?' she says.

As I am pulling my trousers back on – an operation for which the widow has kindly averted her eyes and turned away – one of the framed pictures catches my attention. It features a painted image of none other than Captain Clarke B. himself, posing in the frogman suit, his trusty paddle at his side, against a backdrop of famous sites of the French capital, including some of the city's newest grand construction projects.

When I am done getting dressed, I go over and hold the picture up.

'What is this?' I say.

The widow, who has had her back turned to me, turns around again and looks at the picture.

'That was made last year to promote a potential event,' she says. 'A part of the *Exposition Universelle*, next month. Clarke was going to perform some stunt or other.'

I consider the picture, holding it at arm's length. It is not a bad likeness of the man, and captures something of his character and attitude, although the details of the suit leave a lot to be desired. And it gives me a thought which I almost dare not express.

'What if it could yet happen?' I ask.

'The event?' says the widow. 'In that case, I would stand to make a reasonable amount of money. But there is a fundamental problem: we are missing a fearless frogman.'

'But do we not already have one,' I ask, 'right here?'

'Ah,' she says. 'Well, then, and in that case: we are missing *The Fearless Frogman*.'

'We are missing the captain, yes,' I say. 'But we have the suit. And the idea. What if that's all the Fearless Frogman ever really was?'

'People will not buy tickets to see an idea, Daniel,' says the widow. 'Even one with you in a starring role – clothed or otherwise.'

'If the idea is powerful enough, they might,' I say. 'If one could give them enough reason to believe in it. Say, with a spectacular enough stunt. Didn't the captain always insist that nothing is stronger than a person's will? If he could invent himself through nothing more than self-belief, then surely we can conjure up his ghost, for a brief period of time at least?'

'Do you really think you could do it?'

'I know I could. And that makes it already half done.'

I can tell she is starting to warm to the idea.

'And besides,' I continue, 'who would need to know that I *wasn't* Captain Clarke B.? I have stood in for him before, and fooled a paying audience. And I can grow a moustache easily enough.'

'There would be a beautiful irony to it,' she agrees, smiling. 'His greatest confidence trick, and he wouldn't even know that he had pulled it off.'

'It's the least that he owes me,' I say. 'And that I owe him.'

She moves to inspect the picture more closely.

'But what about the stunt?' she says.

'Leave that to me,' I reply, for the image itself has already given me an idea. And then I stop, for there's something else important that has occurred to me, too.

'I'll need a cape,' I say.

The Lot of a Provincial Policeman's Wife

And so we begin putting our plan into action.

We travel up to the capital together by train to recce locations, as well as for meetings with commercial sponsors and local officials who are surprised but not unexcited by our idea. I'll say this for the Widow Timmermans: she knows how to open doors, and to grease palms, and to charm or inspire or bully those in need of being charmed, inspired or bullied, and quickly too.

I introduce myself at each meeting as Captain Clarke B.'s assistant, explaining that the great man himself is far too busy with his important scientific and life-saving business for minor logistical meetings such as these, but all the same assuring my audiences that the cap is taking a keen interest in all of this, and that I will be reporting back to him of their excellent helpfulness.

In the centre of the city I catch the widow glancing wistfully into the windows of the hotels and bars and restaurants where, I imagine, she used to sleep and drink and dine.

'Soon they will welcome you again,' I say.

'But perhaps I will not want to be welcomed by them,' she replies.

Having lost so much weight and muscle on my starved journey down the river, I embark on a daily programme of physical conditioning, supported by a heroic attempt to entirely eat the widow out of what remains of her house and home. In return for the widow's agreeing to a dinner with the chief of police, I am granted permission to begin training again with the frogman suit, and every morning and afternoon I paddle endless lengths in the river, much to the interest and amusement of the locals, as well as the delight of their children, who throw themselves into the chilly water and attempt to swim alongside me.

In the evenings I study the maps that the widow has, at some expense, obtained for me, and attempt to learn every inch of my potential route by heart, and then from my heart translate the memories to my muscles, counting out the likely number of strokes between each different required manoeuvre while sitting in a full bath tub with a cloth tied over my eyes to aid my concentration. I write to my brother, this time telling him to expect me home before the end of next month, and describing how much I am looking forward to seeing him at last, and wondering if he remembers this or that funny event from our childhood that I have lately been recalling, and telling him that he could do a lot worse than to settle down with either Helen Dunning or Ada Crook.

And bit by bit we watch the widow's house being taken apart from under her, until there's nothing left but some rented furniture and bare walls.

The night of the widow's dinner date with Monsieur Arnaud, she begs me to join the two of them as her chaperone. I suggest that he is not hoping to make up a trio, but she argues that this is exactly why she needs me to accompany her, and so I agree to tag along.

If the good police chief is disappointed when the pair of us show up at his little house and make it clear that he won't be spending the evening alone with the Widow Timmermans, he is gallant enough not to show it. He has cooked his speciality, chicken in a pot, of which he is justifiably proud, and there is more than enough for the three of us, and room in his small kitchen too for the three of us to sit down at the table.

The two of them spend the evening discussing politics, and war, and religion, and a number of other subjects, all of which they apparently disagree on, but not enough to prevent the flow of their conversation, which I stop trying to keep up with early on. When it's my turn to talk I ask if the chief has ever been married, and the widow translates my question and the reply.

'His wife died,' she says. 'Of cancer. Five years ago.'

He goes on to tell the two of us about the wonderful woman that he was married to, who supported his rise through the police ranks, and gave him five strong children and many happy memories and never asked for a thing in return, nor once complained about the fate she was dealt.

'And who among us can ask for more than that?' he says, almost as if challenging us to argue the point.

'Not us,' the widow and I both agree.

'And what of yourself?' Monsieur Arnaud asks me.

I admit that I have been too busy with my career and various adventures to give much thought to finding a wife, and he nods, understanding how it is to be a young man trying to make his way in the world.

'But don't leave it too late,' he says, and I promise that I won't.

As the widow and I walk back to her home, or what's left of it, at the end of the evening, we review how the night has gone.

'You could do considerably worse,' I say.

'I know,' she says.

'And you are not exactly awash with alternative options at the moment,' I remind her.

'I know that too,' she says.

'And if I fail, the lot of a provincial policeman's wife is not a bad one,' I add.

At that she stops, and puts her hand on my arm.

'Don't fail, Dan,' she tells me. 'Swear to me that you won't fail.'

And so I swear.

Of Poets and Bank Robbers

In the last few days before the event we move the base of our operations to the capital itself, taking a couple of rooms in a small boarding house in an unfashionable area of the city, for which the widow pays upfront in cash, telling me, 'And that's just about the last of it spent right there.'

In anticipation of the great exhibition and the coming new century too, the city seems to be remaking itself from the ground up. New streets and squares and monuments are daily rising out of the ruins of the previous decade, and vast civil construction works are underway to lay gleaming new railway tracks and roads and drains. And over everything, from wherever you are in the city, the monstrous, half-finished gigantic iron tower seems to loom like an awful dream.

At the great fair itself people have come in their hundreds of thousands to see demonstrations of the latest technological and military innovations, including mocked-up houses with indoor plumbing and time-saving electrical devices, and models of futuristic boats and trains and aircraft, and presentations of archaeological and cultural objects from around the world, and strange and exotic animals, and Wild West cowboy shows, and a genuine African village which has been painstakingly transported and reconstructed in the Place du T—, complete with real inhabitants.

There are circus acts, and political debates, and wrestling matches, and talks and presentations by famous explorers and scientists and philosophers, and artistic visions of the better world that awaits us in the coming twentieth century, when war and hunger and disease and unhappiness will be ended, and all people will live forevermore for the betterment of each other.

And, here and there, are the posters advertising the latest daredevil stunt from the famed Fearless Frogman himself, Captain Clarke B. – and oh, how he would have enjoyed being a part of all this – which will involve a never-before-attempted feat of bravery and skill, including considerable risk to life and limb, and the very real possibility of death, in *dangerous circumstances that must truly be seen to be believed*, and for which all advance tickets have now been sold.

The day before the event in question is due to take place, the Widow Timmermans and I are returning through the crowds to our lodgings at the end of our final rehearsal when we hear a cry from a busy pavement café table.

We turn to see a young man excitedly waving at us, who I recognise as the mayor's son from the town of A—, where we spent our first day in France, although he has gained rakishly long hair and a dangerously tall hat in the intervening period. He has his arm dangling over the shoulders of the very young woman who is sharing his table, and who is as happily drunk as he.

'It is the daredevil assistant,' he declares, 'come to the capital exactly as I recommended!'

I bow and introduce the widow, and congratulate our young friend on making it here himself, for which he thanks me in turn.

'And are you a poet now, or a bank robber?' I ask him.

He laughs and invites us to join them at their table for one drink, which we agree to do out of politeness, and I ask after the man's parents and his father's many business interests, including the tooth-powder concern, and we discuss the excited mood in the city, and the cap's upcoming death-defying exploit – 'To men of will!' is the young man's offered toast – while the young woman alternately chain-smokes cigarettes and drums her fingers nervously on the table, until the widow gently reaches across and lays a gloved hand on hers.

'He said he was going to take me to see the monkeys,' the girl says.

'I know,' says the widow kindly. 'They always do.'

When it's time for us to leave I wave to the waiter but suddenly there is the sound of a clanging siren, and everyone on the crowded street is moving to get out of the way, as a horse-drawn carriage on which there are five or six police officers comes rushing around the corner in hot pursuit of two men on horse-back with handkerchiefs over their faces and what look like money bags hanging from their saddles. As people scream and shout in surprise, the mayor's son says, 'Excuse me,' and tips his hat to us, and then stands and pulls a pistol from inside his coat and fires off a couple of shots at the police carriage, which causes the driver to attempt to swerve, and end up crashing side-on into a glass shopfront. The lead horseman then pulls up in front of us just long enough for our friend to swing himself up onto the horse's back, before the two of them set off again, the mayor's son still shooting in the direction of the crashed policemen as they gallop away.

And then all is stunned silence, save only for the groans of the policemen as they stumble out of the destroyed carriage, until the young woman stands up and shouts, 'Pascal, you fucking shit, you did it to me again!'

293

Miracle, Marvel and Monument

Having slept about as well as you would expect in the circumstances, on the day of the event itself I am up before dawn, and decide to walk the four or so miles across the city to the site alone rather than wait to travel by rented cab with the widow, who is anyway sleeping off the results of a big night with a number of new sponsors, which involved her challenging a couple of them to an absinthe-drinking competition, and which she won handsomely but likely at some personal cost.

The city is still dark, and the streets are being cleaned of horseshit and washed down before the morning traffic starts up again, and for a brief while at least the day smells of possibility and hope. It also smells of rain, which could potentially cause me problems, although the barometer in the hotel lobby, which I checked as I left, suggested clear skies.

At the site a small podium has already been set up, and with nothing else to do I put on the frogman suit which I have carried with me, and which includes the new cape that the widow has had fashioned for me, which is decorated with the stars and stripes of Captain Clarke B.'s native country just to further support my disguise. Then I sit for a good couple of hours, stroking my new moustache and smoking a couple of cigars because

I have picked up the habit again, and because the cap is well known for it too, and watching the world get itself started.

By nine in the morning we have a decent crowd of people ready to watch the presentation, and the widow has arrived, magnificent hangover or not, and is charming the throng of local politicians and sponsors and journalists in the VIP area, and so I get up on our little stage and start my patter, which I have learned by heart in my best French, and which I'll roughly translate here as follows:

'Fellow citizens of this fine city and of the world,' I declare, in as good an approximation of the captain's accent as I can manage, 'right now you and I stand, whether we are aware of it or not, above one of the greatest technological wonders of this or any other age.'

Here I pause to let them think about it for a moment, and mentally review the possibilities, and consider the local geography, and think about cellars or crypts or underground caverns, and see them wondering if I could actually be talking about –

'For not yards below our feet,' I continue, 'your feet, sir, and yours, and yes, even yours, madam, there lies a miracle of hygienic science, and a marvel of hydrological architecture, and a monument to man's indefatigable will to improve his lot. I speak, of course, of the newly improved sewer system that runs underneath the city's streets, and which now guards each and every one of its people, at all hours of the clock, from the hidden danger of this overpopulated new era, being all that stands between your beautiful capital and the rising tide of human filth, for which every one of you is responsible, and which threatens to engulf it.'

Well, I've got them interested now, what with the contrast between my lofty talk and the base reality of piss and shit, and I can see there's a ripple of excitement at this thrillingly open discussion of things usually better left unmentioned.

'And in honour of this technical achievement,' I go on, 'it is my plan today to travel, on the water and setting out from this very spot, the entire length of the newest part of the system, including joining halfway through my journey the only recently completed main tunnel, *the largest of its kind anywhere in the world*, before eventually finishing my voyage at the outflow into the River S—, in all a feat never before attempted by man.'

Oh, and they *like* this ...

'Along the way,' I tell them, 'I will have to navigate a multitude of man-made obstacles, including fast-running sluices, chutes, flumes, pipes, weirs, falls, and other various mechanisms employed to ensure the smooth and consistent and safe transportation of the city's waste materials – and these are only the dangers *that we know about*, for who can say what other strange and thrilling challenges and perils I might face *down there* – protected as I am only by this patented waterproof suit ...'

And here I go on about the costume, in the manner that you've already heard countless times before and that I don't need to trouble you with again, then moving on, because the crowd expects it, to recount my (which is to say the cap's) various adventures around the world, before rounding off with a few more words about the promise of the coming century, and the wonderful people of the French capital, and being rewarded for the whole thing with polite applause.

And then it's time, and I nod at the widow, who in turn indicates to the two waiting workmen who come forward through the crowd with long metal pikes, which they use to remove the unassuming iron grate that has been at everyone's feet *this whole time*, and so expose the entrance to the underworld.

I climb down from the podium and then, with a wave, lower myself into the hole, putting my feet onto the metal ladder that leads into the sewer and waving once more at the crowds before beginning my descent into the darkness.

But just before the grate is lowered again there is a shout, and I stick my head back out of the hole to see what's occurred, and a young girl runs forward and hands me – a nice theatrical touch from the widow, this, of which Captain Clarke B. himself would have been proud – a single rose, and kisses my cheek too. This rouses a general, indulgent 'Ahh!' from the surrounding crowd, as if all are suddenly casting their minds back to a time when they might have had to make their own solitary journeys, either metaphorical or otherwise, with only a remembered kiss from a lover to keep them company, never mind that I've never actually met this girl before.

And then I duck my head again, and commence my climb down, and above me I hear the heavy clang of the grate being dropped back into place, and I am alone.

The Underworld

For the first hour or so the journey is as uneventful as I had hoped. The smell isn't as bad as you might expect, and besides I am used to it by now after a week of training. The water is fast-flowing and clean enough, at least in this part of the system, and there is enough light filtering down through the regularly spaced grates overhead to see by, and as I paddle along I note the clean and symmetrical brickwork and the vaulted ceilings of the new tunnels, and the overall fine level of craftsmanship that has gone into the planning and construction of the whole enterprise.

If this is the future, I think, then it is a fine one.

Of course I come across the occasional surprised rat, but nothing larger, and no people either, despite some of the rumours I have heard of entire communities of fugitives and criminals down here, and crocodiles besides.

Halfway through the morning I come to the first tricky piece of navigation, which is a place where the tunnel I am in joins a larger, much deeper-lying tributary via a long, steeply sloping weir, which I have no choice but to shoot down on my back, holding the paddle above my head. This successfully achieved, I find that the water in the larger tunnel is flowing faster, being fed by a number of other streams, and so soon reach the second major obstacle – a set of narrow gates through which the water travels at some considerable force and speed, and which I paddle in front of for a good few minutes before I gather the courage to lie back, tuck in my arms, and let the water pull me quickly through.

Shortly thereafter I come across the first strange sight of the day.

Where the new tunnel I am in is joined by an older passage, a fully grown tree, twenty feet or more in diameter, is growing out of the crumbling brickwork, apparently fed by the shaft of light that makes its way down from a grate far above. But instead of leaves, the tree is draped with what look from a distance like hundreds of rags, but which on closer inspection turn out to be large numbers of sodden banknotes of various denominations which have been caught, filthy but otherwise intact, in the tree's branches – I assume after having been washed into the sewer following a robbery or other unexpected set of circumstances.

After contemplating this odd apparition for a while I move on, but not before grabbing as many of the notes as I can reach and stuffing them, filthy or not, inside the suit.

Around what would be lunchtime up on the surface I start to feel hungry, and stop and sit on a narrow ledge out of the water to eat the bread and meat that I have brought with me, wrapped tightly in oilcloth. As I eat, I can hear the rushing of what sounds like a waterfall, and when I resume my journey I soon come upon the source of the sound. As the tunnel I am in rounds a corner, I arrive at the edge of a vast, cathedral-like vault, hundreds of feet high, where numerous different streams plunge into the main drain from different angles and directions, creating a series of stepped waterfalls which seem to rise all the way to the top of the giant shaft. Making my way carefully down to the pool at the bottom of the shaft via an iron access ladder which is bolted to the shaft wall, and which is slippery with the same green algae or moss that coats everything else in this area, I realise I must already be much deeper underground than I previously thought.

At the foot of the ladder, amid the roar of the cascading water-falls, the newly constructed main tunnel, which I am to follow for the remainder of the journey, leads away under an arch fully fifty feet high. And there I find a dead body, pale grey but not yet much bloated, floating face down in the water, slowly going round in a circular current caused by the plunging cataracts.

For some reason I am suddenly and utterly convinced that the corpse is the body of the captain, although why he should be in this place and at this time I have no idea, and feel compelled to paddle over and turn it over in order to know for sure. In the event the lower half of the man's face – for it is a man – is missing, taken by what looks like a gunshot or other traumatic injury, although I realise with a shudder that it could simply have been eaten by animals. Either way, by the looks of it he still has two eyes, or did in life at least, which rules out the cap.

I wonder if he was a murder victim, and was dumped into the sewer to avoid detection, or if he fell into a river somewhere and never came out again and eventually floated down here deep under the city, or even if he died by his own hand. I wonder if he had a family who are still looking for him, and if he was someone's father or brother or son, and who might have loved him, and whether he was a good man or a bad man, or a mixture of the two.

I realise that there is no way I can take the body out with me, or even weigh it down with anything to sink it, so I say a brief and silent prayer and mark the spot on my map, and carry on with my journey.

An hour or so later I almost become a corpse myself.

For the last couple of miles, the water in the wide and slow-flowing main tunnel has been incrementally thickening to a soup or sludge made up of materials that I don't want to think too much about, and it's for this reason, as I know, that a system of parallel rotating propellers has been built across the tunnel, in order to separate out the silt and so remove the viscosity from the fluid. I have planned for this, and know that the propellers will be rotating at a slow enough speed for me to slip through – and sure enough when the vast wheels come into view this looks like being the case.

But then, as a result – as I later find out – of the sudden rainstorm that I had been worrying about earlier this morning, the water level in the tunnel suddenly begins to rise, and the speed of the current increases too, and with it the rotation of the propellers, and having no way to gain any purchase on the perfectly smooth walls of the new tunnel I find myself frantically trying to paddle against the flow as the rushing water tries to drag me to my doom.

As I am pulled towards the spinning contraption I wonder if this is really the way I'm going to go out, and how I'll be remembered, and what will be said at my funeral by my brother, and whether Andrea will somehow be there, and how I'll go down in history as a man who I'm not. But at least I won't go without a fight, I decide.

At the last second before I am sliced in half I jam my paddle into the track of the propeller blade, which holds for just long enough before snapping in half – breaking my bad arm with it as it goes – to enable me to slip through the mechanism, the reactivated propeller missing the top of my head by less than a hair's breadth.

And then I am through, and racing down a rapidly narrowing chute towards the light, gritting my teeth and holding one shattered arm against my body with the other, before I am fired out into the open air in a stream of water alongside the rest of the gushing effluent, to fall the ten feet or so into the dirty, wonderful River S—, which is lined, would you believe it, with amazed and suddenly cheering crowds.

And so, after being dragged out of the water by a couple of surprised boatmen and delivered to the crowd on the embankment, who carry me immediately on hundreds of hands to a waiting cart, onto which I am strapped for the journey to the hospital, where I am stitched and bandaged and plastered up, it turns out that I have survived.

I still have the shit-stained money on me too.

The Journey Home

The journey home takes three days, and if we're not exactly returning in triumph, then at least we're doing it in a reasonable amount of comfort, as we cross the channel by steamer rather than sail and paddle, which I think would have been a sacrifice too far even for the redoubtable Widow Timmermans, and even taking into account the fact that she is now the manager of a world-famous daredevil adventurer.

With the fearless Captain Clarke B. seemingly back from the dead – or self-imposed exile, or bout of amnesia, or kidnap by anarchists from which he barely escaped with his life, or contemplative, monastical retreat on some uninhabited Mediterranean island (I like this one the best), or wherever he has supposedly been these whole past few months, the widow having been thrillingly vague about the entire business in her interviews with the press – the offers of new appearances and sponsorship and commercial opportunities have come in quickly, including the possibility of a Scandinavian tour along the magnificent fjords towards the Arctic Circle, and a crossing of the B— from Europe to Asia, and a trip down the mighty River V—.

But first we are to put on a couple of presentations in England, and at the sight of white cliffs making themselves apparent through the clearing drizzle as we stand on the ship's deck, the widow asks me how I feel.

'Old,' I say, aware of the ache in my re-broken arm, and the miles, nautical and otherwise, now under my belt. 'How about you?'

'Young,' she says, and puts a friendly hand on my shoulder. 'Younger than I have perhaps ever felt.'

In fact, how I am actually feeling is excited but nervous about seeing my brother, who I haven't heard from in months, as well as somewhat concerned by the prospect of setting foot back in the village where I grew up, and did so much to escape from, and apprehending it for the first time through the eyes of someone new. I wonder – and not for the first time – what Andrea would have made of it, and of all of this, and where he might be now, and hope he is happy with his lot one way or another.

Of course, both the widow and I are aware that there's no way my impersonation of the cap, no matter how good from a distance, will ever be able to stand up to close scrutiny – which is why the new Captain Clarke B., we have decided, is a man very much changed, humbled even, by his near-death experience or exile or kidnap or retreat. He is a man who, most conveniently for us, would these days much rather shun the limelight than stand in it, and who prefers to let his actions – and his new manager, the Widow Timmermans – speak for him, particularly when it comes to relations with members of the world's press.

And this, of course, only adds to the mystery of the fellow, and makes those same members of the press, not to mention our sponsors, even more intrigued. Which is why it is agreed that the captain won't be taking up any of the numerous offers we have received for him to hobnob with London society while back in the country, but instead will be staying outside the capital, at a secret training camp, to ensure his newly desired privacy. And why he is making his own secret way there, possibly alone, probably in disguise, likely under cover of darkness, and almost definitely not by passenger ship, and so isn't seen disembarking at Dover later that day along with the widow and I, or accompanying us on the train up to London, or joining us in our hired horse and carriage as we head out eastwards from the capital the next morning, bound for parts out in the territories unheard of in high-ceilinged Marylebone drawing rooms, or racy Chelsea salons, or even Fleet Street newspaper offices.

'It's as if we've thought of everything,' I say to the widow, as we roll across a wide-open country under the racing shadows of spring clouds, watching the villages speed by outside the carriage window, and coming ever closer to my former home.

'It almost is,' she agrees.

But of course we are wrong.

HERE I AM, NOW

The spit, at least, looks the same as it did when I left it. The same dirt road, the same falling-down houses, the same shingle banks filled with upturned boats, and grey mudflats beyond, on either side.

Riding through the village, we pass the church and the schoolhouse and come to Giant Pete's inn, where the carriage pulls up and we are unloaded. Giant Pete and his wife are nowhere about, but Little Pete takes the widow's bags inside with much bowing and scraping, having failed utterly to recognise me, perhaps on account of my new moustache, while the Widow Timmermans and I walk the quarter-mile or so to my old house.

'There's no need for you to accompany me,' I tell her.

'After that journey I need the air,' she says, rolling her stiff neck. 'And I also admit to being more than a little intrigued.'

Once we are past the protection of the street, the wind blowing up off the estuary hits us hard and the widow is forced to hold on to her hat as we cross the exposed beach. Out on the water beyond, a couple of boats are fighting the weather. I point out the oyster beds, and indicate the direction of Holland across the sea, in order to make the widow feel more at home.

But at the house, or the place where the house used to be, I am shocked to find little more than a ruin, with a caved-in roof, which looks like it has been uninhabited for months. Inside, the place is gutted, and it stinks. Most of our father's gear is gone, and the kitchen and what furniture we had has been stripped out too. On the low shelf where the bed used to be I find one of my brother's flattened lead soldiers, but no other signs that anyone has been here in a long time. Outside the house my vegetable garden, which I so carefully dug out of the shingle, has been completely scoured away by the wind.

'What happened here?' asks the widow.

'Perhaps he has absconded again,' I say.

'Looks like he absconded quite some time ago,' she says.

Returning to the inn, we are shown to our rooms by Little Pete, who I don't disabuse of the notion that I am some rich traveller up from London, and we unpack our things and wash our faces and so on. I look out of the second-floor window of my room and get a perspective on the village that I have never had before, and note how low and crouched and small the place really is, cowering as it does in the face of the elements. It occurs to me that in sixteen years – seventeen now, in fact – I have never once got a look inside any of the bedrooms at the inn, those being reserved exclusively for the use of people with money and so *not from our village*, until today.

'Well, here I am, now,' I say to no one in particular, before heading downstairs.

I find the Widow Timmermans already seated in the bar, where she is reviewing some paperwork pertaining to the next stage in Captain Clarke B.'s fabulously revived career, including invitations to swim in the lakes and private rivers of various lords and minor royals, and requests for interviews and personal appearances, and agreements for the cap to endorse numerous products from potted meat to men's girdles, all for sums of money that I would not have believed possible a few months ago.

'Constipation relief tablets,' says the widow, shaking her head at it all. 'Hair-loss remedies. Tonics to return male vigour, if you would believe it. Had I known he was sitting on such a potential goldmine all this time …'

'You would have lectured him on the evils of capitalism, all the same,' I say.

'Well, yes. But still: God bless you, Clarke,' says the widow. 'Wherever you are.'

The widow then asks shy Little Pete, who is simultaneously trying to make himself look busy and useful while also hiding from his only two customers, what there is good to eat today, and he says that there's only one thing, good or bad, and so the widow tells him that we'll have a couple of servings of that, then. And so we are served some of the fish stew from the kitchen, which is authentically tasty enough that I start to feel a little less guilty about having dragged the widow so far away from civilisation. Besides, there is a fine, roaring log fire in the bar which counteracts the effects of the cold North Sea wind coming in under the door, and a decent wine cellar, all things considered, and an absence of prying eyes from the big city who might otherwise find us out and expose our caper for the frogman-less sham that it actually is.

In fact, there seems to be an absence of anyone at all about today, and I am just about to ask Little Pete where everyone is when the door opens and here's Giant Pete coming booming into the bar now, with his apparently pregnant daughter in tow – I do a quick mental calculation to discount the possibility that the cap might have been involved in this situation – and then he's shouting, 'Daniel Bones the daredevil!' and lifting me off my feet, before complimenting me on my moustache and shaking the widow's hand and asking her if everything is to her satisfaction.

The widow agrees that everything is fine, and that this place surely compares favourably to some of the finest hotels on the continent, and Giant Pete declares himself delighted to hear it, and then goes behind the bar and pours the two of them a pair of large gins in honour of her native country, though there is not one offered to me.

'Obviously we are used to having celebrity here,' says Giant Pete, clinking his glass against the widow's.

'Obviously,' says she.

'And not just the famous captain, mind,' he tells her. 'We once had a woman prize-fighter who could knock out a cow with a single punch.'

'A praiseworthy talent indeed.'

'Who was that actor we had the other year, Maude?'

'I don't know, Dad,' says his daughter sullenly, and then excuses herself to go to her room.

Ignoring her, Giant Pete asks me, 'And have you been to see your brother, yet, Dan?'

'I don't know where he is,' I admit.

Giant Pete looks momentarily confused at this, and turns to Little Pete, who is hanging around in the doorway, for help, but gets nothing more than a shrug in return.

'Well …' says Giant Pete. 'He's in gaol is where he is, Dan. Up in C—. We thought that was why you came back.'

'Why is he in gaol?' I ask, expecting some story about a stolen horse or boat, or perhaps a fist fight, or maybe even something to do with the customs and excise men.

No.

'Killed the old man, didn't he?' says Giant Pete. 'And in his own boat, too. Then weighted the body and threw it over the side. Only the weights didn't take and the body washed up a month later, your brother's knife still in his neck.'

'They think Will murdered our father?'

'Not much to think about, by all accounts.'

'But … what are they going to do?'

'Well,' says Giant Pete, before knocking back his gin and placing the glass back on the bar, 'most likely they're going to hang him, Dan.'

A Matching Pair

That evening the widow writes a letter to her lawyers in London, telling them to send someone over to see what they can do for us, and I arrange a trip up to C— in the morning to go and visit Will, and meanwhile try to find out what else I can about what has gone on from Giant Pete, which isn't much.

We establish that my father's body was indeed found just as the innkeeper described, and that it didn't take long after that for the authorities to come for my brother – 'And he didn't try to run, either,' says George Baines, who claims to have been there that morning, and gives his version of the story for the price of a drink, but doesn't add much to the general understanding of events.

And he's not the only one. In fact, the bar is soon full of people – and not all of them locals – who claim to have some knowledge of what went on, either in the run-up to, during, or in the aftermath of, the event in question, although all end up being equally light on useful details. And of course no one in the village has any idea of what happened to the contents of the ransacked house afterwards – although I bet that the most cursory search would turn up at least one of my father's tools inside every one of the homes on the spit.

I also learn in the course of my investigations about all of the other comings and goings of the village over the last year, and receive a number of conflicting versions of who has died, or got pregnant, or married, or moved away, or come back again.

Susan the vicar's daughter even does me the honour of personally filling me in on the story of her year, after crashing into the table that the widow and I have been sharing in the bar that evening and interrupting me as I attempt to introduce her.

'I'm the one who got caught fucking two brothers,' she declares to the Widow Timmermans, defiantly. 'And is there anything wrong with that?'

'Well not in my personal experience, no,' says the widow.

I stand up, gently taking Susan by the elbow and guiding her towards the door.

'Do you mind if we …?' I ask the widow.

'Please,' she says.

Outside we lean against the wall of the inn and Susan lights two cigarettes and hands me one.

'I thought you'd been sent away,' I say.

'I reached an agreement with my parents,' she replies.

'What kind of agreement?'

'I married Joseph Parsons.'

'Is he the one who catches –'

'No, that's the brother. Jeremiah.'

'Of course.'

Far off we hear someone shouting. A drunken fight some-where. A dog barking at a seagull. Just like in the good old days. And then Susan lets out a big lungful of smoke and sighs.

'I think I married the wrong one, Dan,' she says.

'Well I can see how you might make that mistake.'

'He's drunk all the time.'

'That's hardly strange behaviour round here, though, is it?'

'No, but he's a nasty drunk.'

'Ah.'

I feel her hand reaching for mine, and our fingers twining together.

'And where is he tonight?' I ask.

'Oh, who knows?' she says.

And then she leans over and kisses me, more in a friendly way than anything else. It goes on for quite a while, though, and I kiss her back too. When it's finished she leans back against the wall, and takes another drag of her cigarette.

'It would have been funny if you and I had ended up together, wouldn't it?' she says.

'Funnier than you know.'

She looks at me sideways in the dark and squints, as if trying to spot someone else standing in my place.

'What happened to you over there?' she asks me. 'You're different.'

'In a good way?'

'I don't know,' she says. 'I'm not sure it suits you.'

'Is it the moustache?' I ask.

The next morning I'm up early to take the coach to C—, and the castle-like prison there, where I discover that my money easily buys me an interview with prisoner William Bones, which takes place in a small tiled room with a wooden table and two chairs, plus an attendant guard.

The look of my little brother when they lead him in is a shock. In a prison uniform and chained at the wrists he already seems bigger and more muscular than I remember, with a face starting to widen like a tomcat's. His cheek is bruised, and he has a swollen lip, and an only half-healed black eye. It's hard to tell how much is down to his injuries and how much is just the

313

difference a year makes, but he looks older and harder too – which, I suppose, is inevitable given the circumstances.

Nevertheless, as he sits down at the table it's him who says to me, 'Well, you've looked better.'

I hold up my plastered arm with a smile.

'I thought we could be a matching pair,' I say. 'But it seems yours has healed.'

'It's been a year,' he says, then, gesturing at our surroundings, 'A lot has changed. I even smoke now.'

And with that he gets out a pouch of tobacco and starts rolling a cigarette.

'So I see.'

'You know that he deserved it, Dan,' he says, without looking up. 'And worse too.'

'I know.'

'If you'd been there –'

'I know that too.'

'Hey,' he says, as the guard leans over to light the cigarette for him, 'do you remember that time we stole Bill Draper's boat only it was just me who got the blame?'

'Why didn't you write and tell me?' I ask him.

'I did,' he says, blowing out smoke. 'But the last address I had for you was a hotel in V—, in Italy.'

'But the money I sent …'

'What money?' he says. 'I've been in here since November, Dan. The only gifts I've received are cakes from Helen Dunning and Ada Crook. And Davey Cooper offered to get hold of a gun and break me out, but then he lost his leg.'

'How did he lose his leg?'

'Oh, you know Davey Cooper.'

He rotates his wrists, trying to get some relief from the metal cuffs.

'Mrs Pritchard the vicar's wife comes to see me once a week and reads the Bible to me. That's a sort of comfort. She brings Susan sometimes. Do you remember much from the Bible, Dan?'

'I almost became a monk in France,' I say. I don't tell him about my experience with the travelling Bible salesman. Things are complicated enough as it is. He looks at me for a long while then, as if trying to place me, and match me to the person he used to know.

'We're getting you a lawyer,' I say, and he nods. He puts out his cigarette and immediately starts rolling another one.

'Is there anything else you need?' I ask.

'Well I could do with getting out of here before they hang me,' he says. 'That would be good if you can arrange it.'

'That's the basis of our plan, yes,' I say.

'Susan was asking after you,' he says.

'I know.'

'You could still do a lot worse.'

'I'll keep that in mind.'

Seeing the tears in my eyes he moves his hand across the table and pats mine.

'I'm glad you're back, Dan,' he says.

'So am I,' I lie.

The Logistical Details

There is a heavy swell on the grey water the day I borrow the boat from Giant Pete's cousin Giant Charlie to sail myself and the widow out to the old fort that lies off the coast, and it's not long into the five-mile round trip that my passenger starts to look almost as green as I remember Andrea once looking.

'Technically we are more in the North Sea here than the river estuary,' I tell her, apologising for the rough conditions, and the motion of our little boat. 'And it can get a lot worse than this.'

'But can you do it?' she asks, as we approach the giant circular stone building that stands alone above the waves, its ramparts still armed with rusting canons, guarding the access to the river and so the country itself.

'With the suit and a bit of luck with the weather?' I say. 'Yes.'

'And if we aren't lucky?'

'Then I'll just have to rely on the suit alone.'

We've been working on the plan for the cap's next stunt since before we left France, but it's only in the last week that we've been able to start dealing with the logistical details, including reconnoitring the actual location, which I haven't visited since I used to come out here as a boy, and lining up publicity and promotional opportunities.

'And we're sure it'll be empty?' the widow asks, trying in vain to keep the hair that has escaped her cap out of her face in the high wind.

'It's been empty for nearly half a century,' I say. 'It was built to stop Napoleon's fleet from sailing up the river, and that's not been a worry for about seventy years.'

I tell the same story about the fort to the sponsors we meet when the widow and I take the carriage to London for the day, and we all sit drinking tea in a very fancy hotel that looks out onto an even fancier park, and I pretend to be offended on the cap's behalf when the group of businessmen question his abilities.

'He can do it,' I say, firmly. 'Be in no doubt.'

'And what about personal appearances?' they ask. 'Photography? Speeches? An address to the Houses of Parliament?'

'In the suit: yes,' the Widow tells them. 'Out of the suit: no.'

Notes are then taken to be written up later into legal contracts, and further sit-downs arranged, and hands shaken all round, and it is agreed that the issue of a five-night residency at the London Palladium will be put off for further discussion at a later meeting.

'And now, I wonder,' the widow continues, 'have you gentlemen considered the strategic placing of the names of your products *on the actual frogman outfit itself?*'

Unfortunately, the meetings with the lawyers for my brother have not gone so well as those with the sponsors, being more concerned with minute legal details and precedents and other complexities that go mostly over my head. The upshot here seems to be that the widow's representatives are doing what they can, and that these things take time, and that we are to be patient – but also that, based on the evidence and Will's flat refusal to deny responsibility for the act, this is not an un-challenging case.

I agree to relay as much of this as I can to my brother at my next prison visit, though I determine to present it to him in a rather more positive light.

Meanwhile, the widow and I have settled into our headquarters at Giant Pete's and the day-to-day life of the village itself, in which we have no choice but to take part, including work and friendships and gossip and fallings-out and the occasional minor acts of violence or revenge. Susan the vicar's daughter quickly attaches herself to us, having decided that the widow will make an ideal mentor, and potential ticket out of here. She enthusiastically attempts to make herself useful as a fixer and organiser and general secretary, while insisting what a fine gang the three of us make. I think the widow sees something worthwhile in her too, and not just on account of her unfortunate marital situation.

But the fact that the more time Susan spends with us, the less she has to endure her husband's presence, doesn't escape anyone, not least the old (eighteen years of age) man himself, who manages to incur a ban from Giant Pete's, as well as a slap from the Giant's hand, after drunkenly insulting the Widow Timmermans in public, and threatening me besides.

Giant Pete himself is clearly very taken with the widow, and announces that the two of us are to be his most special overnight guests (luckily, we are also his only overnight guests for the moment), and will receive his personal attention in all eventualities and at all times of the day, which does not go down that well with his wife – although, as he points out, no one has forgotten how *she* behaved when Captain Clarke B. was in town.

And in return for his hospitality I entertain Giant Pete's customers every night in the bar with tales of the cap's adventures in Europe and elsewhere, including the occasional minor cameo by yours truly, as well as teasing some details of the upcoming stunt.

'And so will you and the cap be breaking young Will out of the prison, then?' asks Giant Pete.

'I think that might be beyond even the cap's powers,' the widow tells the giant innkeeper, gently.

'And perhaps we should let the legal profession do what they're best at,' I add.

'I'd fancy the lad's chances a lot more with the cap, to be honest,' says Giant Pete.

'I'll let him know,' I say. 'The next time I see him.'

'Do so,' says Giant Pete. 'And tell him we all stand ready to help in whatever way the captain needs us to, wherever and whenever he needs it.'

'These are strange people you come from,' the widow tells me, as the two of us review our situation, while forging the cap's signature on various documents late into the night.

'And yet, still, they are mine,' I tell her.

'And do you trust them?'

'I think I do, yes,' I say, surprising even myself.

'Good,' says the Widow Timmermans, 'because we might yet need to rely on that trust before too long.'

European Practices

The next day the widow is off to town until the evening to tie up a couple more deals, and I have the day to myself to check over the suit and the tide charts for the tenth or eleventh time, and to brood on everything.

I am returning from a rainy walk on the mudflats, where I have gone to think about my brother and what might be done for him, and the challenge ahead too, and what's to come after that – for now that the widow has seen the promise of our new business venture, I doubt she'll want to give it up too soon – when I spot the two men who are seemingly setting out to try to walk the Angel's Road. This is a low stone causeway, little more than a cobbled pavement, that crosses the flats between our spit and one of the tidal islands.

I've had the feeling that I may be being watched – and not just by the eyes of the curious townsfolk – for a few days now, including spotting a rider on horseback out among the dunes who seemed to be observing me from a distance, and who turned and rode away when I tried to approach. But this time I am sure of it, and walk towards the pair, who I finger as pressmen up from London likely trying to get the scoop on Captain Clarke B.'s secret training methods, as one is carrying a camera mounted on a tripod over his shoulder, and both are wearing entirely inappropriate shoes for the muddy conditions.

'If you go out there you'll likely not live to tell the tale,' I tell them.

'And why would that be?' says the taller of the two.

'Tide's turned,' I say, indicating out across the flats towards the sea. 'You'll get about halfway out, perhaps, and then when you realise how fast the water is coming in you'll turn around. But you won't make it back.'

They look at each other, and one nods to the other.

'Perhaps we'll leave it then.'

'A wise choice,' I say, then bid them good morning, for I have a pressing appointment back in the village.

Over the last couple of weeks Susan the vicar's daughter and I have drifted, almost accidentally it seems, into a sort of friendly love affair. Or, at least, a series of daily romantic adventures which take place in my room at Giant Pete's – and occasionally in the bed she shares with Joseph Parsons at their two-room cottage, while he is out at sea, which I have to admit adds an illicit thrill to the proceedings.

'You've picked up a trick or two that I never taught you,' she tells me happily that dark afternoon as we lie in my bed, our breath slowing, listening to the rain fall on the roof.

'Thank you,' I tell her, thinking of what other European practices I might surprise her with before we are done.

'Jeremiah still can't fuck worth a damn, despite my best efforts,' she says. 'He's sweet though.'

'You mean Joseph, surely.'

'No, Joseph can fuck. He just isn't very nice.'

'Oh,' I say. 'I didn't realise that you were still ...'

'You're the one fucking another man's wife, Dan,' she says lightly. 'I don't think you have a right to judge me or anyone else.'

'That's fair,' I agree.

'By the way, my mother has invited you and the widow around for dinner this evening. Along with Joseph and me. And possibly Jeremiah, too.'

'Won't that make for quite a strange night?'

'More than likely,' says Susan. 'But then what isn't strange around here?'

And so, after the widow has returned from the day's business, and we have caught up on things, we all spend a stilted evening at the Reverend and Mrs Pritchard's, where I answer many questions about my European journey, and discuss my brother's unfortunate situation, and learn how much the noble Mrs Pritchard herself has been doing to help him. I also discover a possible answer to what happened to the money I sent my brother, and the other things besides, after I notice the collection of familiar-looking French lead soldiers that grace the shelf above the reverend's writing table, and learn that they were a late Christmas gift from his remarkably generous wife.

And then Joseph and Jeremiah Parsons, who have been at each other's throats all evening – which has fortunately kept their attention away from me, and Susan's hand on my thigh – round things off nicely with a drunken fist fight in the lane behind the house.

When the widow and I return to the otherwise empty bar of the inn at the end of the evening, we are greeted by the sight of the two gentlemen I took for journalists earlier in the day, as well as a third man who I also recognise, and who smiles when he sees me and gestures for the widow and I to join them at their table, where two extra wine glasses are already set out.

'We're glad to see you alive, Dan,' says the man as we sit. 'We were all very surprised when we read about that stunt in P—. Are you hiding the captain somewhere around here too?'

He makes a show of looking under the table.

'I haven't seen the cap since Italy,' I tell them, truthfully.

'So he really is retired?' says the man. 'In which case it must be you who'll be making the swim out to Fort Gallow. Well, that works fine, too.'

'Let me guess,' I say. 'You want someone to blow it up.'

'Ha, no. Not this time. Actually, the first thing we'd like you to do is help us strike against the *other* side. A little job up in the Frisian Islands. If you're not too busy, of course.'

'Which other side?'

'There's always another side, Dan,' says the man, pouring wine for the widow and me. 'Just like there's always a war coming.'

'And why would I help you?'

'Well, because we own you. How's that for a start? And this is just the beginning of what could be a very fruitful partnership.'

'I don't owe you anything. I'm not the captain.'

'But you are, Dan,' says the man, raising his glass to us. 'You have been ever since you chose to put the suit on.'

'We have a lot of friends in this village,' says the Widow Timmermans quietly. 'If we say the word, you'll never get out of here alive.'

The man shrugs.

'We're replaceable. More men like us will come. You of all people know how this works, Frieda.'

I look at the widow then, and she looks down guiltily.

'What if I run?' I say.

'And leave your brother to be hanged? Come on, now.'

I pick up my glass of wine and finish it off in one swallow.

'It seems as if you've thought of everything,' I say.

'It does, rather,' says the man, the duelling scars on either cheek lifting as he smiles, 'doesn't it?'

A Bad Bunch to a Man

It's a bright spring morning when I next set out by carriage to visit my brother, this time with Mrs Pritchard for company, and we make good time on the dried-out roads.

All the same the reverend's wife manages to spend the whole journey explaining to me her vast disappointment in her daughter Susan, for whom she had such high hopes, and who is still too good for the men of our village, and the surrounding ones besides, despite all the evidence to the contrary.

'The men of these parts are all the same, Dan,' she tells me. 'No offence to you and your brother. Although look where he has ended up.'

I agree that we are indeed a bad bunch to a man, who drink and swear too much, and go off on strange adventures, and do our best to squander every opportunity handed to us.

'Well,' says Mrs Pritchard, surprised but appreciative of finding such a receptive audience, 'yes.'

I don't ask about what happened to the money I sent my brother, or the strange case of the set of lead soldiers posted over from France, either.

At the prison it is the formidable moral force of Mrs Pritchard, rather than money, that secures us access this time, and I am

324

pulled along in her slipstream as she blows through the echoing corridors. When they bring my brother into the little room she dismisses the guard, telling him, 'You may leave us now,' and embraces the prisoner, and then insists that the three of us say a prayer before we begin.

While this is going on I crack open an eye, to see both Mrs Pritchard's and Will's earnestly shut tight, and am touched in spite of myself. With his eyes closed my brother looks like the determined little boy I remember, never mind the surroundings and circumstance. He has been beaten again since my last visit, and looks like he is missing a couple of teeth. His interlaced fingers as he prays are bruised and cut at the knuckles too, which suggests that he at least gave as good as he got.

The liturgy over, Mrs Pritchard asks after Will's health, and his diet, and daily life in the prison, and the extent of his latest set of injuries.

'Ah, I had worse than this growing up, Mrs Pritchard,' says Will, and winks at me.

'And have you, perhaps, made any friends yet?' his friendly interrogator asks.

'It's not really that sort of place,' he replies.

'You are a brave boy, William,' Mrs Pritchard tells him, 'and you need to trust that the Lord has a plan for you.'

'That I do try, for sure,' he says. 'And maybe he'll start putting his trust in me too, and soon.'

When it's my turn to talk I catch Will up on the latest gossip from the village, though obviously steering clear of the situation with Susan, and the current state of our plans – 'That is, the *captain's* plans,' I add, for the benefit of Mrs Pritchard – for the upcoming performance.

'It's a tricky stretch of water,' Will agrees. 'Remember when we almost drowned trying to break into that fort?'

I hurriedly move on, and explain the most recent developments in his case, reviewing my meetings with the lawyers and attempting to paint a positive picture of things, but I can't deny that events are proceeding more slowly than we would like, and I can offer little in the way of a timescale for resolving them. It breaks my heart to see my younger brother's face fall, despite his obvious determination not to show his despair.

'God will provide,' says Mrs Pritchard.

'I hope he hurries up,' Will replies, managing a half-laugh, I think mainly for my benefit.

When it's time for us to leave he embraces me and holds on for a very long time, before clearing his throat and offering me a goodbye.

The next day I travel to London to the offices of the cap's creditors, alone, and noisily demand an audience with them.

I am shown into the wood-panelled boardroom, where a junior member of the organisation listens patiently to what I have to say.

'And why should we agree to help?' he asks me, when I have presented my case.

'If my brother dies,' I say, 'then what have I got to live for anyway?'

And I leave them to ponder that, while showing myself out.

CALLING IT SQUARE

The wind has been blowing for almost a week now, and everyone in the village is on edge. Up and down the main street there are shouting matches and hysterical outbursts and fallings-out and fist fights even between the oldest of friends, and Joseph and Jeremiah Parsons have taken to trying to kill each other in increasingly elaborate ambushes. As the wind whistles under the doors and around the windows, Giant Pete and his wife spend all their time at the inn either arguing or noisily making up, often not even getting as far as their bedroom before falling passionately into one another's arms – to the point that it becomes customary and sensible to knock before entering any room at the inn with a closed door, store cupboards included.

'People have used wind-madness as a defence for murdering their spouses, you know,' Giant Pete yells at Mrs Pete.

'Murder?' she shouts back. 'They'd give me a medal!'

Out on the mudflats a weird foam whipped up from the waves clings to the asters and the seablite, or breaks away in giant clots and bounces across the shingle. At high tide the water almost reaches the main street, and various ships carrying both legal and illegal cargoes are run aground or wrecked in the estuary. In the church the Reverend Pritchard delivers apocalyptic sermons against fornication and bearing false witness, which I note nicely covers both his daughter and his wife.

Even Susan has become somewhat introspective, although this doesn't stop her from keeping our daily appointments, which we conduct to the accompaniment of the howling wind. After one fantastic coupling she idly muses about what it might be like to bed myself, Joseph and Jeremiah all at the same time, but, remembering my time in southern France, and the consequences of that, I politely decline the offer.

The steadily deteriorating weather also threatens to have an impact on our planned stunt, with the giant waves making it impossible to carry out rehearsals on the water, or even safely get within more than a hundred feet of the fort. Still, the size of the sponsorship deals in place mean that cancelling would likely ruin us all over again, never mind the expense of hiring the boats and support crew, and the arrangements with the press, and the various backhanders that have been paid to other interested parties.

And so we carry on with our preparations.

I spend most of the night before the event out on the spit helping a party of village men secure the roof on Colin Wright's house, which has been partially blown off by the wind. In the darkness we can hardly hear each other over the booming of the giant waves and the noise of the storm, but I am surprised by how much I enjoy the work and the company.

When I get back to the inn most of the lamps have blown out and Giant Pete is up and down the stairs re-lighting them, so it takes me a moment to spot the new customer sitting at a table in the half-darkness, huddled in a waterproof cape. But then he stands up and turns towards me and I recognise the eye patch.

'Hello, Dan,' says the cap as I approach, and that's as far as he gets before I catch him with a fine right hook, which sends him to the floor.

'Well,' he says, lying there, 'I should say I deserved that.'

I hold out a hand and help him to his feet, but then decide to hit him again, with the left this time, and he falls to the floor once more. He doesn't try to defend himself, even when I lift up a stool, fully intending to smash his face in with it, so I put the stool back down.

'Are you finished?' he asks warily.

'For now,' I say.

I help him up again and sit him back at the table, and I take the chair opposite.

'I heard about your stunt in the sewers of P—,' he says, rubbing his jaw. 'It must have been quite a spectacle.'

'And is that why you've come back?' I ask. 'To take the credit again?'

'Well, not to argue the point, but it does seem to be you who is taking the credit for my name, at the moment.'

'I think I've earned it,' I tell him. 'And that's before we take into account the money you stole.'

He reaches into the bag under his chair and takes out a purse full of money, which he slides across the table towards me.

'Can we call it square?' he says.

I push the purse back across the table to him.

'And who's going to square things with your creditors?'

His eyes narrow at that.

'What did you agree with them?' he asks.

'That I'll be their man,' I say. 'For as long as they want me. If I survive tomorrow.'

'And in return?'

'In return they get my brother out of prison and save his neck.'

'And what happens to him if you don't survive tomorrow?'

'They're getting him out and bringing him to me before the stunt,' I tell him. 'Because I'm smart, remember?'

'I am impressed,' he says.

'Why are you here?' I ask.

He studies me for a moment, as if only truly seeing me for the first time in a very long time. Perhaps it's the first time ever. Then he opens his bag again and unrolls a nautical chart onto the table. I recognise it immediately.

'This is the fort, here?' he asks, pointing to the familiar location.

'You can read a chart as well as I can,' I say.

'That I can. And I can read the papers too. So: sheer walls, no breakwater, no landing stage since the old one collapsed years ago. And, what, thirty-foot waves on a night like this?'

'There or thereabouts.'

'But you think a man could swim to it, and climb to the ramparts, and let off a rocket to show that he has succeeded?'

'That's the stunt.'

He looks up and smiles, then considers me again.

'Let me have it, Dan,' he says.

I laugh in his face.

'To reclaim your throne?'

'Or say a final goodbye to it.'

'One last stunt?' I say. 'And then you can retire happily?'

'If you like.'

'No.'

'Well then, if you prefer, let me have it because I don't want you to die.'

'And what would save you in my place? The indefatigable power of your will?'

'Either that or luck.'

'Oh, you do have that, for sure,' I say.

I get up and go to the bar and, since Giant Pete is nowhere to be found, pour myself a drink of rum and then pour one for the cap too, and put it on the bar top so that he has to come over to get it.

'I read the story you invented about my religious retreat,' he says, and takes a sip, 'or was it a kidnap?'

'There were a few different versions,' I tell him.

'Do you want to know where I went?' he asks.

I shrug.

'I got on a boat to New York,' he says. 'Obviously I wanted to get as far away as possible. But also some part of me still knew I could make use of the experience. A lecture tour. A warning to others of the Dangers of European Travel. Something like that. Because I'm good with a crowd. I was already putting plans together when we reached the Azores. But then I got off the boat and I never got back on.'

He finishes his drink and indicates for me to refill his glass.

'I didn't have any kind of a plan, beyond drinking myself to death, perhaps. And when that didn't work I tried to gamble the money away in the bars at the docks, but I kept winning more back. I even tried giving it away but somehow it kept finding its way back to me. And so eventually I began to wonder if I wasn't destined to do one last heroic thing, after all. One final great performance. And then one morning, as I was cursing my fate and my latest hangover, I saw the newspaper story about the stunt in Paris, and knew fate had something more in store for me.'

'Are you done?' I ask him, sourly.

'That's my piece said, yes.'

We look at each other then, and I have no idea what will happen next. But then the door opens and here's the Widow Timmermans, who has just been woken up by the wind, and come down to get herself a nightcap.

'Hello, Bunny,' says the cap.

331

ᎮLANS

No one gets much sleep that night, although at least in the case of the reunited Captain Clarke B. and Widow Timmermans there's some joy had out of it when they finally retire to bed together for an hour or so around dawn. Until then the three of us, along with Giant Pete who has come in to find the cap being righteously yelled at by the widow, are up together into the very smallest hours putting a plan together, and running it backwards and forwards, and passing it between ourselves and turning it round to try to find the holes in it.

And in the morning we're all up early again and out and about in the wind to see to our various allotted parts and duties. The cap and I are to check the suit over and examine the barometer, and then to meet with Giant Pete's other cousin, the infamous Giant Arthur, to look at a couple of boats, while the widow has numerous appointments with sponsors and business partners and members of the press.

The rain that has held off for the last few days has come back in earnest, and along with the wind and the tide it brings the high waterline up to most people's doorsteps by late morning. When I meet Susan at her small cottage she's still standing at the front door armed with a broom, watching the water recede with some suspicion, as if it might change direction again at any moment, and ready to somehow hold it back if that were the case. And I'm not sure she wouldn't succeed, either.

When we're finished and are lying naked in her marital bed, and she is on her back smoking a cigarette, and I am once again marvelling at how different a woman's body is from a man's, and how different they all are, I suppose, from each other, I make her the offer.

'Marry me,' I say.

'I'm already married,' she tells me, 'and besides, we don't love each other.'

'Well, no,' I agree, 'but we are good friends. And we do fit together very nicely in bed.'

She looks at me askance.

'Hey, you're not bad, Dan, but you're no Davey Cooper.'

'I think you take my point, all the same.'

'Can I mull it over?' she says.

'Of course,' I tell her. 'But I will need a decision by the end of today.'

And then I see that the sky outside is growing darker, and Joseph Parsons will likely be home soon, though I doubt he's had any kind of day out on the water today, that is if he hasn't just spent it holed up somewhere with a bottle. And so I kiss Susan the vicar's daughter, Mrs Joseph Parsons, on the mouth and then in a few other places besides, which starts things off all over again, and then when we're all done I get on my way.

As I stand in the rain with the captain on the wooden jetty behind Giant Pete's inn, the tide is so far out that the little boat sits a good ten feet below us. Out on the mudflats even the birds are taking cover from the weather. I admit that I am wavering, and having second or even third thoughts about the operation we are commencing, but the cap puts a hand on my shoulder and gives me a cigar and lights one for himself, and we both struggle to smoke in the wind-blown, horizontal rain, and that takes my mind off things for a bit.

We go over the various timings and repeat the points on the map that we have both memorised, and the arrangements for what will happen afterwards, and back-up meeting plans and so on.

'This is the only way to get them off our backs, Dan,' says the cap.

'I know.'

'And besides, think of the story we'll have to tell.'

'I know.'

'Not to mention that it is the right thing to do, in the circumstances.'

'In the circumstances,' I agree. 'Yes.'

'If you are in doubt, remember what we have on our side, Dan.'

'Willpower?' say I, throwing away the sodden cigar. 'Or luck?'

Captain Clarke B. smiles sadly.

'I was going to say "love".'

And then we embrace, and go our separate ways, towards our individual destinies.

By the time the carriage that I am sharing with Giant Pete and two of Giant Arthur's men has reached the crossroads half-way between our village and the town of C—, it's already dark, and out on the estuary the tide has started rising again. The driver stops by the stand of trees as instructed, and we wait in the rain for the arrival of the other carriage, which appears out of the shadows soon enough, and pulls up some thirty feet from our own cab.

We watch the two overcoated men step out into the rain, one carrying a lantern, which he waves around as we have been told to expect.

'Let's see him,' I shout from our carriage, and my brother's confused face is presented at the window.

'All of him, please.'

And so Will is brought down and stands in the mud looking scared and cold, still in his prison outfit and shackles, a man on either side of him and another on top of the carriage, all with pistols now pointed in his direction.

'Good enough?' shouts one of the men.

I find that my mouth has gone dry and try to imagine how Andrea would act in this situation, and feel my grief at the loss of him all over again.

'Good enough?' the man shouts again.

'Excellent,' I manage to shout, and then wait, as nothing at all happens for a couple of seconds.

'Excellent,' I shout again, just as the rest of Giant Arthur's men emerge from the trees on the far side of the crossroads and open fire on my brother's captors, and make short work of killing all three of them, and then their driver besides, because you can never be too careful in their business.

And then I embrace my surprised brother, who has now been in two ambushes tonight, having earlier been sprung during his hastily arranged prison transfer, and we put him in our carriage, and run the other one off the road and into the rising sea, and then we hightail it back towards the village where Giant Arthur's best ship will be waiting for us, knowing that all the while, somewhere out in the darkness, the cap is paddling for dear life against the monstrous swell.

'I admit I am still confused,' says Giant Pete to me, as I hold my shivering brother, a blanket wrapped around his shoulders, against the bouncing of the carriage along the rutted, muddy track.

'Go on,' I say.

'As far as your sponsors and the world's press know, it's the captain who is undertaking the swim out to the fort.'

'Yes.'

'However, the plan all along was actually for you to impersonate him, which is what the cap's creditors still believe is happening.'

'Correct.'

'But now, in fact, the captain is out there impersonating you impersonating him …'

'That's it exactly, yes.'

'So who,' says Giant Pete, 'is the actual real Fearless Frogman?'

Goodbyes, Again

In the village the water level is already higher than it got this morning, and will get higher still before the tide turns again. A couple of houses out towards the shingle have already been washed away, including the remains of our old shack, and four more will go before the night is out. Five lives will be taken with them, including the unfortunate Davey Cooper, one-legged lovemaking machine, who sadly didn't get to play a bigger part in this story. Which is a shame as you would have liked him, I think.

As Will and the Widow Timmermans are led down to Giant Arthur's steam-powered fishing boat – the pride of his smuggling fleet, no less – I go off in search of Susan, the vicar's daughter, but at her cottage find only her husband, drunk and face down in the kitchen, which is already filling with water. After failing to wake Joseph Parsons by shaking and slapping him for a full two minutes I decide that he can take his own chances, and leave him there.

Fighting my way through the now ankle-deep waves, I am aware that I only have a short amount of time before the boat leaves without me. At Susan's parents' house no one is home, and the church and the schoolhouse are closed for the evening.

337

Eventually I find my quarry at the house that Jeremiah Parsons still shares with his parents, where she has gone to tell him that she loves him far more than his brother, and would rather be married to him, and to suggest that they try out some of the continental tricks I have shared with her.

Standing at the front door I tell her that I'm happy for her, and in truth I am, but suggest that the whole family might want to think about climbing onto the roof while they still can.

'Goodbye again, Daniel Bones,' she shouts after me as I wade away through the floodwaters. 'You weren't a bad man.'

By the time I get to the jetty the boat is almost as high as the roof of the inn that looks out over it, and Giant Arthur himself is at the wheel with his men, getting ready to cast off. I am dragged aboard just as the wooden landing stage is smashed in half and we swing out into the estuary, under conditions no sane boat captain would ever set out into. As we head out to sea we sail past the flotilla of hired boats carrying sponsors and members of the press which are desperately trying to get back into port, or the next best thing.

Out on the North Sea the waves are mountainous, and only Giant Arthur's skill and experience keeps us from being swamped or smashed to pieces. He stands at the wheel laughing and singing to himself, and I do believe he has one of the best nights of his life. Will and I stand in the cabin with him, on the lookout, and if anything Will is in even higher spirits than our pilot. The Widow Timmermans, clinging to a bunk below decks and reconsidering her relationship with God, is less thrilled with the state of things.

And then eventually, just as I am beginning to wonder if this whole operation was always doomed to failure, Giant Arthur spots what our untrained eyes couldn't see, and he shouts, 'There she is, boys!' and sure enough we glimpse the giant white shape of the fort looming out of the darkness and the roaring sea, long enough to confirm that it is real, before it's lost again behind the waves.

A minute later we have it again, even closer now, and this time we also see what could be the impossible figure of a man on top of the ramparts, illuminated by the light of a flare.

'He's done it!' shouts Giant Arthur.

And so, it seems, he has, as the figure then launches a rocket into the sky, although there are no pressmen or independent adjudicators still around to see it and so confirm the cap's success, and it is quickly lost in the stormy night sky.

'Now what's he doing?'

The three of us watch as Captain Clarke B. – for who else can it be other than him? – stands with his arms outstretched against the elements, though whether his pose is in celebration of his ultimate victory over the fates, or in surrender to the destiny that has finally caught up with him, it is impossible to tell.

Either way, it is not an unpleasant image of him to remember, if it is to be the last I ever have of him, and I will ultimately be glad I was there to see it over the months and years to come – to see him defying the odds, including those he had endlessly stacked against himself, for one last time, before the giant wave, taller even than the fort itself, comes down on top of him and takes away with it every trace that he was ever there.

ℰNDS

We waited there in those horrifying seas, as was the plan, sweeping the water with lamps and calling out into the darkness despite the deafening roar of the waves, for as long as we could, and for far longer than was necessary to declare Captain Clarke B. lost. Eventually even Giant Arthur decided that it was too dangerous to stay any further, and told us that there was nothing more to be done unless we all fancied joining the cap at the bottom of the sea, too. And for himself, he said, he'd rather vote against that eventuality.

And so we all gathered as best we could in the ship's cabin, even the widow gamely struggling up from below decks, where my brother impressed everyone with a few good words from the Bible about man coming up and going down that he had studied with Mrs Pritchard the vicar's wife, and I added a couple of lines from Psalm 37 that I remembered about how the blameless would spend their lives under the Lord's care, although I had no idea who among us could be counted among their number, except perhaps Will himself. And that done we all shared a cigar in the captain's honour, then threw another one into the sea after him.

And then we set course for Holland, as I had always promised my brother we would someday do, sailing through the night and the next day to reach the Dutch coast, where the three of us – the Widow Timmermans, my brother and I – were smuggled ashore in the grey dawn light in a small rowing boat, and unloaded unsteadily into the thunderous surf off the beach at S—, where I remembered the cap once challenging me to a race, a hundred or so years ago.

'Well, he always was an idiot,' said the widow, as we stood on the wet sand watching the boat struggling back through the breakers.

When I didn't say anything, my brother added a quiet 'Amen', and we were done with that part of our life forever.

From the small seaside town we travelled with our few bags by train to the widow's now mostly boarded-up house at D—, where we holed up for a couple of days while getting things in order for our next moves. 'I didn't know people lived like this,' my brother admitted when I showed him to the room that we would be sharing, and I told him, 'Oh, you have no idea …'

That first night over a candlelit dinner made out of what we could find left in the pantry cupboards, the widow explained her plans to liquidate the rest of her business interests, including selling off the remains of her continental property portfolio, and to disappear from her old life for a while.

'Where will you go?' asked Will, who had already become quite attached to our formidable friend over the last couple of days.

'I think I might travel the world, Will,' she told him. 'I feel I owe it a few favours in return for what it has given me.'

Little did we know then about just how much the widow's extensive art collection was worth, or about the revolutionary activities that it would fund over the next few years across Europe and Africa, or the legends that would grow up around the Famous Widow Timmermans, radical, adventurer, sometime gun-runner and champion of international workers' rights, before she was eventually shot dead at the age of sixty during the failed revolution in Russia in January 190—, and given a funeral that almost caused an international incident.

For our parts, Will and I used the money that the widow gave us to buy a little barge, and a business moving things and people from here to there along with it, and set ourselves up as sailors of the canals and rivers of the continent, including transporting coal to the misty medieval towns of Belgium, and carrying passengers on pilgrimages along the R— in France, and occasionally taking people down the romantic River Rh—, and sometimes across Lake C—, and now and then into Italy, although we have not yet managed to find Andrea for all that we continue to look for him. We have travelled further afield, too, navigating the E—, and the T—, and even sailing the length of the D—, and the V—, and we are at it still.

As for the Fearless Frogman, who as Giant Pete pointed out may have been either Captain Clarke B., or myself, or perhaps someone else altogether, well he officially died along with the cap.

But.

But I have it on good authority that not two years after the captain's death in that great storm, a new tourist attraction was opened in Coney Island, New York. A water park containing various thrilling rides, including patented chutes and flumes and pipes and falls, down and along and over which visitors could ride, in barrels and boats and special rubber suits designed just for that purpose, all for the price of entry – plus an hourly show including feats of daring and skill by the park's resident daredevil, with excitement and exhilaration and astonishment all personally guaranteed by the proprietor, a certain Captain *Paul* B.

And I still plan to visit him there, too, one day.

ACKNOWLEDGEMENTS

Thanks to Hayley Webster, Richard Smyth, Julia Silk, Helen Garnons-Williams, David Southwell, Amber Burlinson, and always to Arthur, Emma and Stan (thanks for the diving bell!)